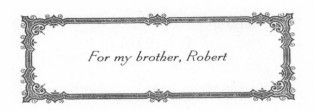

For my brother, Robert

CAT ROYAL SERIES

The Diamond of Drury Lane — Cat in London
(On the trail of a diamond mystery)

Cat among the Pigeons — Cat goes to school
(Pedro comes under threat from his old master)

Den of Thieves — Cat in Paris
(Cat takes up a new career in revolutionary France)

Cat O'Nine Tails — Cat at sea
(Our heroine takes an unplanned journey
across the Atlantic)

Black Heart of Jamaica

of

JULIA GOLDING

CAT IN THE CARIBBEAN

EGMONT

EGMONT

We bring stories to life

First published 2008
by Egmont UK Ltd
239 Kensington High Street, London W8 6SA

Text copyright © 2008 Julia Golding
Cover illustration copyright © 2008 Tim Spencer

The moral rights of the author and cover illustrator
have been asserted

ISBN 978 1 4052 3757 4
1 3 5 7 9 10 8 6 4 2

A CIP catalogue record for this title is available from
the British Library

Typeset by Avon DataSet Ltd, Bidford on Avon, Warwickshire
Printed and bound in Great Britain by the CPI Group

www.egmont.co.uk
www.juliagolding.co.uk

Maps courtesy of Bodleian Library, University of Oxford: G1 A1
(1) index map, (2) survey map, (3) passage map

Lyrics from Edward Braithwaite, *The Development of Creole Society
in Jamaica 1770–1820* (Oxford 1971)

'Give Cat Royal your vote and I'll kiss you!' – GEORGINA, DUCHESS OF DEVONSHIRE, POLITICAL CAMPAIGNER

'Another book from Cat Royal? She's always worth a gamble.' – JOHN MONTAGUE, THE FOURTH EARL OF SANDWICH

'I prophesy great things from this girl before the advent of the millennium' – JOANNA SOUTHCOTT, PROPHETESS

'Her words weave a pleasing serpentine line through the landscape of the imagination' – HUMPHRY REPTON, LANDSCAPE GARDENER

'She gives me a heady dose of laughter, as potent as my own nitrous oxide' – JOSEPH PRIESTLEY, NATURAL PHILOSOPHER, DISCOVERER OF LAUGHING GAS

'On reflection, I think I've heard quite enough from this representative of the swinish multitude' – EDMUND BURKE, POLITICIAN

INDEX

❧ Note to the Reader ❧

Reader,

In polite company, it is expected that a guide introduce themselves. Allow me to do so now. My name is Cat Royal, daughter of parents unknown, formerly a ward of the Theatre Royal, Drury Lane, London. Imagine we have bobbed curtseys, bowed, shaken hands – now, Reader, we can be friends and I can take you into my confidence.

Until a year ago, I knew little about the world beyond the confines of Covent Garden; now I find myself in the New World, visiting people and places I barely knew existed. I have discovered as rich and colourful a society as that which I am used to back home, also with its underclass hidden from upper class eyes. If you wish to follow me on this adventure into the black heart of Jamaica, you must promise not to make assumptions about people due to class, language or colour of skin. I am confident you can manage this: after all, by now you will have learned not to judge me.

Cat Royal

PRINCIPAL CHARACTERS

IN PHILADELPHIA

Miss Cat Royal – Fledgling actress and your guide

Mr Pedro Amakye – African violinist, former slave, a good friend

Frank (The Earl of Arden) – son of a duke, reluctant to take up his title

Mrs Lizzie Fitzroy – sister to Frank, now wife to…

Mr Johnny Fitzroy – ex-British lord, American citizen, artist

Miss Catherine Fitzroy – their daughter, and *my* goddaughter

Mr Syd Fletcher – old friend with a powerful punch

IN JAMAICA

Mrs Peabody – fearsome manager of acting ensemble

Miss Hetty Peabody – her untalented but pretty daughter

Miss Georgina Atkins (Georgie) – friendly mulatto actress from Antigua, my friend

Mr Jim Brown – Bostonian flautist

Mr Billy Shepherd – old enemy turned planter
Captain Bonaventure – unreliable French captain of the *Medici*
Mr Kingston Hawkins – Pedro's old master, and a nasty piece of work
Miss Jenny – a slave with a new mistress
Mr Moses – her father, slave on Billy's estate
Obeah man – wise man of the black community
Mrs Cookie – kindly slave in Mr Hawkins' household
Miss Rafie – capable nurse
Mr Dawlish – deeply unpleasant overseer

ON THE *MERRY MEG*

Captain Ol Tivern – smuggler with a soft heart
Mr Kai – Chinese cook
Mr Mickey – bloodthirsty bosun

IN SAN DOMINGO

Mr Caesar – courageous driver of the mules
Colonel Deforce – rebel leader of the arms train
Mr Pitt – fatally obstinate mule

Jamaican theatre-goers, rebel soldiers, drunken sailors, etc., etc.

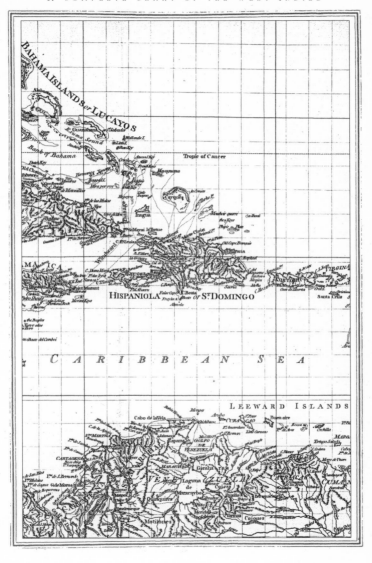

**Philadelphia, United States of America,
June 1792** – Curtain rises.

PROLOGUE

AUDITIONS

This is the story of how I, Cat Royal, became a pirate.

Reader, before you throw up your hands in horror at this scandalous confession or call the constable, I rush to assure you that my piracy was entirely accidental. When my adventures in the Caribbean began, I had absolutely no intention of pursuing this path; unfortunately events conspired against me, resulting in this most unexpected twist of fate.

The beginnings of my West Indian tale were impeccably correct, which makes the descent into piracy even more surprising, not least to myself. It began with the search for employment. Having foiled a plot to do away with Lord Francis, the son of the Duke of Avon, my friends and I had ended up in Philadelphia on the east coast of America.* It was now high time I decided what to do with my future. Should I head home to England with Lord Francis (that's Frank to you and me) and Syd, both of whom had their lives to resume after the unplanned adventure aboard His Majesty's ship *Courageous*? Or should I stay in America with Frank's sister, Lizzie, and her husband, Johnny? As the weeks passed, I realized that I had no desire to be at a loose end in their household. Quite under-standably, they were absorbed in each other and their newborn and did not need me underfoot. But neither was I ready yet to return home to England. I felt as if my true life waited but I was not sure where.

'Cat, if you're determined to work,' declared Frank as we sat in the parlour of his sister's snug little house on Market Street one sunny afternoon, 'you'll need to decide on a career.'

He was a pretty sight, nursing his one-month-

* For full details of that fiendish plot, see my fourth adventure, *Cat O'Nine Tails*.

old niece on his shoulder as her tiny fists gripped a lock of his curly dark hair. With his long limbs and twinkling blue eyes, I predicted that my noble friend would break many hearts on his return to England – particularly if they saw how good he was in the nursery. The Mamas would be moving heaven and earth to wed their daughters to one of England's most eligible young bachelors.

Yet while his future was certain – to be the fox to all the husband-hunting debutantes for the next few years – mine was far less settled.

'But what can I do?' I asked, throwing aside the newspaper. I'd been skimming it for news of the revolution in France.

'Well, let me think.' Frank gave me a smug smile as little Catherine drifted off to sleep under his soothing touch. 'You can pretend to be a boy convincingly, you dance well, sing passably, write amusingly; I've seen you climb the rigging like a seasoned salt, and ride bareback like a native – Cat, there really is no end to your talents. And you also speak at least two foreign languages.'

Entering from the kitchen, Lizzie kissed her

brother on the top of the head; Johnny followed carrying the tea tray.

'You've a masterful touch with babies, Frank,' she commended her brother. 'What I shame I can't hire you as a nursemaid.'

Lizzie looked very pretty with her long chestnut locks caught up in a practical chignon and a white apron protecting her light blue day dress. Her new role as American wife and mother was quite a climb down from her days as a British duke's daughter with hundreds of servants at her beck and call, but the change seemed to suit her. She'd never been one to stand on ceremony; after all, she had befriended me.

'Sorry, Lizzie, but as much as such skills are worthy of a duke-in-training, I feel a perverse desire to take up my place at Cambridge instead.' Frank rubbed his cheek against the soft hair of the baby. 'Tempting though the offer is.'

'And Father wants you to assume your proper title now you're at an age to go out into society,' Lizzie reminded him.

Frank groaned.

'The Earl of Arden?' I prompted, remembering his title from our time in Bath.

'I much prefer "Frank" but it won't do back home.' Frank sighed at the thought. 'Mama delayed the day as long as possible for me but now I'll have to resign myself to answering to a name that sounds like a coaching inn.'

'A very superior coaching inn,' I consoled him. 'Do you want me to call you Arden, or would you prefer Lord Dog and Duck, or perhaps Lord Jolly Boatman?'

He chuckled. 'None of the above, thank you, Cat. And the day you refer to me as Arden is the day I start calling you Miss Royal. I insist that you at least stick with Frank.'

The matter of titles settled to our mutual satisfaction, Johnny returned to the conversation that had been interrupted by the entry of the tea service.

'So what were you saying to Cat about talents?' he asked as I cleared a space for the tray among the litter of his drawing things.

I rolled my eyes. 'Frank seeks to persuade me that I am eminently employable.'

To my surprise, Lizzie nodded her agreement. 'Quite right too. You have many skills; you just need to find a suitable situation.'

'Not that you have to work,' Frank chipped in. 'You know my parents will look after you.'

My pride bristled at the suggestion. 'I don't need looking after – well, not much,' I added, remembering how the Avons had taken me in after Drury Lane had been demolished.

Johnny chuckled. 'I'm sure you don't, Catkin. You are a very capable young lady – you've proved that on the high seas and in the wilds of America. But you should also know that you are welcome to stay here as long as you have need.'

'And don't forget that Syd wants you to go home with him,' Frank said quietly for my ears only as Lizzie rattled the tea cups.

I knew full well what he meant. Syd, my oldest friend from Covent Garden, was determined not to let me out of his sight again, not since I had jumped ship from under his nose and given him months of heartache when he believed me lost for good. But his plans for me led to a future marriage and life as a butcher's wife, something I was not remotely ready to consider – not yet anyway.

'I'm sorry, but I don't want to be wrapped in cotton wool and that's exactly what Syd will do to me; I want to stand on my own two feet – prove to myself that I can make my own way.'

Lizzie poured the tea with efficient grace. 'Speaking of which, where are Syd and Pedro?'

'At the docks,' said Frank, helping himself to a biscuit that he somehow managed to eat without getting crumbs on Catherine. 'I asked them to find out which ships are in harbour. If I'm to go up in Michaelmas term, I have to leave as soon as possible.'

'And what about Pedro? Has he decided to go too?' Johnny asked, toying with his pen. His long fingers never bearing to be idle for long, he picked up a piece of paper and began to sketch his brother-in-law with his baby daughter.

'He's waiting for Cat's decision,' Frank replied. 'Make sure you catch my best side, Johnny.'

'You don't have one, Lord Dog and Duck,' Johnny replied with a wink at me. He was taking his role of teasing older brother-in-law to heart. 'So, Catkin, what's it to be?'

I spread my hands empty in front of me. 'Any suggestions?'

'You're far too young for a governess,' mused Lizzie as she stirred cream into her tea.

'And the strain of behaving would probably kill you,' muttered Frank. Lizzie swatted his leg, but from her smile I could tell she agreed. For that matter, so did I.

'I would've thought the answer was fairly obvious,' said Johnny, scrutinizing his quick drawing.

What could he mean? There were few professions open to women: teacher, maid . . .

'Surely not a seamstress!' I gasped.

'No!' my three friends said in unison. Then we all laughed. My sewing skills were infamous.

Johnny laid aside his portrait and flipped the newspaper over to the classified advertisements. He pointed to an announcement with the end of his pen. 'Take a look at that. You have years of experience at Drury Lane, Cat. A theatrical company here would welcome you with open arms.'

I studied the page. Philadelphia had a lively social scene with a number of companies providing drama and musical entertainments. Indeed, only last week I had been to a passable production of Dryden's *All for Love*. Now it seemed that one of those companies was taking on new members:

The Peabody Theatrical Ensemble

Is proud to

Announce its Summer Tour

Engagements already secured in the West Indies. Ladies and Gentlemen of outstanding abilities sought.

Recruiting now.

It sounded very grand, but I had my suspicions. Even the top theatres of the world like Drury Lane and Covent Garden were somewhat – all right, *very* – moth-eaten when examined in the light of day. This ensemble was likely to be three stage-struck fools and a cart of props. I read the advertisement again with greater care. Or perhaps not. If they already had engagements organized abroad, that suggested proper management: the Peabody Ensemble might be worth a closer look.

'You think they'll take me on?' I asked dubiously.

'I'm sure you stand an excellent chance,' Johnny confirmed. 'You have experience both on and off stage; you're just what a small company like that needs for a tour, able to turn your hand to anything. And it's not forever. It'll give you a taste of the life and you can make a final decision as to whether it's the career for you when you return here in the autumn.'

He was right. It was the perfect opportunity for me to test the waters. I had always seen my future as being bound up with the theatre, but the closure of Drury Lane had prematurely cut off those hopes. Now I had a chance to get back into that life.

My face must have betrayed my excitement for my friends exchanged pleased looks.

'Well, that's settled then,' said Frank, stroking the baby's back. Catherine gave a most unladylike burp. 'I imagine it will suit you down to the ground, but I hope you don't decide to stay away from England forever, Cat.'

'Just for a few months,' I reiterated hesitantly.

'Yes, that's right,' said Johnny, returning to his sketch.

'A chance to find out if my talents really do lie on stage?'

'Absolutely,' nodded Frank. 'But I for one have no doubts on that score.'

'All you need to do now is persuade them to take you on,' concluded Lizzie.

Easier said than done.

'That won't be difficult.' Pedro had returned unnoticed and must have been listening from the doorway. He leaned against the jamb, his arms crossed, fingers tapping restlessly as if itching to return to his instrument.

'I'm pleased you have so much faith in me,' I smiled.

'That wasn't what I meant.' Pedro took a step towards the sofa and leant across Frank to steal a biscuit. He waved it in the air like a baton. 'Not that I don't have faith in you, of course.'

'Thanks.'

'But if we offer ourselves as a duet – you with your talents and me with mine – then I doubt they'll be able to resist.'

I jumped up and hugged him, making him drop his biscuit. 'You'll come with me?'

He hugged me back. 'Of course. You're not getting rid of me so easily, Cat Royal. Not this time.'

My grin must have stretched from ear to ear. The future seemed far less daunting when not faced alone.

'If they turn down the best violinist in the world, and the star of the Paris Opera,' I performed a perfect pirouette, dipping into a curtsey, 'then they are not worthy of us.'

'That's the spirit,' agreed Pedro, rubbing his hands together. 'So when do we start?'

The auditions took place in the Man Full of Trouble Tavern on Little Dock Creek, a humble inn that offered not much more than warm beer and warm beds to sailors passing through port.

The Peabody Ensemble had to cut their cloth to suit their purse and I took this as due warning that this was going to be no luxury theatrical cruise of the West Indies. Yet the modesty of the surroundings did not deter those dreaming of stardom. As we approached we found that a line of hopefuls already stretched around the block. Though I had never joined one before, I'd seen such queues in Drury Lane – gatherings of the talentless multitude and the talented few, all desperate for their moment centre stage. My confidence took a little dent: with so many trying for a place, would we really be so irresistible? Shoulders back, head up, I steeled myself for the ordeal. We would never find out unless we tried.

Pedro and I attached ourselves to the end of the queue, resigned to a long wait. Syd stood with us, frowning at an inept juggler practising a few places in front. My boxing friend attracted admiring glances from the girls thanks to his muscular frame and handsome – if a little battered – face, but today he was oblivious to them.

'Are you sure about this, Cat?' he grumbled,

rubbing his chin. He hated the idea that I intended to stay in the Americas without him. I knew that, if he hadn't had a swindling boxing manager to pursue, he would have abandoned his plans to go home.

'I'm sure, Syd.'

'And you'll come 'ome when you've done this tour?' The anxious note in his voice made my heart ache for him. He was so desperate not to lose me forever, but what could I say when I didn't know what was going to happen?

'I make no promises, Syd. There's nothing for me in London now Drury Lane is closed.'

'Nothink, Cat? There's me – and the lads.'

I squeezed his hand. I could at least provide him with some comfort.

'Syd, I can't imagine living the rest of my life away from London. No doubt I'll be drawn back one day. It's my home after all.'

He nodded.

I tugged on his waistcoat to get his full attention. 'But you promise not to wait for me? It might be years before I return.'

He refused to meet my eyes, instead gazing fixedly at an advert for McLackland's tooth-powder. 'What I decide to do is my own business,' he said stiffly – meaning he fully intended to wait.

'Next!' bellowed a man taking names at the door. Pedro and I shuffled forward a pace. I glanced back but Syd had disappeared into the crowd.

'Pedro Amakye, violinist and dancer, and Catherine Royal, actress, singer and dancer,' Pedro informed him.

The man raised an eyebrow at us both, hearing the unusual accents.

'Both from Drury Lane, London,' Pedro finished.

The man's eyes lit up. 'Well now, ain't that just fine and dandy. I was thinking you'd say you were from Africa.' He eyed Pedro speculatively, taking in the contrary signals of his dark skin coupled with fine clothes. 'My, my, Drury Lane. Mrs Peabody sure will be pleased to meet you two. Go on in, boy.'

Mrs Peabody – now that was a surprise. A

woman running a theatre company? She had my immediate respect.

We stepped into the audition room. The juggler had just been summarily dismissed and a pale-faced girl had taken his place.

'Name?' barked a woman seated by the pianoforte.

'Charlotte Potter, Mrs Peabody,' the girl whispered, intimidated by the grim-faced lady of indeterminate years who was glaring at her. Dressed in black, the company manager looked rather like a bald eagle poised to swoop on any theatrical failing, ready to rip reputations to shreds.

'Go on then, Miss Potter, do your worst.' Mrs Peabody nodded to the accompanist. The pianoforte began to tinkle. The girl opened her mouth to sing a ballad in a quavering voice.

The response was ruthless.

'Next!' bellowed Mrs Peabody. 'I suggest you try another profession, Miss Potter, one that doesn't involve singing, and stop wasting my time.'

The poor girl was led away in tears. Mrs

Peabody might be worthy of respect but she also inspired in me a creeping case of stage fright. I glanced nervously at Pedro, but he seemed unruffled by the humiliations inflicted on others — so secure was he in his own talent.

'Who are you?' Mrs Peabody enquired with an exasperated sigh as Pedro and I made our way forward. She was evidently tired of the whole business after a morning of disappointment. I was tempted to slip away without trying her patience further.

Before we could introduce ourselves, the man who had greeted us at the door called out:

'Thought you'd like to know, ma'am, they're from Drury Lane.'

Mrs Peabody's face relaxed into an unexpectedly fond smile. 'Ah, Drury Lane!' She waved her notes languidly in front of her face as if the memory had summoned up a warm flush. 'My, my. I was once Mr Garrick's favourite, did you know? Miss Dorothea Featherstone, famed for my Desdemona and Cleopatra.'

Strange, I'd never heard of a Miss Featherstone

and I thought I knew all the names of the great actresses of the past.

'He said no one could match my deportment and diction. My success was certain. That was before I married the late Mr Peabody, of course.' Her mouth wrinkled into a bitter line.

Pedro and I exchanged looks.

Mrs Peabody flapped the memories away. 'Well, well, let's see what you can do then,' and she sat back to judge our pieces.

Pedro went first. To begin with those waiting in the queue did not give a black boy the courtesy of silence, chatting and laughing loudly at the side of the audition room. That was until he completed his first musical phrase. I was delighted to note the open mouths and pleasantly shocked expressions as the lively piece by Bach wove its spell. Pedro finished to an awed hush, then enthusiastic applause.

'I think he's hired,' muttered the rejected juggler in my ear, not sounding the least bit jealous. 'She'd be a fool not to snap him up – and Mrs Peabody is no one's fool.'

I nodded politely but could not answer as nerves had set in: my turn. I couldn't let Pedro down.

My friend gave me a grin, summoning me forward.

Imagine you're back on the *Courageous,* I told myself. They're just shipmates wanting to be entertained.

So why did I feel more like a Christian about to be thrown to the lions?

Pedro ran through the introduction to *Blow the Man Down.* It was now or never. Taking a breath, I began to sing the sea shanty.

I cannot claim the instant success that followed Pedro's performance, but I sang my heart out. The superior quality of Pedro's playing always brought out the best in me. I slipped back into the familiar place with him – the easy partnership of music. As I made eye contact with my audience, I felt opinion shift in my favour. Many smiled, some tapped their toes, others gave me encouraging nods. When I finished I closed my eyes for a second, then turned to face my judge.

'Well, Miss Royal, I congratulate you: that was very sweetly done.'

My relief at her praise was greater than my pleasure.

Mrs Peabody's stern face cracked into a smile. 'Thank the Lord I haven't completely wasted my morning on nobodies without an ounce of talent!' 'At least there are two young people in Philadelphia with skills worthy of the Peabody Theatrical Ensemble. Report to Penn's Landing on Monday. We're sailing on the *Running Sally*. My stage manager will give you a list of what is required and settle your wages. I'm delighted you have joined us.' She waved us aside; and with a hunch of her shoulders, her bird-of-prey stance was back in place, ready for the next victim.

Act I - In which things turn

out not as you like it . . .

ACT I

SCENE 1 – CARIBBEAN SUNSHINE

Penn's Landing was bustling with people as we alighted from our hired carriage. Neither Pedro nor I had much luggage to encumber us. My most prized possession, Sasakwa, a Creek Indian pony, had been entrusted to Frank to transport home. I felt she would be happier running free on the green pastures of his family's estate, Boxton, than confined in the livery stable in the poky backstreets of Philadelphia. I certainly couldn't take her to the Caribbean, so England it would have to be until we could be reunited. My farewell with her had been easy: a rub on the nose and an extra carrot. I did not think I would escape as lightly from the rest of my friends.

'Look after each other,' Lizzie said, holding baby Catherine up for a kiss. 'Write soon.'

Johnny ruffled my hair and shook Pedro's hand. 'Mind you don't get split up! I'm only happy knowing you're watching out for each other.'

Frank gave me a hug, then pushed me away as if embarrassed he had let it last so long. 'I expect you to visit me in Cambridge, Cat, so we can go rattle the dons together. My life will be far too staid without you around. Pedro, keep an eye on her, will you?'

'Two eyes,' promised Pedro.

Syd didn't say anything but there was no need: we both knew what the other was thinking. He folded me in a bear hug, crushing my head against his chest. His heart was beating fast.

'Goodbye, Syd. You *will* see me again.' There, I'd made my promise.

'I'd better, or there'll be trouble.' He cleared his throat and nodded to Pedro. 'You know what I expect from you, Prince.'

'Yes, Syd. I'll look after her or you'll punch me.'

Syd gave a grim smile. 'That's right. Glad you understand. Now get along with you, Cat Royal. Go impress the 'ell out of your punters.'

I wiped the tears from my eyes. 'I'll try.'

'And you'll succeed, Kitten. I 'ave faith in you.'

He brushed my cheeks with his thumbs where the salt trail had crinkled them. 'They'll love you. Everyone does.'

'It's no good,' I moaned two weeks into the voyage, 'I'm going to have to kill Mrs Peabody. I can see no other option.'

I had slipped away after Sunday prayers and found Pedro enjoying the fine morning on the main deck of the *Running Sally*, a trading sloop on which we had secured passage for Jamaica. Pedro was waxing his bow with rosin and chatting to some of the gentlemen in the ensemble. All of them looked relaxed and happy. How different from the cabin where we women were packed together like sardines in a barrel. The very managing Mrs Peabody had absurdly strict notions of propriety and had refused me permission to wander the deck.

'We may be actresses, Miss Royal, but that does not mean we need not worry about our reputations,' she had snapped when I'd begged leave to get some fresh air.

I was prepared for her to run the ensemble, but I drew the line at her organizing my life too.

The women's quarters were unbearable for more reasons than close confinement. Mrs Peabody had brought along her empty-headed daughter, Hetty, expecting me to be company for her. We had nothing in common except the desire to throttle each other after an hour spent in the same room. A blue-eyed, golden-curled girl of my age, she infuriated me by making sheep's eyes at every man. As a ginger-haired green-eyed runt of the litter, I'm afraid, Reader, I envied her luscious beauty. Perhaps her mother was right to be concerned for her with the sailors, but I couldn't understand why I had to suffer because Hetty did not know how to behave. Besides, I had sailed across the Atlantic dressed as a boy for heaven's sake; I rather thought it too late for me to worry about such petty social rules, particularly if it meant being separated from my only remaining friend.

My death threat against our employer produced only a patient sigh as Pedro prepared to hear yet more of my complaints. But if I couldn't moan to him, to whom could I speak on this interminable voyage?

I let out my main grievance. 'And she's cast Hetty – Hetty of all people! – as Rosalind. The girl can't act, barely can speak the verse. It's going to be a disaster.'

'And you?' asked Pedro, looking amused as he squinted up at me in the bright light. I spun my parasol to shade him. I knew better than to venture on deck without protection; my freckles were already rioting across my nose at the merest hint of Caribbean sunshine. A breeze kept the heat comfortable out here, unlike the cabin.

'I'm to be Phoebe, the brainless shepherdess.' It was a humiliation, a complete waste of my talents. I'd never rated myself all that highly, but surely even I scored better in this company than that! 'Actually, I've changed my mind. I'm going to rip up the script and make Mrs Peabody and her daughter eat *As You Like It* page by page. They do not deserve to be entrusted with Shakespeare.'

'Let me get this straight, Cat,' said Pedro. He ran his fingers lovingly over his bow. 'Are you going to feed these items to Mrs Peabody before or after you've done her in?'

'Does it matter?'

'Of course it does. Before would be a little easier, I would say.'

I waved my hand. 'Details, details. I think you understand the sentiment.'

'Completely. Can't say I particularly like the woman myself, but she's the master and we all have to dance to her tune.'

I slumped next to Pedro on his coil of rope and scanned the rigging with a professional eye.

'Seems to me we could pack on a little more sail in this breeze,' I commented, watching the men up on the yardarm. 'I never thought I'd miss being a sailor, but anything is better than being a lady on Mrs Peabody's terms.'

'Can't you team up with her daughter?' suggested Pedro. 'Though unable to act, Miss Peabody seems a pleasant enough girl. If you both appealed for a little more freedom, perhaps she would listen.'

I gazed out at the unbroken blue of the

horizon. 'Pleasant fiddlesticks! Don't tell me she's been making eyes at you too? All the men in the ensemble think she's an angel when in fact she's a shallow creature far too used to getting her own way. She treats poor Miss Atkins like dirt.'

'I like Miss Atkins,' Pedro said, a little off-subject in my estimation. 'She loves music.'

'Yes, she's a sweet mouse but now she's got to be Celia to Hetty's Rosalind. Her life is going to be hell: all those scenes together with Hetty upstaging her by simpering at the audience.'

'Miss Royal!' The strident tones of Mrs Peabody floated down from the stern.

'Hide me!' I said desperately, ducking behind Pedro.

'Cat, I think she can see you,' Pedro said calmly. 'You'd best go at once.'

'Come here directly, Miss Royal.' Mrs Peabody strode forward, hooked my arm and towed me back into the cabin. Hetty and Miss Atkins looked up from their prayer books to stare. 'I told you not to wander off on your own. Your behaviour is a disappointment. You of all people should know that as an actress one hint of impropriety and people will quickly assume you are ruined. Mr Garrick never allowed his actresses to conduct themselves in such a scandalous manner.'

I doubted that very much. According to my theatre friends who had had the privilege of working with the famous actor-manager at Drury Lane, David Garrick had not interested himself in the private lives of his actresses, only in their public talent. I was steadily growing more and more suspicious that Dorothea Featherstone had never trod the boards there.

'My apologies, Mrs Peabody. But surely you do not require me for a rehearsal on the Sabbath, our day of rest?' I said sweetly, taking a stool next to Miss Atkins.

Our theatrical manageress gave me a sour smile. 'No, Miss Royal, but you remind me of my duties. I do think we should prepare some appropriate entertainment suitable for Sundays. The pious folk of Jamaica may well require it of us. As you seem at a loose end, you, young miss, will spend the rest of the day memorizing Psalm One Hundred and Nineteen, all one hundred and seventy-six verses.'

Our eyes locked.

'It is your job to entertain, is it not, Miss Royal?'

'Very well. Psalm One Hundred and Nineteen it is.'

The other women left the cabin to take a turn on deck. Flinging a few unsabbath-like words at Mrs Peabody's back, I settled down to the challenge. I had only reached verse thirty when Miss Atkins returned.

'How far have you got with the psalm?' she asked, patting her honey-blonde hair in place after the dishevelment of the sea breeze. When unbound it sprang into tight cork-screw curls. I had noticed that she kept herself to herself when the Peabodys were present. I imagined she found that life was easier if she did not attract attention; perhaps this was a lesson I should learn.

I reeled off the first segment of the psalm word-perfect.

'Excellent.' Her cheeks dimpled as she smiled,

making her even prettier. 'I admire your memory, Miss Royal.'

'Please call me Cat when she's not around. Everyone else does.'

Miss Atkins nodded. 'I'd like that. Still, I'd also like to know your secret of learning so fast. Celia's part is quite daunting.'

'I learned the trick from Mr Kemble and Mrs Siddons,' I said, naming the brother and sister acting duet at Drury Lane, well known to you, Reader, I am sure. 'It's like exercising a muscle: once your brain is warmed up, it's surprising how much you can retain with the right kind of concentration.'

'What else do you know?'

'Oh, bits and bobs. Speeches from plays, poetry, English, French and Latin.'

She laughed. 'I can see your talents are wasted on a small part like Phoebe.'

I gave her a cheeky grin. 'And I also know lots of sea-shanties, not all of them decent.'

'Perhaps you should teach me some.' She leaned forward with a wicked smile. 'But not on a Sunday.'

I sat back and fluttered my hand in a missish gesture often employed by Hetty. 'You shock me, Miss Atkins.'

'Georgina, or Georgie, please. When *she's* not around.'

I gave a conspiratorial nod. 'Georgie it is, then.'

Feeling the ice had been well and truly broken, I yawned and threw the Bible aside. No need to pretend with her.

'Tell me about yourself, Georgie. How did you come to be part of Mrs Peabody's hen-pecked ensemble?'

The actress shrugged and took a place on the narrow bunk beside me. 'She's not so bad. I've known worse. As for me, there's not much to tell. My quiet life in Antigua ended when my father died.'

'Antigua?'

'It's one of the islands in the West Indies – we might be going there later on the tour.'

'Do you have family living there still?'

She shook her head. 'My mother passed away years before, taken by the yellow fever. Father was in charge of supplies for the Naval Dockyard but left me with little – too honest for his own good when everyone else was lining their pockets. I was thrown upon my own resources, and being an actress was one of the more desirable options.'

'What about marriage?' I couldn't believe that a pretty woman like her would have been without offers from the officers who passed through the island.

Georgie tweaked her hair. 'Did you not realize, Cat? I'm a mulatto. No man of decent family is going to offer for me, and the other sort of men I prefer to keep at a distance.'

'A mulatto? Doesn't that mean you have mixed blood?'

She nodded.

'But you look white.'

'The memories of many people out here are very long. My grandmother was a slave – that makes me a quadroon.'

'A what?'

'A quarter African but, to many people, that's the part that matters.'

'That's absurd.' Not to say insulting: as if one kind of blood was better or worse than another!

She smiled bitterly. 'Isn't it? You would not believe the minute categories they dream up on the islands to account for blood. You have to reach octoroon before you're automatically free.'

I gasped. 'You're not a slave, are you?'

'No, no. My grandfather freed my grandmother and married her. But the taint remains, acceptable for an actress but not for a wife of a European planter or an officer.'

'Does Mrs Peabody know?'

'Of course. I would never hide such a thing from my employer. She hired me last year when the troop came to Antigua and I've been with the Peabodys ever since. They're not bad sorts: infuriating but not cruel. So here I am.' She spread her hands wide. 'One very boring life. This voyage is the most exciting thing that has ever happened to me and even I recognize that it has been pretty uneventful. Nothing by your standards, I'm sure.'

'My standards?' I asked, puzzled.

'Pedro's been telling me stories at dinner while

you've been discussing the finer points of sailing with the bosun.'

I laughed. It was true: I had been milking the crew for information about the ship at every opportunity.

Georgie kicked off her shoes. 'I must say it is very odd to be cabin-mate with a girl who, though younger than me, has seen far more of life.'

My smile faded. I wondered if she meant that as a veiled insult. In our society, girls were not supposed to be worldly; we were supposed to be sweet innocents without an original thought in our head. But as her face glowed with genuine interest, I decided she had not meant to censure me.

'Everything that's happened to me has always been a bit by accident,' I confessed. 'My friends think I attract trouble.'

Georgie clasped her hands to her chest. 'How wonderful!'

'Not always. Sometimes it can be terrifying.'

'But still, you're really living, not drifting as so many of us do. How I would like to live an adventure, not just act in one!'

I laughed. Miss Georgina Atkins was quite a surprise.

'In that case, I think we should make a pact against the forces of dullness and decorum,' I suggested, nodding towards Mrs Peabody's chair. 'Though we outwardly conform – or at least you do,' I amended, 'inside we will know that we are free; we'll grab our adventures before they pass us by!' I spat on the palm of my hand in a true Covent Garden gesture of deal-making. 'Agreed?'

Georgie hesitated for a fraction then spat delicately before shaking my hand. 'Agreed.'

Sailing with the Turk and Caicos Islands to the east, two hundred and fifty miles north of Jamaica, the *Running Sally* continued to make good progress. When not required for rehearsal, I often stood watching the slow unfurling of the wake behind the ship and once was rewarded with the glimpse of the stately wave of a whale's tail before it slapped down on to the waters and disappeared. Inside the reef protecting the islands, the sea glowed turquoise; out in the channel where we were sailing it was a deeper blue. The sun shone in a sky smudged by only a few puffs of cloud like powder marks on an azure gown. Revelling in this chance to travel, I fell in love with the boundless horizons and sense of freedom you can only find on the ocean.

Our first port of call was approaching. The captain hailed a passing trading vessel and the two ships drew in canvas for an exchange of news. Our route to Jamaica would be taking us to the troubled French colony of San Domingo and he did not want any unpleasant surprises when we called in to off-load some cargo. Whatever the other captain told him was clearly a matter of great concern.

'Apparently the whole island of San Domingo is in uproar.' Pedro filled me in on the details during a lull in our morning rehearsal. 'The mulattos are fighting for their rights, the slaves are demanding their freedom; it's revolution, Cat, and the French masters can hardly complain because the people are only following the example set in Paris.' Pedro grinned. 'I can't tell you how proud it makes me to hear that some of my people have finally done what we all wanted. They've taken their freedom rather than waiting for it to be handed to them.'

I bit my lip, watching Mrs Peabody going through Hetty's part with her for the hundredth time. The girl had a brain in which no words would stick. 'I don't know, Pedro. What if the masters get back in control? Their revenge will be terrible.'

'Then the slaves must not lose.'

'I hate to sound pessimistic, but when have you ever heard of a successful slave revolt?'

'There always has to be a first.' Pedro's tone was brittle. He was taking my doubt personally. 'The main point is that Le Cap where our captain had thought to make port is too dangerous with all these different groups running wild. He's making for the Ile de la Tortue.'

'Where?'

'Tortoise Island – you might have heard it called Tortuga. It lies to the north, just off the mainland of San Domingo, so he thinks it will probably have escaped most of the turmoil. He's dropping off some cargo there and then will take the Windward Passage to Jamaica.'

Tortuga I had heard of, yes. It sounded a most intriguing destination. From what the old tars on board had told me, the island had been the centre of piracy in the early days of our century. That was the heyday of buccaneers: a time when you might've met Blackbeard and William Kidd drinking at a local Tortugan tavern. Since then, the French and British Navies had imposed some order on the Caribbean, but there were still plenty of disreputable privateers ready to walk on the wrong side of the law when no one was looking; and I had heard that Tortuga was still a notoriously lawless place. I very much doubted that Mrs Peabody would let us girls go ashore.

After weeks of travel, the temptation to put foot on dry land was strong. I hadn't come on this voyage to spend my time staring at the walls of my cabin. As we drew into the main port on the island, I squinted into the shafts of evening sunshine. Cayonne was a ramshackle place in the shelter of the turtle-backed mountain, a jumble of taverns and shops serving the sea-going vessels, but to me it didn't look very threatening – no worse than the places I'd visited on Bermuda on my voyage out from England. I sighed. No point getting myself thrown out of the company for disobeying Mrs Peabody without good reason.

When Pedro returned from shore-leave at dawn, he was a good deal richer but I sensed that the visit to Tortuga had disturbed him profoundly. Lucky, then, that the *Running Sally* was not lingering; cargo unloaded, the captain was already making preparations to sail.

Pedro stood at the ship's side, drumming his fingers on the rail.

'What was it like?' I asked curiously, tugging him out of the way of a sailor busy with the task of casting off.

My friend drew his hand over his brow. 'The usual collection of dirty inns and drunks.'

'So why the long face?'

'I just feel as though I should . . .' He paused, searching for the right words. 'Everyone's talking

about this rebellion on San Domingo; I think . . .
no, I *know* that it's a cause I would give my life for
and I can't say that about anything else, except
perhaps for my friends.' He squeezed my hand
then let it drop. 'Just think: if they succeed here it
could mean the end of slavery across the West
Indies as rebellion spreads from island to island.'

I was taken aback by his vehemence. I'd never
seen Pedro in this mood before. 'What happened,
Pedro? Who did you meet?'

'Am I so easy to read?' Pedro gave me a
fond smile.

'Only to me.'

'Well.' He slumped down with his back to a
barrel, rubbing his head with both hands, elbows
on knees. I sat down next to him. 'There was a
man in the second inn we went to – an escaped
slave. I got talking to him about San Domingo.
He told me that people of my colour were
gathering around a leader called Toussaint. He's
hiding out in the interior; he's training up an
army of slaves.'

I whistled. 'A risky venture.'

Pedro shrugged. 'Of course. The slaves won't get freedom without sacrifice.'

'That might be true, but it sounds as if there's going to be a lot of blood spilt.'

'What about the blood being spilt already – every day on the slave plantations?'

I didn't have an answer to that.

'I think this Toussaint is right,' continued Pedro, fists clenching. 'We have to grab freedom rather than wait for white men to grant it to us. The masters will squeeze work out of the slaves until they no longer have use for them. Only then will they think about giving us our freedom – too late.'

'But you *are* free, Pedro.' I took his hand in mine, smoothing out his fist and feeling the calluses on the pads of his fingers from his violin-playing.

'Yes, Cat, but don't you want to do something to help?'

'Maybe. But what could I do?' I caught his eye, guessing what he was thinking. 'And what use would you be to a soldier?'

'I don't know.' He looked longingly at the San

Domingo mainland just a few miles off our bow. 'I don't know. As you said, I'm free but I feel I've got to use my freedom well. I owe it to my people. It seems wrong not to try.'

'What about your promise to stay with me?' I said lightly.

He bent his head. 'You're right. It's just a mad dream of mine – a way to slay the dragons of my past.'

'I thought you'd slain them when you won your freedom?'

'So did I, Cat. So did I.'

SCENE 2 — KINGSTON, JAMAICA

By tacit consent, we avoided the tricky subject of the San Domingo rebellion for the rest of the voyage. A favourable breeze blew us down the Windward Passage as the ship sprinted the sea miles to Jamaica. The disquieting scenes in Tortuga fell behind as the island slipped below the horizon. The ensemble enjoyed watching the dolphins leaping in outrageous display alongside the ship. What a shame we couldn't put them on stage: we'd be guaranteed a sell-out. Pedro appeared to settle into the familiar routine of rehearsals and forget his desire to fight for the slaves. We had plenty to keep us busy. He was providing the accompanying music for the ballads in *As You Like It* and I had been given a couple to sing. In my humble opinion, our contribution was the best part of the play. Nothing could disguise the fact that Hetty Peabody had not inherited her mother's talent for acting, if that even existed.

Hetty had the figure to carry off the costumes, but what use was that when she had all the acting ability of a tree stump?

We had a number of other plays in preparation, but *As You Like It* was supposed to be our grand debut in Kingston. I feared that if things went ahead as planned, we would have a very unprofitable tour playing to empty houses. I wondered how long it would take Mrs Peabody before financial realities outweighed parental blindness. Reader, I had no desire to be left destitute in the West Indies because she had lost all her money puffing the hopeless cause of her beloved daughter.

At least Pedro and I had the camaraderie of the other members of the troupe to sustain us. He had palled up with a couple of musicians: a young Bostonian called Jim who was a skilled flautist, and Douglas, a Scot, who played the trumpet. I had made a good friend in Georgina Atkins and was very soon able to be of service to her when she abandoned efforts to rehearse her lines with Hetty – the girl could not remember her own, let alone cue in another player. Instead, I found myself playing Rosalind to Georgie's Celia in spare moments. I was already familiar with the part, having seen numerous productions in Drury Lane. The famous comedy actress, Mrs Jordan, had made the role her own, not least because she looked very dashing in breeches, so I modelled my performance on hers. Georgie and I had such fun together; it brought home to me just how much I loved this life and how right it felt to slip into the role of actress. I knew what we were doing was a feeble echo of the brilliance of a London production; as the days passed I found that acting did not satisfy but rather sharpened my longing for home.

This pleasant holiday from reality was but a brief interlude. The moment of truth was fast approaching when the Peabody Ensemble would face the verdict of the Jamaican public. In the last week in June the island appeared on the horizon, giving me my first glimpse of one of Britain's richest colonies. Our destination of Kingston sat on one side of a natural harbour, a settlement of brightly painted houses, fringed by lush mangroves, set against the backdrop of the Blue Mountains of the Interior. Across the bay on a protective spit of land lay Port Royal, a naval base and centre of shipping. The bay was a thicket of masts as ships waited to off-load the 'black ivory' of slaves and take on cargoes of sugar, coffee, tobacco and other plantation goods. Small boats plied the water between the sea-going vessels, offering fresh goods for sale. The sea sparkled blue under a cloudless sky; the wind was warm and spicy. I felt as if I could purr with happiness at the tantalizingly exotic scene before me. It lived up to all my dreams of foreign lands: dramatic scenery, strange sights and sounds, the promise of adventure.

The *Running Sally* slipped into her mooring with a rattle of the anchor chain, our long voyage finally over. I couldn't wait to set foot on dry land.

As we gathered our belongings in preparation to disembark, the strains of singing floated across the water from an approaching canoe. I rushed to the side, charmed by the harmonious female voices coming from the boat, punctuated by rhythmic clapping.

'Can you hear that, Pedro?'

Pedro plucked at my sleeve, his face sombre. 'Come away, Cat. You don't want to listen to them.'

I laughed, surprised that my musical friend did not want to linger. 'Why ever not? They've got beautiful voices.' I strained my ears to make out the unfamiliar words sung by the black women.

'New-come buckra,
> *He get sick,*
He tak fever,
> *He be die*
> *He be die.'*

The tune ended with the girls bursting into gales of laughter at the passengers' bemused faces.

'That's not a very happy song. What's a "buckra"?' I asked.

Pedro had once been the property of a Jamaican slave owner and was familiar with the local Creole language. 'That be you, Cat – and all the white men.'

'Oh.' The women were still laughing at us, holding up melons to tempt the sea-wearied passengers. I hadn't considered that I might fall sick on this adventure. I knew that Jamaica was infamously bad for European constitutions, but I'd never thought of myself as delicate, having grown up on the streets of London and come safely through most infant maladies from chicken pox to scarlet fever when other children had succumbed. But the West Indies was home to the far more lethal yellow fever, as well as malaria, caused by the foul air of the swampy ground. Newcomers were said to drop like flies.

Still, I refused to accept that coming here was a death sentence. With a defiant smile, I turned to face Pedro. I wasn't going to let anything dent my pleasure today.

'Well, good for them. I'm glad they're teasing us buckras. It seems mild compared to what white men do to them.'

Pedro offered me his arm to escort me to the disembarkation point. 'Quite so. And I wouldn't worry, Cat: I can't see a fever getting the better of you. It wouldn't dare.'

'Now gather round, everyone,' called Mrs Peabody brusquely. 'Once we've been cleared for landing, I intend to take us straight to the theatre in North Parade. My agent should have secured us lodgings nearby. The first performance will be the day after tomorrow, all being well.'

As she was speaking, a boat carrying the customs officials arrived, backed by a small party of soldiers. One man went apart with the captain to discuss the ship's manifest, a second officer took up the passenger list. He began a roll-call of names, checking our paperwork and ticking us off against the list.

'Seems to be more or less in order, ma'am,' the official announced to Mrs Peabody, handing back a sheaf of papers. 'All of you are cleared for landing, with the exception of Miss Georgina Atkins and Mr Pedro Amakye.'

'What!' I burst out. Pedro elbowed me in the ribs to make me shut up. The soldier closest to us shifted the butt of his rifle.

'And what is wrong with Miss Atkins and Mr Amakye?' Mrs Peabody asked with icy hauteur.

'I'm afraid, ma'am, that no free black or coloureds are allowed to enter Jamaica at this time.'

'Since when, sir?'

'Since March. By order of the governor.'

I couldn't contain myself. 'But why ever not?'

The official narrowed his eyes at me. 'Are you Miss Atkins?'

'No, sir, I'm Catherine Royal.'

'Then you are welcome to disembark.'

'But my friends –'

'Your friends will have to remain on board. We can't take the risk of contamination. We have to take steps against the spread of the madness currently ripping San Domingo apart.'

'Contamination!'

Mrs Peabody motioned me to hold my tongue. 'I can vouch for both these young people.' She drew a purse from her pocket and chinked it suggestively.

The official cleared his throat. 'Let me see the two in question.'

Blushing, Miss Atkins stepped forward, Pedro standing proudly at her side.

The man looked back down at the passenger list. 'I believe you docked at Tortuga. Did either of you go ashore?'

Pedro nodded stiffly.

'No, sir,' Miss Atkins murmured. 'I did not, as the ladies remained aboard.'

'In that case, I can make an exception for you, young woman, as you are unlikely to be infected with dangerous ideas. A quadroon, I believe?'

Georgie nodded. 'From Antigua, sir.'

'Well, just you remember the loyalties due to three-quarters of your blood, rather than the unfortunate fraction.'

The insufferable man! How dare he insult her so!

The official next sized up Pedro. My friend did himself no favours by his defiant stance. 'But I'm afraid the boy will not be allowed to land under any circumstances. That is my final word.'

'No!' I grabbed Pedro's arm, dragging him with me. 'You can't do that to him. He's friends with the Earl of Arden and he's a star at Drury Lane!'

The official looked at me with distaste. 'I doubt that very much, young lady. In any case, the law is the law. If you don't want to be parted from your friend, I suggest you resign yourself to a long stay aboard this vessel. Good day to you all.'

With that, he returned to his boat.

Mrs Peabody stood with her arms akimbo, watching the official's departure. 'Well, I like that! Not so much as an apology for ruining my plans for our debut! This place really has gone to the dogs since last year.'

But what about Pedro? I wanted to scream.

She patted my friend on the shoulder. 'I'm sorry, Mr Amakye, but I have to release you from your contract. If this is the law in Jamaica, I fear that there will be no theatre open to you in the West Indies. I had no idea things had changed so much recently, but then we live in strange times. I'll have words with the captain about your passage back to America. Perhaps you can work your way home?'

Pedro gave a curt nod, but his eyes were shining with outrage. I squeezed his hand.

'I'll come with you, don't worry,' I whispered.

'I'm afraid not, Miss Royal,' Mrs Peabody interrupted. 'You are still under an obligation to me and I cannot afford to lose you as well as your friend.'

'You can't keep me here against my will!'

'No, but if you run out on me at this point I will seek payment for your passage out, food, lodging and so on – that comes to at least twenty dollars. Do you have such a sum?'

Mutely, I shook my head.

'Then I'll be forced to have you arrested for debt.'

I was fuming: how dare she!

Pedro pulled me aside, out of earshot of the others. 'Don't worry about me. We can't do anything about this law and it's not Mrs Peabody's fault. Don't spoil your chance with her.'

He was right, of course; but that didn't stop me cursing her and the world in general. 'But what are you going to do, Pedro?'

'Nothing – for a few days. And don't worry: I won't do anything without letting you know.'

'Will you go back to Lizzie and Johnny?'

He gave a non-committal shrug. 'Probably. But it does seem a waste of a long journey just to retreat with my tail between my legs.'

'You're not thinking of going to San Domingo – tell me you're not.'

He gave me a hug. 'I'm not thinking anything at the moment. I need to catch my breath and work out what this all means. Just promise me you won't worry about me and you'll enjoy yourself.'

I frowned. 'I'll try, Pedro. But it won't be the same.'

'No, it won't.' He pushed me away. 'But remember, Cat Royal, the show must go on.'

It was an order no theatrical person could ignore. I gave him an ironic salute. 'Yes, sir.'

I hated leaving Pedro behind on the *Running Sally* as the rest of us disembarked for Kingston. Resigned to his fate, he watched us depart in our little flotilla of boats transferring us to the mainland, a lonely figure on the empty deck. I waved until he was out of sight.

Jim the flautist tapped my wrist to get my attention. 'Don't worry about Pedro, Cat. He'll be fine, you'll see. And he asked me to keep an eye on you.'

'But who will keep an eye on him?' I asked mournfully.

We had nearly reached the quayside. Most of the wooden houses on the dockside were gaily decorated, somehow in tune with the bright colours of the sea and sky. White birds with enormous bills, sagging like overstuffed portmanteaus, fished from the shore. Pelicans, according to Georgie. The streets bustled with people going about their tasks. The majority of the black people I saw – slaves, I supposed – were dressed in simple linen dresses, shirts and trousers, a sober background of whites and blue to the peacock-rich planters and their wives and daughters. These fine folk were dressed European style. The ladies appeared to favour bright tropical colours, silks and satins rather than the insipid muslins in fashion in London. I was intrigued to see two gentlemen in tight buckskin breeches lounging on the veranda of the customs house smoking fat rolls of tobacco – or 'segars' as Georgie called them. In London men generally took snuff or smoked pipes; this was the first time I'd seen them spouting smoke directly from the tobacco leaf – it looked most barbaric.

But the beauty of the scene was destroyed by a stark reminder of the other ugly reality on which the wealth of Kingston was built. As I watched, a party of newly arrived slaves shuffled along the quayside. They were dressed in rags and chained together at the neck. No one paid them any attention, oblivious even to the disgraceful nakedness of the women.

I nudged Georgie. 'How can they treat people like that?'

'Like what?' she asked, wondering what had caught my eye.

'Those slaves. The poor women have nothing to cover themselves but they're being paraded in public. They're not cattle; they must feel their shame.'

Georgie watched the slaves tramp out of sight. 'You mean the guinea-birds, fresh caught from Africa?'

'I mean those men and women, those people, Georgie.'

'You don't have to persuade me they're human; you forget my ancestry.'

I blushed. 'Sorry. I'm just not used to seeing my fellows being treated like beasts.'

'You're lucky. I'm so used to it, I'm no longer shocked. If it's any comfort to you, the women are probably used to being lightly clad.'

'Lightly clad! They're practically naked.'

'And when they're sold, their master is obliged to provide them with suitable clothes – that's the law.'

'Hurrah for the law.' That sounded no comfort to me.

Georgie tweaked one of my stray curls. 'Cat, don't tell me you're here to take on the institution of slavery? You won't last long if you do. The whole place depends on it and has no tolerance for abolitionists. Growing sugar is difficult work: the planters could not manage without many hands.'

'Many unwilling hands. Why can't they pay wages like the rest of the world?'

She shrugged. 'Don't ask me – ask a planter.'

'I will,' I muttered, vowing to do just that.

*

The theatre lay on the far side of a parade ground, a brisk walk from the pier. A string of porters followed with our luggage, before being rapidly despatched to our lodging house by Mrs Peabody's agent, Mr Barker. Tanned and somewhat rumpled in his best jacket, he seemed an efficient enough sort of person. I noticed that bills for *As You Like It* were already prominently on display so he had not been letting the grass grow since hearing news of our approach.

I pointed one out to Georgie. 'See there: we've only ourselves to blame if we don't get an audience.'

'And why shouldn't we?'

'I fear that the sailors from the *Running Sally* might spill the secret of Hetty the Tree Stump. They were treated to far too many of our rehearsals to still be ignorant.'

Georgie laughed. 'Don't worry. It will be all right, you'll see.'

'Will it?' I feared I had far more experience of theatrical disasters than her. And I knew a flop when I saw one. In London, an angry audience threw orange peel and rotten fruit; I wondered what the good people of Kingston used to convey their displeasure. Melons? Pineapples? I made a mental note to improve my dodging skills.

The theatre was a small house by my standards, comfortably seating some three hundred or so. Walking through the quiet corridors backstage was an unsettling experience as it had the same smell as Drury Lane – wood shavings, varnish, perspiration, powder and paint. If I closed my eyes, I could almost believe I had been transported home. If only . . .

'Miss Royal, are you quite well?' Mrs Peabody's concern was belied by the sharp dig in my ribs. She just didn't want any more casualties to her line-up.

'Yes, ma'am. But smell that – doesn't it take you back?'

Mrs Peabody looked at me as if I were mad. 'Take me back where, child?'

'Mr Garrick's theatre – London – Drury Lane.'

'Oh. *Oh*,' she said a second time with more emphasis, reminded to claim her credentials. 'I suppose it does.' She stood beside me and sniffed. 'An unmistakable odour to be sure.'

'Were you friendly with Mrs Abington or Peg Woffington?' I probed, naming some of Mr Garrick's most famous leading ladies.

'Er, only in passing. Bit before my time.'

That did not wash: no one backstage ever had a 'passing' friendship, not if they were in the same productions.

'So when *was* your time, Mrs Peabody? Perhaps I know some of your acquaintances?'

'I'm sure you do, but I'm afraid we don't have time for that now, Miss Royal. Come, come.' She clapped her hands twice. 'Let's go to our lodgings to take a well-earned rest. Rehearsal tomorrow morning at nine.'

I noted that Mrs Peabody's expression was far from friendly as I followed Georgie back out into the sunshine.

'I don't think I should do that,' I said with a sigh.

'Do what?' asked Georgie, giving a soldier a cold look as he made to approach her. In Kingston as in London, actresses had to be very careful about encouraging the right sort of attention. She hooked my elbow firmly in hers as we trailed after Mrs Peabody and Hetty.

'Test her on her origins. If that Mrs Peabody ever starred at Drury Lane then my name's Sarah Siddons.'

'You think she's lying?'

'Without a doubt. I know my own family history, and she isn't in it.'

Georgie giggled. 'That would make sense. There's many a person making a silk purse out of a sow's ear here – black sheep of aristocratic families, fallen women, bankrupts. It's not a bad place to make a new start and embroider it as you will.'

'Then you think I should leave her to her little deception?'

'Why not? It's not harming anyone, is it?'

'No, I suppose not.' I grinned, my spirits improving for the first time since having to leave Pedro behind. 'But that won't stop me teasing her: it's just too much fun. She can be insufferable.'

Georgie smiled. 'She might think the same about you.'

'I'm sure she does. Pedro was always the better part of the bargain she made with us and now look what's happened. She's stuck with me and he's not able to set foot on dry land.'

Georgie scanned the harbour, seeking the *Running Sally* among all the other ships at anchor. 'Do you think he'll be all right?'

'I don't know. I can only hope so.'

To our delight in the allocation of rooms among ensemble members, Georgie and I were given a room together at Mrs Edwards' lodging house on Harbour Street. A tiny chamber, it faced on to a quiet yard at the back where a few chickens scratched in the dirt and a housegirl was hanging out the washing. But as I had been afraid of being billeted with Hetty, I thought our room a slice of heaven.

Tired out by travelling, Georgie said she would pass the time till dinner sleeping. I was too restless to settle. Worried for Pedro, I decided to take a turn to the waterfront to see if the *Running Sally* was still where we had left her. Perhaps I could persuade a boatman to take a message. Thanks to my wages as an actress, I was in the unusual position of actually having some money in my pocket for once.

'I'm just going out for a few minutes,' I announced.

My friend already had her eyes closed. 'Is that wise?' she asked languidly.

'I'm not going far.'

She was asleep before I left the chamber.

I know, Reader, Mrs Peabody had warned us of the danger to unescorted females wandering the streets of Kingston. But it was three in the afternoon: what possible harm could befall me? Completely unafraid – except of a tongue-lashing if caught – I slipped out the front door on to the blazing heat of the pavement and headed to where the water danced in the sunlight. A little adventure suited to an intrepid traveller, nothing more – that was what I told myself.

What a fool I am! I failed to notice that my emergence on the street was of great interest to two sailors lounging opposite. Blithely unaware of any threat to my person, I tripped down the sidewalk, lured on by the gleam of the sea. I passed the entrance to an alleyway . . .

Whoosh! All went black as a sack was thrown over my head. Before I could cry out, I was bundled on to a man's shoulder. He set off at a run – in what direction I could not tell, but as no one protested I guessed we had left the main road. Heart pounding with shock and fury, I screamed and kicked to no effect. Changing tactic, I listened to my captor's voice: he was speaking French to his accomplice.

French? In Kingston?

I went as limp as a dead fish, my mind whirling.

Noticing my lack of resistance, the second sailor asked, 'Is the little one all right, Claude?'

My abductor poked me in the ribs, forcing an indignant squeak from me.

'*Oui*, the little cat is fine. Not long now, *ma petite*.'

That gave me more food for thought. How did they know my name? What on earth was this about?

Footsteps thumped up what sounded like a springy gangplank and I was taken into a cabin and placed carefully on the floor. Though it was reassuring to find that no immediate harm was intended, I still could not work out why anyone would go to the trouble of snatching me off the streets.

'Did you get the right one?' a man asked.

'*Bien sur, mon capitaine*. I remember the little red-head very well.'

'*Bon*. Let us see her then.'

The sack was untied and whisked away. I found myself looking up at Captain Bonaventure, master of the *Medici*, the very vessel I had sailed aboard when I escaped from Paris the year before. A handsome man, his white-blonde hair was neatly fastened back with a black ribbon and his skin tanned by months of sailing. His fine clothing was a little more weather-stained than I remembered, a natural consequence of such a long journey.

'Mademoiselle Royal, it is a pleasure,' he said, offering his hand. His smile, as always, was calculating. I'd last seen this expression on a stallholder in Covent Garden known for cheating his customers with his smooth talk.

I withheld my hand. I wasn't moving until I knew what was going on.

'Captain, the pleasure is all yours. Could you not have invited me aboard for a friendly chat rather than pluck me off the sidewalk?'

'Perhaps.' He waved the suggestion away with a flutter of his beringed fingers. 'But we thought there was a danger you might refuse.'

'*We*?' I had a sudden flash of hope. 'Is J-F with you?' I had first made Captain Bonaventure's acquaintance thanks to a friend of mine who enjoyed the rank of King of the Palais Royal Thieves in Paris. If by some twist of fate he was here, then there was no need for me to be afraid of the notoriously unreliable captain.*

* For my previous adventures with J-F and Captain Bonaventure, please see *Den of Thieves*.

'*Malheureusement*, mademoiselle, he remains in Paris. *Non*, a business associate of his asked me to find you.'

'Not the Bishop of the Notre Dame Vagabonds, surely?'

'*Non*.' Captain Bonaventure withdrew his hand and sat down in his chair, prepared to enjoy my little interrogation.

'No, I thought not. Ibrahim has doubtless not spared me a second thought since I escaped him.'

'You underestimate yourself, Mademoiselle Cat. I'm sure he remembers you most fondly: you were a very lucrative venture for him. As you are for me today.'

I frowned. 'Then who's paid you to find me?'

I heard a chuckle behind my back. I'd been so intent on the captain I had not registered that there was another man leaning on the bulkhead by the door.

'No!' I moaned. 'This isn't fair. This isn't happening to me.' I closed my eyes at the injustice of life. There was no need to turn to look: I knew that voice. Curse J-F for going into business with him after all my warnings!

'Hello, Cat. Where've you been?' asked Billy Shepherd.

SCENE 3 – SEARCH FOR THE LOST SHEEP

I feel I owe you, Reader, a brief word of explanation about Billy Shepherd. If you are familiar with my adventures in London, you will have a shrewd idea why I was not overwhelmed with joy at meeting my old acquaintance from Covent Garden. Billy was a cutthroat who had made a number of attempts on my life, tried to trap me into working for his criminal gang, and, worst of all, kissed me at a ball in Bath! Quite what he was doing in Kingston was anyone's guess, but if the past was anything to go by, it was unlikely to bode well for me.

'Not you!' I groaned.

'I'm afraid it is me, Cat. Did you miss me?' he asked, taking a step further into the cabin. Taller than I remembered and with more colour to his usually pasty face, he looked like a bronzed snake, ready to strike.

I got up and scurried to the far side of the desk,

putting my back against the wall. It was never good to offer Billy too easy a target as he is skilled with all manner of blades.

'Strangely enough, Billy, I have not spared you a thought since last we met.' *Liar.*

His grey-green eyes sparkled knowingly. ''Ow unfair. I've been quite eaten up with anxiety ever since I got wind of you bein' set up by Dixon. Knew someone 'ad to come after you and 'ere I am.' I noted that he felt no need to put on his carefully learned rich man's drawl for me.

'That's an awfully long way to come on a mission of mercy, Billy, and so out of character. What's in it for you?'

Captain Bonaventure laughed, steepling his fingers and rocking back on his chair. 'She understands you well, Monsieur Shepherd.'

'Yeah, you're right. That's why I'm 'ere.'

I smoothed my skirts nervously, thinking hard. 'Well, as you can see, Billy, I am in no need of rescuing. It was a kind thought but I managed to look after myself.' I made a move to leave but Billy headed me off.

'Good for you, Kitten. But the least you can do is take a seat and tell me 'ow you did it. I was prepared to take on 'Is Majesty's Navy to get you out.' Billy picked up a chair and placed it in front of the desk, flicking it mockingly with his silk handkerchief. 'There you go, fit for a lady.'

I sat down, trapped between the amused gaze of the eminently unreliable Captain Bonaventure and the shrewd observation of fiendish Billy Shepherd: enough to make most girls fall into hysterics. Tempting, but not my style. I just wished I knew what they planned for me.

I folded my hands neatly in my lap, trying to look unconcerned. 'I'll satisfy your curiosity if you tell me why you're here.'

Billy perched on the edge of the captain's bunk. 'Let's say I just wanted the adventure, like you, Cat.'

'Stow it, Billy. Your life is exciting enough trying to stay one step ahead of your rivals – not to mention the law: you've no need to travel for adventures.'

'P'rhaps you're right. As you don't believe any

of my explanations, why don't *you* tell me why I'm 'ere.'

I glanced at the captain, wondering if he'd give me a clue, but he was watching us, fascinated by the exchange. Few people dared to stand up to Billy – that made me a rare and endangered species.

'I imagine it suited you to come to the West Indies.'

'True. I'm lookin' into various investment opportunities.' He took out a knife and began to clean his nails. 'But that's not the 'ole story.'

'Let me guess: your marriage plans went belly up and you're fleeing with a broken heart?'

He guffawed. 'Now that's a good'un. My fiancée and I never 'ad our 'earts as part of the bargain. Nah, the wedding's still on. I'm just makin' the old cow wait while I deal with a more pressin' matter.'

'I imagine she's relieved. All right, I give up. Tell me why you're here.'

Billy helped himself to a glass of the captain's rum, toasted me and tossed it down in one gulp. 'You're the lost sheep.'

'Billy, I think you need to lie down a bit.'

'Don't you ever go to church, Cat? The Good Shepherd's lost sheep.'

I spluttered at 'Good'. 'Well, that's the first time I've ever heard you quote scripture at me, Billy. You must be sickening for something.'

He grinned and refilled the glass. 'Long ago, I decided where you go and what you do is my business. I don't want no sharp cove like Dixon messin' with you.'

'You may think of me as part of your flock of bleating cutthroats, but I certainly don't.'

He waved my objection away. 'When I 'eard 'e'd press-ganged you, I admit I didn't sleep easy in my bed for a few nights.'

'My heart bleeds for you, Billy.'

'So I decided to follow you. Monsewer Bonaventure was persuadable that a trip to the West Indies was in order.'

The captain bowed an acknowledgement.

'Trail went cold when the *Courageous* turned up in Jamaica without you, but I 'ad your mates tailed to Philadelphia and finally got word you were on your way 'ere.'

So he had really come all this way for me. From anyone else that would have been a sweet thought; from him it was alarming.

'Now you've seen that I'm in one piece, Billy, you can rest easy. Go back to crow on your dung heap in London.'

'We'll give you free passage; get you 'ome before the end of the summer.'

'Thanks, but no thanks. I've got engagements here.'

'Oh yeah, the theatre. Well, the offer's on the table.'

But what about Pedro? He could do with a ticket out of here. Could Billy actually for once in his life be of use to me? I quickly weighed up the likely outcomes if I revealed the situation and decided I couldn't bring myself to trust him.

'And there the offer will lie for all eternity, I'm afraid. I'd rather paddle back to England in a washtub than travel with you.'

Laughing, Billy raised his glass to me. 'Good to see you're still on form, Cat. I've missed you.'

I rose, determined to escape this time. 'Excuse me, gentlemen, I must return to my lodgings.'

'You 'aven't told us your tale.'

'Oh, er, yes.' Blast it, I had promised.

Billy winked at Bonaventure. 'Maybe another time. We're plannin' to stick around for a while. Let us know if you change your mind.'

'I will – I don't mean that I'll change my mind, but I'll let you know if I do . . . er . . . did.' With that piece of semi-coherent babbling I backed out of the cabin, surprised that no one made any move to stop me. 'Good afternoon.'

I ran for it, elbowing my way through the rascally crew of the *Medici* to the relative safety of the shore. I didn't stop until I was safely back in my bedchamber.

'Pleasant stroll, Cat?' murmured Georgie from under the covers, still half-asleep.

I had never before so welcomed the distraction of an impending theatrical disaster, as its imminence helped turn my thoughts from that disturbing interview. I knew I had to come to terms with this development and what it meant for me, but not just yet. Had Billy Shepherd really travelled all this way out of concern for me? I couldn't think about it. I plunged myself into the dress rehearsal. Pedro's absence required a number of adjustments. I now had to practise my songs accompanied by Jim the flautist. A gangling man with a prominent Adam's apple, when he played he reminded me of a heron perched on a riverbank, silver fish in beak, dipping and swaying into the stream of music. With his slow manner and gentle sense of humour, he made the time pass easily. I was touched to discover that he had made the effort to check on Pedro and was able to report that our friend was still safe on board the *Running Sally*. Apparently, Pedro had become a firm favourite of the skeleton crew that remained behind, his music alleviating the boredom.

Up on stage, Hetty was tripping through the first scenes, supported by Georgie's prompts like a drunk lurching home on the shoulders of his drinking companions. I closed my eyes against the insult to Shakespeare.

'Lovely, dear,' called Mrs Peabody from the pit,

'but the name you assume as a boy is Ganymede, not Gunnymuddle.'

'Planning where to hide tonight?' Jim asked me softly.

'You mean when the audience tries to lynch us?'

'Uh-huh. I reserve the prop cupboard but I'll give you a leg-up to the chandelier first if you like.'

'You're on.'

We exchanged pained smiles and returned to the song.

That night, the good people of Kingston filed into the playhouse, unsuspecting of the dubious feast we had in store for them. Behind me, the gentlemen actors checked each other's costumes and tweaked wigs, laughing too loudly at feeble jokes. We all had a serious case of pre-performance nerves. Ready well in advance, I peeked out from behind the curtain, watching the benches fill. Unlike other segregated entertainments, the theatre attracted a mixed crowd, but everyone appeared to know their place: white people in the lower boxes and pit, people of colour in the upper boxes and gallery.

The audience was as divided on skin colour as at home we are on class.

'Oh lord, they're here,' I groaned as Billy and Captain Bonaventure took their seats in the pit near the front. I wasn't really surprised but would have preferred the approaching humiliation to take place before total strangers.

Georgie was striding restlessly up and down the stage, muttering her lines and wringing her hands. '*Who's* here?' she asked.

'No one.'

She was too nervous to press the matter.

My part did not come till well into the play so I could linger in the wings to watch the opening scenes. The curtain rose to friendly applause. There was nothing to fault in the performance of the men, but when Georgia and Hetty made their entrance I knew it was going to be worse than even I had feared. Hetty looked terrified. Her appearance drew a few murmurs of appreciation and whistles, but these soon died when it was evident that she was frozen, clutching Georgie's arm. Jim appeared at my shoulder.

'What you reckon, Cat, chandelier now?'

Mrs Peabody was frantically hissing her daughter's cues from the prompt's chair on the far side of the stage but to no avail. Realizing that Hetty's few remaining wits had finally fled in the face of a real audience, Georgie began a strange conversation, telling 'Rosalind' what she would have said if she had not been too upset by the banishment of her father.

'She can't keep up the whole play acting two parts,' I murmured.

My eyes met Mrs Peabody's across the stage and I saw that she had finally – belatedly – acknowledged her error. She then pointed to Hetty then at me, mouthing something. I shook my head, not understanding what she meant. Get her off? Do my song now while she shook some sense into her daughter?

Before I could fathom what was going on, Mrs Peabody herself signalled for the curtain to be brought down and strode on to the forestage.

'Ladies and gentlemen,' I heard her announce. 'Unfortunately, Miss Hetty Peabody has been taken ill and her part will now be played by her understudy, Miss Catherine Royal.'

'What!' I exclaimed, backing away.

Jim grabbed the back of my skirts to stop me fleeing. 'Go get changed, Cat.'

'But I'm not her understudy.'

'You are now.'

Mrs Peabody was still talking. 'There will be a short delay before the performance recommences.' She swept back through the curtain and hooked her daughter by the elbow, pulling her to the wings. 'Take your dress off and give it to Miss Royal.'

Georgie dashed over and began unlacing my peasant costume.

'No,' I moaned, feeling cold dread. 'I don't know her moves, I won't fit the costumes.'

'But you do know the lines,' said Mrs Peabody ruthlessly, thrusting the gown over my head. 'That's one better than my daughter.' Rosalind's dress trailed on the floor and gaped at the bodice. Mrs Peabody pulled the fastenings tight and clucked her tongue at the length. 'I'll whip up a new hem after this scene and see what I can do about your Ganymede costume. Just try not to fall over. Hetty, go fetch the sewing box.'

It was like one of my worst dreams: I was about to be humiliated and Billy Shepherd was there to witness it.

Georgie squeezed my hand. 'Don't worry, Cat. I'll help you.'

'You're on!' With a firm shove between my shoulder blades, Mrs Peabody pushed me on to the stage and gave the signal for the curtain to rise. There was a smattering of applause, less friendly than before.

'I pray thee, Rosalind, sweet my coz, be merry,' said Georgie, giving me Celia's first line.

For a nightmarish moment, my mind went blank. I knew exactly how poor Hetty felt, exposed to all eyes with a brain as empty as a beggar's bowl. I pasted a smile on my face and turned towards Georgia, planning to appeal for help, but suddenly it happened.

A miracle.

Standing in the pool of light on stage, hearing the rustle and murmur of an audience, it all came back to me. It was as if something clicked into place, letting the familiar words flow from my lips. 'Dear Celia, I show more mirth than I am mistress of.'

I was back in Drury Lane, imagining myself in the role, enjoying the rapier-sharp wit of one of Shakespeare's loveliest heroines. For years I'd longed to play the part and now I finally had my chance. I forgot my baggy dress and lack of rehearsal; I ignored the fact that I very often ended up on the wrong side of the stage; none of that mattered: I was caught up in the spell of performance. The audience laughed at my witty ripostes, my absurd mock-courting by my sweetheart Orlando; they even applauded my song. Mrs Peabody read in my abandoned role of Phoebe but no one seemed to mind the clumsy casting because, at the curtain call, we were given a standing ovation. As I curtseyed, my eyes found Billy's, sitting only a few feet away. His uneven teeth glinted wolfishly as he joined in the applause. Putting two fingers in his mouth, he whistled.

Revelling in the applause, I realized that this

was what I had been looking for. I felt almost drunk on the praise and acceptance of the audience, delighted that I, an orphaned nobody from the streets of London, could please them.

'Bravo, Cat!' Billy yelled, then laughed because he saw I was blushing.

Ten minutes later, in the dressing rooms, we were still bubbling with excitement as we removed our costumes and makeup.

'You were brilliant!' enthused Georgie. 'I can't get over how well you managed.'

'I couldn't have done it without my wonderful partner,' I repaid the compliment, 'dragging me to the right spot when I wandered off in the wrong direction.'

'Yes, Orlando was most surprised when you gave him the cut direct for his most romantic speech.'

I giggled. 'Yes, he saw rather a lot of my back, didn't he?'

I felt a cold touch on my arm. 'Well done, Miss Royal. You can safely assume that you are to continue in the role for the foreseeable future,' said Mrs Peabody, offering me a tight smile before progressing through the female performers to dispense parsimoniously her thanks and praise. She really was the most rigid woman I knew, her natural feelings under strict control like her grip on the ensemble's finances.

Just then, my eyes fell on Hetty sitting quietly in a corner altering Rosalind's costumes. I gestured slightly in her direction. 'Do you think I should say something?' I asked Georgie.

My friend shrugged and wriggled out of her dress. 'Up to you.'

Taking a breath, I crossed the room and knelt down at Hetty's side.

'Are you all right? You're not angry with me for taking your part?'

Hetty looked up, her limpid blue eyes more friendly than of late.

'Oh no. I can't tell you how relieved I am. Mama has been pushing and pushing for me to make my debut and I always knew I was going to disappoint her. I know I can't act. I've been out of sorts just imagining how bad it would be.'

That was a revelation. I now wondered if

Hetty's haughty manner had been a protection from unavoidable hurts. I sat down and toyed with the end of Rosalind's court dress. Close to, it looked like a tatty old curtain; on stage, under the lights, it appeared magnificent. 'So why did you agree to do it?'

Hetty gave a smug smile, the expression of someone finally let off the hook. 'Nothing short of total humiliating failure would convince Mama that I didn't have a hope of making our fortune on stage and I thought a little place like Kingston the best venue for the disaster. I really can't remember the lines.' She leant closer. 'You see, Miss Royal, I have great difficulty reading – the words just don't behave for me like they do for other people. I'd much prefer to sew.' She snapped the thread efficiently and held up a beautifully hemmed gown. 'That's one talent I have inherited from Mama. You can have the part of Rosalind and welcome.'

'Delivery for Missy Royal and Missy Atkins!' announced the porter at the door. He was weighed down by an enormous bunch of exotic blooms. I rushed to relieve him of it, but he held me back.

'No, Missy, dese be for dat one.' He gestured to Georgie, unburdening himself into her arms.

Georgie fished out a card. 'To the enchanting Celia, from Captain Bonaventure.' She waved it around. 'Who's that?'

I shook my head. 'You really don't want to know.'

'A friend of yours?'

'An acquaintance. A French pirate if ever there was one.'

Georgie's eyes sparkled with interest.

'Don't even think it,' I warned her. 'You've been reading too many romances – he is not a dashing, heroic fellow. Well, I suppose he is a bit dashing, but definitely not heroic. Mercenary is the right word.'

Georgie grimaced. 'Lovely flowers though.'

The porter was still waiting to give me his second gift. My experience of presents being so limited, I couldn't help a rush of excitement as I held out my hand for the small box. No card.

'Who gave it to you?' I asked.

'De young massa out dere.' The porter pointed to the stage door.

A gentleman? I had an inkling who might be the sender. Not putting it past Billy to send me a scorpion, I gingerly opened the box.

'Oh my word!' exclaimed Georgie. 'Someone really likes you, Cat.'

Nestled on a white satin bed was a gold chain with a cat-shaped pendant. If I was not mistaken, the eyes were little emeralds – the genuine article.

I shook my head in disbelief. 'I think he must've gone mad. He never gives anything to anyone.'

'Then maybe you're not just anyone. Put it on, put it on!' urged Georgie, getting very excited on my behalf.

I lifted up the chain and let it ripple through my fingers. Oh so tempting. I'd never owned a piece of jewellery and it was unquestionably of the highest quality, but to put it on would seem to allow Billy some claim over me.

'No, I can't,' I said, putting it back in the box with great reluctance. 'I can't accept a present – it's not decent.'

Georgie snapped her fingers. 'Decent fiddle-sticks! What about our vow to confront the forces of dullness and decorum? It's anonymous – you don't have to acknowledge the giver. You're in debt to no one. If you don't put it on, I'll beat you over the head with my flowers.'

I held out my hands to restrain her. 'No, don't do that. That prickly one looks quite vicious.' I caressed the necklace again. 'Oh, all right. It is too lovely to waste.'

Smiling knowingly at my short-lived resistance, Georgie lifted my hair up at the back and fastened the clasp.

'See? It wouldn't suit anyone else.' She rested her hands on my shoulders, admiring our reflections in the mirror. 'Now are you going to tell me about your admirer?'

'I think . . . not.'

She swatted me playfully. 'Tease! I'll get it out of you, never you fear. Come, let's go home.' And with our shawls wrapped over our street clothes, we said our goodbyes and made our way to the stage door.

As soon as we emerged, Captain Bonaventure stepped out of the shadows.

'Mademoiselle Royal, would you do me the very great honour of introducing your lovely companion to me?'

I wanted to tell him to take a long walk off a short plank, but Georgie did seem to want to meet him so I completed the formalities.

'May I have the pleasure of escorting you to your door?' the captain continued smoothly, holding out an arm.

Georgie cast a look at me over her shoulder as if for permission. I shrugged.

'Don't mind me,' I muttered.

She took his arm.

'Cat?' I was not surprised to find Billy at my side, offering me his arm.

Deciding it was best not to make a fuss about walking two hundred yards with him, I took up the offer.

'Did you enjoy the show?' I asked, preferring to set the tone if we were to be forced into conversation.

'Yes – though I thought the first Rosalind easier on the eye than the funny little thing they brought on as an understudy. She looked as if she was wearing her older sister's togs.'

Trust Billy to make fun of my big moment. 'I don't think she had much say in the matter,' I said primly.

'I s'pose not.' Then he squeezed my arm in an almost companionable gesture. 'Seriously, Cat, you did well.'

I could feel the hair on the back of my neck prickle. 'This isn't right, Billy. Why are you being so kind to me?'

He chuckled. 'Makes a change, don't it? I think we've reached somethink of a truce, 'aven't we? And I'm relieved to find you alive and flourishin' at what you do best. Some'ow that makes the world feel right – everythink in its proper place.'

This philosophical mood was so out of character. My instinct was to be very wary.

'You've never taken much interest in my comfort before, Billy. I seem to recall that most of our acquaintance has been a decidedly unpleasant experience for me – perhaps for us both. Even when we were little, you bullied me something terrible.'

'I did, didn't I?' He seemed almost proud of the memories. 'You see, no one gave me as much amusement. Bullyin' you was like a high yield investment, bound to pay out more than I 'ad to put in.'

I fingered the pendant surreptitiously. No, I wasn't going to mention it, I decided. Thankfully, Mrs Edwards' lodging house was in sight.

'Then truce it is, Billy. Thank you for your escort.'

'Anythink to keep you safe, Cat.'

'I only start worrying for my safety when I don't know what you're up to.' Like now.

He paused at the threshold and held my gaze for a moment. His eyes dipped to my neck and his smile broadened when he caught a glimpse of the gold chain. ''Ow about a ride in the country with me? Tomorrow's an 'oliday for you, ain't it?'

'I . . . er . . .' It would be pleasant to see a bit more of the island but could I trust him?

'Miss Atkins can come too, of course.'

'In that case –'

'Good. I'll fetch you at ten.' He bent over my hand. 'Goodnight. You did Drury Lane proud, Cat.'

Perhaps Billy Shepherd wasn't *all* bad, I thought as he walked away.

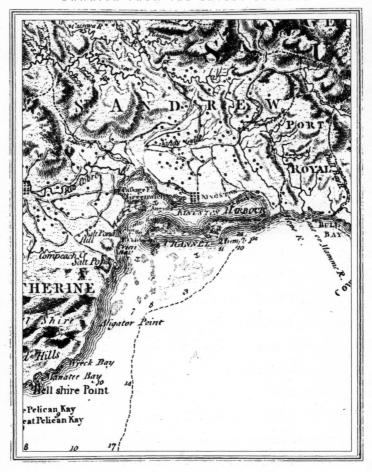

Act II – In which Billy

shows his true colours . . .

ACT II

SCENE 1 – SUGAR CANE

Billy Shepherd is without a shadow of a doubt the worst, the foulest, the most evil person currently blighting the world with his presence.

What has caused this sudden change of heart, you ask, Reader? You sensed that for a brief moment I was indulging in warmer sentiments towards him, inspired by kind words and beautiful presents? Well, you would be right – but they did not last very long. To be precise, they lasted only until we reached our destination on our little sightseeing excursion.

'What do you think, ladies?' Billy asked Georgie and me as we gazed at the stunning scenery from the front seat of his curricle. I was squeezed rather uncomfortably close in the middle but still could relish the exuberant green of the cane fields sweeping down to a white sand bay, the turquoise waters beyond. It was very warm in the morning sun, but a sea breeze made it a comfortable sort of heat.

'Very pleasant, sir,' replied Georgie politely. 'Whose penn is it?'

'Penn?' I queried.

'Estate,' Georgie explained.

Billy tapped his lovely pair of brown-sugar pacers into line with the end of his long whip. Then he flicked the reins, making the curricle jerk into motion.

'Shall we see the house?' he asked.

'If the owners do not mind,' said Georgie, thoroughly enjoying our adventure.

I kept quiet, employed in chewing my lip thoughtfully. I didn't like being out here with Billy, even with Georgie as a chaperone. He was up to something.

The house came into view around the next bend: a single-storey wooden building erected on a foundation of stubby raised pillars. Venetian blinds barred all the windows, giving the house a secretive appearance. The gardens looked well tended, despite there being no one in sight. Some distance away over to our left, I could see a cluster of buildings. Billy pointed towards them.

'That's where the workers live – and the sugar mill, boiling house and distillery. Not good to have it too close to home, eh, Miss Atkins?'

I noticed Billy was making an effort to sound more refined for my friend's benefit.

'No, I suppose not,' she replied, smiling prettily at him over my head.

'By workers, you mean slaves,' I muttered mutinously. 'Oh yes, keep the ugliness of forced labour out of sight, then the planter can forget his fortune is built on the blood of others. How very civilized. Who owns this place?'

Billy cracked his whip. 'I do – as of last Thursday.'

'You – a planter! A slave-owner!' I was so shocked by this revelation, words failed me.

Billy smiled at my gaping expression. 'Catching flies, Cat?'

I clamped my lips together, curling them in disgust. 'I thought you'd stooped low in your career, Billy, but this is the very bottom of the barrel! What was it you said once? "I don't hold with no slavery?" I remember as if it were yesterday.'

He laughed. 'You're so naïve, Cat. Ain't she, Miss Atkins?'

Georgie squirmed in her seat, knowing she should be loyal to me, but clearly agreeing with Billy.

'I think it's just that she has been brought up somewhere where freedom is taken for granted,' she replied, trying to be diplomatic.

'It doesn't matter where I was raised: slavery is wrong and no sugar-coating of that pill can take away the bitterness!'

'But, Cat, it's how things are done here,' Georgie continued patiently. 'I wish it were otherwise, but these farms could not be profitable without the slaves.'

'So? I won't cry if a few heartless businessmen like Mr Shepherd here can't make money.'

'But the slaves would be destitute. At least now they are housed, clothed and fed.'

'And beaten – and separated from family – and

abused by their masters!' Everything that Pedro had ever told me about the horrors of slavery bubbled up in my hot outrage. I felt close to exploding.

'Calm down, Cat,' Billy said patronizingly. 'Save it for your abolition friends. Your words are wasted out here.'

'Not if San Domingo is anything to go by. It could happen here too!'

'All the more reason to shut up. You'll make no friends if you go shouting out things like that in Kingston.'

'As if I care.' I folded my arms across my chest, ignoring them both.

We drew up at the front steps. Billy applied the carriage brake, leapt down and offered his hand to Georgie. I slithered down on the other side. Calls were heard inside the house.

'It's de Massa. De Massa he come!'

Two blinds rattled open and the front door was thrown wide. A grey-haired house slave stood in the entrance.

'Refreshments for the ladies, Thomas,' said

Billy, handing him his hat and gloves.

'Yessir,' the butler responded eagerly. Relieving us of our parasols, he darted away to execute his orders.

Accepting Billy's arm, Georgie stepped inside. I trailed reluctantly behind. It was beautifully cool in the house. We entered a long room that ran all the way down the front of the building. Instead of carpets, the floor was an expanse of polished mahogany wood. The slats on the blinds were angled to allow the breeze to pass through but keeping the glare of the sun out. Potted plants added a touch of lushness in the corners. Several clusters of chairs and sofas gathered around little tables signalled that this was a place for entertaining. Against my inclination, I had to admit it was a lovely room, decorated with more taste than I associated with Billy.

Then again, he'd only owned it since Thursday so had not had time to spoil it.

'So, Billy, you've turned slave-owner.' I ran my finger lightly over a windowsill and came away with a layer of fine dust blown in from the cane fields. 'At least that has the merit of keeping you out of London. Perhaps it's time I returned after all.'

He sat in a chair, balancing one booted foot on his knee, completely at ease in his new domain.

'No, I won't be staying. Few gentlemen do.'

'Gentlemen!' I snorted.

'My agent will run things from here.'

Thomas returned with a tray of iced lemon water. Georgie took the glass from him with thanks.

'Who will you be using?' she asked Billy.

'Mr Wynter, an attorney in Kingston. He comes highly recommended by the Middletons.'

Georgie nodded as if this was all perfectly clear to her.

I leaned back on the sill and sipped my drink. 'So let me get this straight, Billy. You take on an estate with scores of slaves –'

'One hundred and nineteen field slaves,' Billy supplied.

'Quite. You loll about pretending to be a planter for a few weeks then sail off back to England leaving it all in the hands of someone else

– not even a farmer by the sounds of it but a pen-pushing lawyer.'

'That's right.' His eyes sparkled with amusement as he watched me battle with my indignation.

'So how will you know if this Wynter person is treating your slaves well?'

'I won't. What I'll know is the yield and turnover. If we're getting through too many slaves, I'll come back and sort it out.' He was so calm; I felt like wringing his neck.

'Did I hear you correctly? You'll only worry when slaves dropping dead from exhaustion and ill treatment begin to affect profits?'

'Yes. They're damned expensive – about sixty pounds for a healthy man and you can only expect seven years' good service from him.'

I ignored the exorbitant price for the moment. 'Why seven years?'

Billy shrugged. 'They get worn out. Cultivating cane is a hard business. Why else would we use slaves?'

I thumped my fist to my forehead. 'I can't believe it! You talk about them as if they are machines for the scrap heap or horses for the knacker's yard.'

'You're wrong, Cat. They're an investment. I'll leave instructions for them to be treated well.'

'Oh, well done you.'

'After all, a happy worker produces more than a sullen, ill-fed one.'

I couldn't bear it any longer. I thumped my drink down on a side table and strode out of the door.

'Where are you going?' called Georgie.

'For a walk. Alone. You two can sit cosy and discuss yield and profits and sugar cane.'

Billy chuckled. 'Jealous, Cat?'

'No, furious.'

Stamping down the steps, I marched out into the sunshine, heading for the buildings that housed the slaves. It was a hot walk and I had foolishly abandoned my parasol, but righteous anger propelled me onwards. I found a cart track running between cane fields leading in the right direction. Either side of the road the sugar plots were protected by raised boundaries planted with prickly penguin shrub. Sweat ran down my nose and between my shoulder blades.

Just think what it is like to work all day in these fields, I told myself, not allowing any self-pity for my discomfort.

As I approached the settlement, the sound of singing reached my ears. A deep bass rolled across the countryside, with a resonance that made my spine tingle.

If me want for go in a Congo,
Me can't go there!
Since dem take me from my tatta,
Me can't go there!

Intrigued as to who could possess such an astoundingly rich voice, I slowed down for the last hundred yards, looking for the source. I spotted my singer working on a little garden out the back of one of the slave huts: a big man of forty or so, he had a swirl of tribal marking on his cheeks and arms like bird tracks on a sooty windowsill. Unaware that he was being watched, he continued with his song, chuckling with self-deprecating humour as he listed all the places he could not go. A girl of about my age with braided hair emerged from the hut and leaned against the post to watch. I noticed that she held herself gracefully, somewhat like the ballerinas I knew. Before I could duck out of sight, she spotted me.

'Tatta!' she exclaimed, pointing in my direction.

'Blast!' I muttered under my breath as my free concert ended abruptly.

The man stood up straight, a silent reproof to my spying.

'Er, sorry. I was only enjoying your singing.'

'De Massa send you?' the man asked stiffly.

'Definitely not.' I tried a friendly smile. 'You've a lovely voice, did you know?'

He ignored my flattery. 'What you be doin' here, missy? You be lost?' Even if my new acquaintance wasn't being overly welcoming, I couldn't help but like the way he spoke and sang English. He made the language feel somehow more generous, stretching the sounds and sprinkling in unfamiliar words, transforming it into his own. Even the irregular grammar he used seemed like a refusal to submit to the shackles of an imposed tongue.

'No, I'm not lost, just walking.'

He shook his head as if the idea of a white lady wandering through his village was too much to believe. He picked up his spade again, deciding it was best to pretend I wasn't there. The girl watched me warily.

Trying to appear unthreatening, I leant on the fence. 'Tell me about your song.'

He paused and raised an eyebrow.

'Please. I'm interested – I'm a singer too. I came here with the Peabody Theatrical Ensemble but we don't have anyone with such a fine voice.'

He grunted. 'Noting special 'bout dis voice of mine.' He turned over a spadeful of soil.

'It sent tingles down my spine, I can tell you. My friend, Pedro, would love to hear you but they wouldn't let him land.'

That piqued his interest. 'Mulatto boy?'

'No, he's from Africa. We met in London.'

My singer smiled and launched into another verse:

'If me want for go in a Kingston,
Me can't go there!
Since Massa go in a England,
Me can't go there!'

I plucked a leaf from a bush and rolled it between my fingers. 'Actually, the new massa is sitting in the house.' Then I suddenly had what I considered a brilliant idea. 'Do you want me to ask him if you can audition for Mrs Peabody? She is always on the lookout for new talent.'

He stopped digging again and looked over at the girl.

'You hear dat, Jenny? De buckra gal make me a big massa – dat no problem for her.' He chuckled but the girl glared at me.

'Why you tease him?' she asked, flapping her apron at me as if I were a goose she wanted to drive off the vegetable patch. 'We not want you here.'

'But I'm serious!' I exclaimed. 'I meant no offence.'

'Leave de buckra gal. She have too much of de sun.' The man tapped his head.

It was true I'd stormed off without my parasol, but that was the extent of my madness and I did not like anyone to suggest otherwise.

'I'll ask Mr Shepherd today,' I announced, refusing to be discouraged from doing my good turn. 'He'll listen to me.' Turning on my heels, I took a step towards the big house.

'No!' A warm, rough hand the size of a dinner plate grabbed my elbow, swinging me round. The singer let go of me immediately, holding up empty palms to show me he meant no harm. 'Me no lay finger on you, missy, but you must not do dat. You make trouble for Moses if you go tellin' massa me want to leave.'

'But you have an amazing voice! It shouldn't be wasted.'

'No matter what voice Moses have, Moses is good worker, not trouble-maker.' He must have read something of my confusion for he added in a lower tone. 'Dey kill trouble-makers, missy.'

I realized at last that I was only distressing the man for whom I had thought to do a favour. 'All right, if you really do not want me to say anything, I won't.'

He patted me heavily on the shoulder, then dropped his palm quickly, concerned he had taken too much of a liberty. 'Tank you, missy,' he said, clasping his hands behind his back.

'Come, sit in de shade,' called Jenny, trying to make amends for her earlier hostility. 'Your nose is as red as de chilli pepper.'

Taking heed of her vivid if somewhat unflattering description, I came through the little wicket gate and accepted a stool in the shelter of the back wall.

'I'm sorry if I upset you,' I told Moses. 'It's just when I hear a talent like yours, I can't help but want to bring it to the attention of other people. My best friend Pedro is a violinist; it didn't occur to me that you would not be allowed to be a musician too.'

Billy had been right: I was hopelessly naïve about some things – what it meant to be a field slave for one.

'Your Pedro, he be lucky.' Moses took a draft of water from a half-coconut shell. 'Is he free?'

'He is now. He used to belong to a Mr Hawkins.'

Moses shuddered. 'Dat Mr Hawkins – he be old massa.'

'Is Hawkins still in Jamaica?' I gasped as I imagined a most unpleasant reunion.

'Massa Hawkins lose crop in de hurricane, and so he had to sell de penn to de new massa from London to pay debts. He go now to his other penn in Trelawny Parish, a much poorer man.' Moses chuckled at the thought.

That explained how Billy had come to be involved in this particular estate.

'Hawkins is a nasty piece of work: you're well rid of him. I can't imagine Mr Shepherd will be worse. He told me he wants to make money out of the estate so I don't think he'll ill-treat you.'

Moses shrugged. 'Me no can do noting if he do mistreat us.'

Feeling we had reached an understanding, I returned to my earlier question. 'So, Mr Moses, will you tell me about your song?'

'*Mr* Moses – you hear dat, Jenny! Me be Moses, just Moses, missy. But my voice – dat noting special. Many of us sing. What else be dere for us? It keeps de soul alive.'

'Yes, it would; I can see that. Will you teach me the words?'

He looked hard at me. 'You no laugh at Moses?'

'Absolutely not. I'd be grateful. I heard a song when I first arrived but I want to add some more to my repertoire.' I sang the mocking ditty the canoe women had sung to greet the *Running Sally*. Jenny joined in, surprising me with a rich alto.

'Can everyone sing here?' I grinned at them both.

'No, Old Barney have de voice like de sawmill,' said Moses with a matching expression. 'Birds fall from de sky when he sing. Me take you to him one day and he show you.'

Jenny poked her father. 'Tatta, don't be cruel to poor Missy Red-nose.'

'Cat Royal,' I supplied, thinking it far better to drop the 'red-nose' from her vocabulary.

'Oi, Cat!' called a voice from the lane.

My new friends sprang to their feet.

'Yes, Billy?' I replied wearily.

He marched into the garden as if he owned it –

which he did, of course. 'When you've finished spreading rebellion among my slaves, it's time to go.'

Moses and Jenny stood nervously behind me in the presence of their master. I felt a jolt of anger: they had no need to be ashamed in front of a grub like Billy Shepherd.

'Mr Moses and Miss Jenny, may I introduce you to the new master of this estate, Mr Billy Shepherd.' I swept my hand towards him as if this were a drawing room rather than the back step of a hut. 'Mr Shepherd, I don't know if you've had the chance to make the acquaintance of two very important employees of your farm. Good workers, both of them.'

Billy strode to my side and took my elbow. 'What you playin' at?' he murmured in my ear. 'I won't look kindly on any attempt to make trouble 'ere.'

'No need to worry. I did try to turn them to my free-thinking ways and they rejected all my lures. Loyal to the bone, they are. I'm sure you'll treasure them according to their worth. Both seem very good *investments* to me.'

Billy put his hands on his hips, glancing between me and my two new acquaintances. 'That good, are they? I tell you what, Cat: I'll make you a present of the girl.'

My jaw dropped. 'You'd *give* me one of your slaves?'

'Why not? You need a maid, don't you?'

'I've never had a maid; I've only ever been one.' I took a panicked look at Jenny: she seemed as astounded as I by this development.

'But now you're a star of the stage, you'll need someone to look after you, fix your costumes and all that,' Billy continued smoothly. 'You can share 'er with Miss Atkins.'

'That's very generous of you.' My mind began to work through the options: I could give Jenny a new start, restore her freedom, make friends with her hopefully.

Billy held up a finger. 'But there's one condition.'

'Only one?'

'That you don't free her.'

His plan became all too clear. 'You slimy, double-crossing —'

'Now, now, Cat, don't go shockin' my people with your foul language. I want you to be a slave owner. It'll do you the power of good to take on the responsibility, teach you a thing or two about life.'

I couldn't do it. I turned to Jenny. 'I'm sorry, but I don't want to own anyone.'

'And if you refuse,' continued Billy smoothly, 'I'll put Jenny here to work in the fields for the rest of the summer. Been a house slave up till now, 'aven't you, sweetheart?'

Jenny's eyes went wide with shock. She must be cursing the day for bringing me to her back gate. 'Yes, massa.'

'Tell Miss Royal that you want to work cutting cane for the rest of the season.'

Moses gasped and swallowed a protest.

'Me want . . . me want . . .' Jenny couldn't bring herself to tell such a flagrant lie. Her fingers clutched her apron convulsively. 'Please, missy, me be your maid. Me be faithful, good gal.'

I clenched my fists and groaned.

'Yeah, I always knew you'd come round to my

point of view, Cat. She's all yours.'

There I stood, Cat Royal, Drury Lane foundling and now slave owner. I'd never felt more ashamed of myself. I turned to my new maid. 'I'm so sorry that I've got you into this, Jenny. I don't have much money, but I'll make sure you get paid and fed and clothed.'

Billy chuckled. 'You don't need to pay 'er. You seem to be missin' the point of 'avin' slaves.'

'Yes, I do need to pay her. She may technically be a slave but to me she's as good as free and I'll do my best by her.'

Knowing he'd won this round, Billy jerked his head towards the hut. 'Pack your things, Jenny. I want to get back to Kingston.' He looked down at me and cracked his knuckles. 'Well, this 'as been most amusin'. I always said you gave me good value, Cat.'

'I hate you, Billy.' I folded my arms grumpily across my chest and scowled.

He ruffled my hair in an annoyingly patronizing manner. 'Nah, you don't.'

SCENE 2 – EXPLANATIONS

Georgie said nothing to me about our new maid. I guessed that Billy had informed her of his gift and she accepted it as perfectly natural. After all, he'd already given me a valuable necklace; in Jamaica, a slave was not so surprising. Taking the development in her stride, she welcomed Jenny to our little chamber, discussed sleeping arrangements and ran through her duties. Georgie and I shared the only bed, so Mrs Edwards dug out an old mattress for Jenny which could be laid down by the door when we all retired for the night. I expressed a concern that it might be draughty, but Jenny assured me that it was quite comfortable and better than she expected.

When Georgie left us alone for a moment, I seized Jenny's wrist and began apologizing again.

Jenny held up a hand to stay my flow of words. 'Really, missis, me be happy with dis. You kind buckra; me happy slave.'

I slapped my forehead. Missis? If only she knew how much I hated to hear myself called that. 'But I've taken you away from your father, your friends. I've no idea how I'll free you.'

Jenny shrugged and moved to my trunk and began shaking out my crumpled clothes. 'Me trust you to do what be right.'

'And I won't let you down, Jenny; that's my solemn vow.'

'Fine, missis. Now let me mend dese tings for you.'

I slumped on the bed. 'You sew?'

'Yes, missis.'

I now understood how having a maid could become a very seductive idea. My resistance was rapidly turning into gratitude. 'Well,' I hesitated, 'a number of my stockings have holes and the shift is ripped at the hem . . .'

'Don't you worry about dat, missis. Jenny fix all as good as new.'

Despite feeling uncomfortable about my maid doing my chores, I was now left with a few hours on my hands. I decided to spend them with

Pedro, in part because I needed to confess to him what had happened. If he thought I was right to take Jenny, then I knew I wouldn't feel so bad about myself.

As my earlier excursion had taught me that it was not a good idea to venture out alone, I sought Jim to see if he would accompany me on the trip to the *Running Sally*. I found him propping up the bar next door, nursing a brandy, and charming his companions with a stream of witty anecdotes about life back in Boston. Always ready to oblige a lady, as he put it, he needed little persuasion to be my escort.

The sun was low in the sky as the boatmen rowed us across the bay. Lolling with his hat over his eyes to shut out the glare, Jim only sat up straight when we approached our destination.

'Ahoy, *Running Sally*! Two to come aboard,' he called.

Pedro's face appeared at the side. When he saw who it was, he waved back enthusiastically and threw down a line.

'Need a chair, Cat?' he asked with a cheeky grin,

referring to the wooden seat let down for ladies.

'You jest, I hope?' I hadn't spent months in His Majesty's Navy to mess around with equipment for the landlubber. To prove my point, I tied my skirts at the side to stop them billowing in an unseemly fashion and swarmed up the rope.

Jim whistled appreciatively. 'Where you learn to do that, Miss Cat?'

'You wouldn't believe me if I told you,' I called back.

He climbed up more slowly and heaved himself over the rail. 'I brought you a present, Pedro,' he announced, fishing in the bag slung over his shoulder. 'All the latest sheet music I could get my hands on.'

I wished I'd thought to bring such a gift. But then, my resources were very tight just at the moment, what with the expense of fitting out Jenny with a suit of clothes and shoes, extra food . . .

Pedro's eyes sparkled with excitement as he took the parchment. He caressed it lovingly. 'Handel's *Water Music*? Brilliant!'

'And rather appropriate considering the view.' Jim gestured towards the sea. 'The rest are just hymns and such. Good tunes though.'

Pedro shook Jim fervently by the hand. 'Thank you, Jim. They're a godsend. I've been wretchedly bored.'

I gave my friend a hug. 'It's good to see you, Pedro. Are they treating you well?'

He gestured us to take seats on a coil of rope. 'Yes, they're good people. They'll take me with them – if I want to go, that is.'

'Where are they off to next?'

'Mexico.'

'Mexico!'

'I know. I've no desire to go, but what choice do I have?' He rubbed his head wearily, as if tired of this debate. No doubt he had been thinking of little else since being refused entry to Kingston. 'Enough of that – tell me how things are with you.'

Jim lit a pipe and slumped back on the rope. 'Our little Miss Cat here turned out to be the star of the show.'

I grinned and hugged my knees.

'Really?' Pedro wrinkled his brow. 'Let me guess – you had to take over from Hetty?'

I nodded. 'She couldn't get past the first line. I was whisked on as her understudy.'

Pedro punched me lightly on the shoulder. 'Good for you. I knew you had it in you.'

My brief pleasure at impressing him was rapidly clouded by the rest of my news. 'There's something I need to tell you. An old friend has turned up.'

'Oh?' Pedro cocked an eyebrow. 'Anyone I know?'

'Billy Shepherd.'

He choked. 'That's not funny.'

'No, it isn't. He's been looking for me.'

'And found you.'

''Fraid so.'

'And what's he doing?'

'Aside from being worryingly generous to me, he's set himself up as a planter and donated me a slave called Jenny.'

Pedro gave me an uncompromising look. 'You refused, of course.'

'You don't understand. He made it so I couldn't – threatened to make Jenny work in the fields if I didn't accept her.'

'Then you freed her.'

I shook my head miserably. Pedro jumped to his feet and strode away.

'He made me promise I wouldn't.' Pedro's back was rigid: he was furious. 'She's from one of your old master's plantations – Billy's bought it. The work in the fields is cruel. She said she'd prefer to take her chance with me.'

Pedro swung round, hands clenched at his side. 'And your promise to Shepherd means more than her freedom?'

'No, of course not!' I was indignant that he could think such a thing of me. 'But Billy's not given me her papers yet – said he'd take her back if I try to break our agreement. I'm trying to think of a way around it.'

'But for the moment you're a slave owner.'

'Yes.' My voice was a whisper.

'I thought you were different.' His eyes sparkled with cold fury, almost as if he thought he was seeing me properly for the first time.

'I am! You know I am!'

He shrugged and turned away. 'We'll see after you've got used to having someone run after you and look after all your needs. Next you'll say you can't do without her – that you are a kind mistress who knows what's best for a poor ignorant slave girl.'

I gave a snort. 'You really think I'd say anything like that? After all these years as my friend, you believe me capable of that?'

'Don't you like having a maid?'

'Yes, but –'

'You're already falling into the trap, Cat. I expect that's what Billy wants.'

'I expect he does, Pedro, but I won't forget what this is all about. I don't want to own anyone.'

'We'll see.' From his brittle tone, Pedro's disappointment was all too clear. 'Hadn't you better be getting back to your slave?'

'If I've outstayed my welcome, I suppose I should,' I replied stiffly. I felt as if I was being sent away in disgrace and it didn't seem fair. 'But

Pedro, what would you have done in my position?'

He folded his arms and leant back against the side. 'But I'd never be in your position, would I?'

'Oh, Pedro. Don't hate me for this, please! I promise Jenny will be all right – I'll make sure of that.'

'Thanks for coming, Jim.' Pedro held out his hand, pointedly ignoring me.

'Goodbye, Pedro,' I said, offering my palm.

'Mistress,' he replied mockingly, giving me an obsequious bow.

'Don't!'

Seeing my hurt expression, he struggled with himself for a moment then gave me a swift hug. 'Goodbye, Cat.'

Once back in the boat, I gazed up at the hull of the ship looming high over our little boat, water reflections rippling on the wood. At this angle, I could no longer see Pedro – yet another barrier had sprung up between us. Jim jumped in after me, making the boat rock. The oarsmen steadied the craft with their blades and grumbled that he should sit down quickly. With a cheery apology,

Jim obeyed then turned a curious look on me.

'Your friend is very hard on you,' he said, nodding back at the *Running Sally*.

'Yes,' I agreed miserably.

'It's not like him. I thought he was fond of you.'

'He is most of the time, but now he's furious and this is his way of punishing me. I expect he'll come round when he's had time to calm down.'

As the men bent their backs to row us ashore, the sweet sound of a violin drifted across the water from the *Running Sally*. Pedro was playing *Amazing Grace*. I remembered him once telling me it was a hymn written by the repentant slave trader John Newton: an unsubtle reproof to me if ever there was one.

Returning to find my room neatly ordered, my mending done and my night-robe laid out on the bed gave a further twist of the knife to my guilty conscience. I couldn't enjoy being spoiled when I knew to whom I owed the pleasure. Jenny looked up when she saw me on the threshold and leapt to her feet, tugging her apron straight.

'Missis tired? Me fetch your supper?'

'Sit down, sit down,' I answered wearily. 'You don't have to jump up every time I come in. In fact, I'd much prefer it if you treated me like your friend and stopped calling me "missis".'

Jenny obeyed my order and resumed her seat, twisting her fingers restlessly in her lap. 'But you be my missis. You not sorry you take pity on Jenny? You not send her back? You not like my work?'

Somehow I'd managed to upset her with my clumsy attempts to put her at her ease. I now knelt at her side and trapped her hands in mine, making her meet my gaze.

'Look, Jenny, you have to understand that you don't have to prove your worth to me. You're a good maid, I can see that. I just want you to understand that I do not believe in slavery. I can't think of you as my possession. I'll employ you as my maid but I'd much prefer to make a proper friend of you.'

She looked at me warily, suspicious of my intentions.

'I know it's hard for you to understand but maybe it would help if you knew more about me.'

Jenny ventured a smile. 'Missis want to tell story? Me like dat.'

'My name's Cat.'

She nodded. 'Missis Cat.'

It was no good. I had to live with the fact that she wouldn't change the habits of a lifetime on so brief an acquaintance. Searching for a way to make her see me on her own level, I told her how I too had been a maid and worked for no wages but board and lodging. I explained that where I came from there were no slaves and I could not accept that her liberty was something that could be taken from her. At the end of my narrative, Jenny swallowed and looked down on me with scared brown eyes.

'So Missis not want look after Jenny?'

After the upsetting encounter with Pedro, I was finding this explanation almost too much for my depressed spirits. 'Jenny, what I'm trying to say is that I want to be your friend.'

'But buckra not friend.' Jenny got up and walked to the window. 'Useless slave, dey sent into bush, dey starve. Me ask Missis Georgie to care for me.'

I groaned. I could almost see Billy's smirking expression as I backed down. 'You don't have to ask Georgie anything. You're my responsibility, Jenny. You'll have food and lodging as I promised for as long as I have them myself.'

My slave gave a curt nod of understanding. 'You want Jenny now?'

What could I say in answer to such an appeal? Suppressing a groan at the betrayal of myself, I patted her arm. 'Yes, I want you. I'll look after you.'

She clapped hands in relief and spun round. 'Me get your supper now?'

Surrendering to the inevitable, I gestured to the door. 'Yes, Missis Cat is ready for her supper.'

The following day was mercifully busy, spent reworking *As You Like It* with me as Rosalind. When Georgie and I arrived with our new maid, the members of the theatre company accepted Jenny without a murmur. Mrs Peabody found her employment in the wardrobe with Hetty, assisting in the tricky task of altering the costumes from Hetty's statuesque form to my slight figure. From what I could see, Jenny was thoroughly enjoying herself, tape measure draped round her neck like a badge of office.

As for me, with Georgie's help, I had little trouble smoothing out the snags in my performance and I managed to remember my moves, or what we theatre folk call the blocking, after several walk-throughs of the main scenes. I had never been more grateful to the Bard for providing my imagination with something so absorbing that I could temporarily ignore my fall from grace into the ranks of the slave owners. But even without consciously thinking about it, the outlines of a plan began to take shape in my mind. If I could just get Jenny's papers from Billy, it would then be in my power to free her. As Pedro had so forcefully pointed out, my bargain with Billy weighed little in the scales against her freedom. From what Jenny had said, liberty was no use without some means of support. I had hopes that if she made herself indispensable to Mrs Peabody, she might get taken on as part of the ensemble. And there was always her voice . . .

But first I had to get those papers – and that meant seeking out Billy and persuading him that he could trust me with them.

'Georgie, do you know where Captain Bonaventure and Mr Shepherd are lodging?' I asked my friend as we changed back into our street clothes.

A slight blush warmed Georgie's golden complexion at the mention of Bonaventure. 'The captain stays on his ship. But I believe your friend might be found at the Kingston Coffee House when he is not out on the penn. It's where the gentlemen meet to do business.'

I wrinkled my nose. 'Doesn't sound very female-friendly.' I'd had an unfortunate experience in a gentlemen's club and did not want to repeat the experience.* 'Would you mind coming with me, Georgie? I want to ask Billy for Jenny's deed of ownership.'

She tied her bonnet strings neatly under her

---

* Reader, if you wish to relive that particular humiliating experience, please see *Cat Among the Pigeons*.

chin. 'Of course. But I doubt he'll be ready to hand it over.'

'I've got to try.'

Taking my hand and giving it a squeeze, Georgie searched my face for a clue to my intentions. 'I know this is hard for you, Cat, but Jenny's a good girl. You'll do her no favours by freeing her. If you have her best interests at heart, you'll go on as you have, treating her with courtesy and looking after her needs. If you do that, she'll serve you faithfully.'

Her counsel was exactly what Pedro had warned against: the assumption that as the mistress I knew best. I didn't want to argue the point with Georgie so I reached for my bonnet and tied the strings loosely.

'I promise I'll not do anything rash, but I do want those papers.'

Leaving the theatre arm in arm, we strolled down North Parade, admiring the soldiers in their red coats as they marched through their drills. A party of horsemen in blue jackets with scarlet capes rode by, causing heads to turn, though I have to admit most of my interest was reserved for the beautiful horses.

'That's the Horse Militia,' Georgie explained as the jingling bridles and clatter of hooves faded. 'They're the elite force made up of local gentlemen – it costs a fortune to buy a commission.'

'They look like very fine peacocks in their uniform.'

'It's not just for show. Jenny told me they've doubled their exercises since the San Domingo revolt. They fear the same will happen here.'

Bleakly, I wondered how Georgie had managed to get Jenny to chat so freely about such things when all my conversations had been so painful. Perhaps it was because Jenny and Georgie both accepted our situation; I was the only one fighting it.

Arriving outside the Kingston Coffee House, we sent in a message asking Billy to come out to see us. Peering inside I could just make out a long dark room partitioned off into cubicles to give the businessmen privacy for their confidential talks. A waiter wove between the tables serving the customers little cups of black coffee. Georgie tugged me out of the way as three naval officers entered, giving us assessing looks as they passed. After a few moments, the door swung open again, releasing a delicious waft of roast coffee beans, and Billy emerged.

'Ladies,' he bowed. 'To what do I owe the pleasure?'

'Would you care to walk a while with us?' I asked, side-stepping the question for the moment.

With a grin, he offered us each an arm and led us towards the sea promenade. 'You make me the envy of every gentleman in Kingston.'

Suppressing a snort, I kept my eyes on the glittering water.

We paused to allow a fisherman past with his catch of silver fish.

'So, how's that little slave girl turning out, Cat?' Billy asked.

'Splendid, thank you.'

Dropping my arm abruptly, Billy staggered and slapped his heart as if he'd just been shot. 'The fatal day arrives! Cat Royal thanks me for somethink!'

I gritted my teeth. 'Yes, she's a treasure. Now if you could give me her papers, I'll be able to look after her properly.'

'You think me a complete flat?' laughed Billy. 'I know what you'll do the moment you 'ave them in your paws: you'll break our agreement.' He tucked his thumbs in his waistcoat pockets. 'Cat, I think it my duty to keep you on the straight and narrow, a woman of your word.'

'Billy —'

'You can say nothink to change my mind, so give it a rest.'

Georgie flashed me an 'I-told-you-so' look and wandered a little further off to give us some privacy. She fell easily into conversation with a woman selling fruit.

I tried desperately to think of some way of changing Billy's mind, but I had no hold over him. Striking bargains with my wily enemy was a dangerous business and not to be entered into lightly. I was reluctant to risk that again.

Billy's thoughts, however, had moved off Jenny and on to my companion.

'Lovely girl, your Miss Atkins. Bonaventure's quite taken with her.'

It struck me that this was a very strange discussion to be having with Billy Shepherd of all people: he was talking to me as if we were confirmed friends used to sharing such confidences. I did not know how to respond as until now our conversations had largely consisted of an exchange of insults.

'Mulatto, ain't she?' he continued, eyeing Georgie's corkscrew curls. 'You'd hardly tell from her appearance. Limits her opportunities though, don't it?'

'So she says.'

'Shame, but she's right. Knows life that one. Not a dreamer, not like you.' Billy tossed the market woman a coin and picked up a bunch of strange curved fruit, bright yellow in colour. 'Here, try one. It's called a banana.'

I took one cautiously and put it to my nose. It smelt deliciously sweet. I nibbled a corner but found it tough and horrid tasting.

Billy guffawed. 'No, you 'alf-wit: you 'ave to

peel it. Give it 'ere.' Expertly he skinned the fruit. 'Now try.'

After my earlier attempt, I took the banana and inspected the creamy-white centre suspiciously. Something that smelled this good surely couldn't taste too awful. I ventured a small bite. A wonderful taste melted on my tongue, quite unlike anything I had ever eaten.

'That's heavenly!' I demolished the banana enthusiastically. When I finished, Billy handed me another one. From the look on his face, he seemed genuinely pleased at my delight.

He winked. 'You can save that one till later.'

Smiling, I tucked the fruit in my pocket. 'Thanks.'

'Blimey, a second "thank you", Cat: it's turnin' out to be a red-letter day for us.'

Unable to hold on to my annoyance about Jenny's papers, I couldn't help laughing with him. Billy seemed different out here under the Caribbean sunshine, not the scheming cutthroat who terrorized large parts of London with his gangs of boys and his blades. It reminded me that he was only five or so years older than me, for all his worldly ways. He'd grown up quickly on the streets, always tougher and more embittered than the other boys I knew in Covent Garden. This was the first time I'd seen him so playful. If I hadn't known him better, I would've said he seemed almost innocent in his enjoyment.

Innocent? Cat Royal, get a grip on yourself! This was Billy Shepherd: a wolf in wolf's clothing.

It was time to push matters to their conclusion before I got any more ridiculous notions. 'So, Billy, what will it take to get those papers from you?' I asked, throwing the banana skin into the water.

He offered me his arm again. 'I'll 'ave to think about it. For the moment, it suits me to leave things as they are.'

I knew it was pointless to argue. 'You really are the devil incarnate, you know that?'

'So I've been told – mainly by you.'

'You know I hate what you're doing. Are you ever going to stop playing tricks like this on me?'

He paused as if giving the matter serious consideration. 'Nah, I don't think so.'

I groaned and he squeezed my arm against his side.

'Your life would be a lot less interestin' if I left you alone.'

'Some hope.'

He chuckled. 'Tell me, Cat, after all this time, are you still scared of me?'

'Should I be?' This was the man who'd threatened me on many occasions but just now his intentions seemed more or less benign.

Billy scratched his chin in mock-thought. 'You want the truth?'

I nodded.

'I really don't know.'

And giving me a wicked grin, he offered his free arm to Georgie and led us back to the theatre.

SCENE 3 — RECRUIT

The week that passed saw little progress in resolving any of the problems facing Pedro and me: he was still at a loose end on the *Running Sally* and I mistress of one very efficient slave, no closer to securing her freedom. The only bright spot in my life was the theatre. After two more performances, the role of Rosalind came naturally and I threw myself whole-heartedly into enjoying my part in the play. We were also rehearsing for Farquhar's *The Recruiting Officer* for the second week of our run in Kingston, so even away from the stage Georgie and I were kept busy learning our lines.

Being part of a touring company made heavy demands on us actors, always expected to have something new to maintain the interest of the crowd. Unlike Drury Lane with its big cast and hordes of stagehands, we all had to double – and triple – up, turning our hand to anything demanded of us by our sergeant major, Mrs Peabody. And when she barked 'Jump!', my, how we jumped! I'd never met so authoritarian a manager. Hunkered down over my dog-eared copy of the script, I wondered wryly when Mrs Peabody was going to call on my hitherto untested ability to recite Psalm One Hundred and Nineteen. I hadn't seen any sign of the good people of Kingston being particularly desirous of such entertainments. From the evidence available, they were as big a bunch of sinners as theatre-goers in London, with more taste for plays than scripture.

We were about to go on stage for the final performance on Saturday night when matters took an unexpected turn. Hat pushed back on his head, coat billowing, Jim rushed in late, straight into a barrage of reprimands from Mrs Peabody. Like a frigate eluding the enemy's guns, he executed a swift tack to change course and dashed over to where I was waiting in the wings.

'Cat,' he said in a hoarse whisper, 'Pedro's gone.'

I clutched at my throat, feeling a twist of panic. 'What! The *Running Sally*'s sailed?'

'No, just Pedro. He's disappeared.'

'But that makes no sense – not without saying goodbye to me. Has something happened to him?' My mind ran through the possibilities: an accident, kidnap, an attack . . .

'I don't know, but the sailors think he slipped away early this morning. They don't think anything bad has happened to him. But he'll be in trouble if he's found here illegally.'

Out on stage the curtain rose to a round of applause.

'I must go and look for him,' I said desperately, turning on my heel. I was already imagining him languishing in some gaol, mistreated by his suspicious captors. Or on the run, skulking in a dangerous part of town, prey to any band of cutthroats. Or run off to San Domingo . . .

Jim seized my forearms and gave me a little shake. 'Have some sense, gal. There's nothing you can do now. You've got to go on tonight. After the show, we can make plans. But we have to be discreet: the last thing we want is the authorities to be alerted to his presence – if he's here, that is.'

'Where else might he be?'

'He could've shipped out. There was no point him sitting about in harbour any longer, was there?'

I shook my head. 'No, I s'pose not.' My heart sank, thinking of his strange behaviour over the slave revolt. But if he'd gone off to fight, surely he would've sent word to me first?

Not if he knew I'd try to stop him.

From the stage, I heard my cue. Jim was right: I couldn't walk out now, letting all my fellow players down. Pedro would not want me to be so unprofessional. 'All right. I'll speak to you after the show.'

Jim nodded and ran to fetch his instrument before Mrs Peabody docked any more of his pay for tardiness. I stepped out into the pool of light, trying to calm myself. There had to be an explanation, and I would not rest until I found it. I forced a smile on my face and fell into role.

Jim advised me that it would be safest to keep his information to the smallest number of people. We decided therefore to make our plans back at the lodging house in the room I shared with Georgie and Jenny, the only place we could be assured of privacy. The three of us listened as Jim ran through what he had discovered from the sailors. Pedro's violin and music had gone, suggesting that he had planned his escape, but he had left no message, not even a note, to let us know his intentions.

Jim rubbed his chin. 'The captain promised he'd say nothing to the Port Royal authorities unless asked a direct question – which they won't unless they get suspicious. You know your friend better than me, Cat, but I'm surprised at Pedro just going off like that.'

I curled up on the bed and hugged my knees. It was the only way to stop myself running out into the street to begin a desperate search. 'Pedro's a very private sort of person, keeps things from even those closest to him.' I brushed a tear off my cheek, unable to stop this tell-tale sign of distress that had been building since I heard the news. 'And you saw how we parted last time, Jim! He must still be angry with me. He must've got so furious with the whole situation – and now he's just snapped and run for it.'

'Come now, it can't be that bad,' said Georgie gently, stroking my arm.

'Can't it?' I had not told her about my last visit to see Pedro.

'Whatever did you argue about?'

'Me owning a slave.'

Jenny put her darning aside. 'Me get you into trouble, missis?'

'It's not your fault, Jenny. Pedro blamed me for getting myself into this ridiculous position. As if I didn't feel bad enough already,' I added in a mutter that turned into a sob. Pedro was my family – my only family really – and now he was gone.

Jenny gave me a pitying look. 'Where he go?'

'Your guess is as good as mine. He has no friends here that I know of, little money, and no firm plans.' I scrubbed my wet cheeks, furious at my display of weakness, determined to get a grip on myself. 'The only person I've heard him mention is his old master, Mr Hawkins, and he'll want to steer clear of him. He might be trying to head back to Philadelphia or London, but I can't think why he wouldn't let me know.' I kept quiet about my fears that he would be trying to reach San Domingo – I'd been here long enough to realize that the Jamaican authorities would have no mercy if they caught him doing that.

Jenny nodded, pondering the possibilities silently. She looked at my face for a long moment, biting her bottom lip, weighing up a big decision. 'If he here, me can ask de brotherhood.'

Georgie sat up with a start, her expression one of shock. 'You know how to contact them?'

Jim gave a low whistle and went to the window, leaning against the frame with his hat tipped back on his head.

'Who or what are the brotherhood?' I asked, confused.

Snipping off a length of wool, Jenny threaded her needle, not looking at us.

'I'm sorry, but can someone explain?'

Georgie glanced at Jenny. 'Cat, as you've probably realized, there are two separate worlds in

Jamaica – planters and slaves. I've always heard that the blacks have their own channels to pass news and messages. If Pedro's joined his own people, Jenny's friends will be the ones to ask.'

Jenny continued stitching. 'We go see tatta tomorrow and ask him.'

Georgie passed her the ball of wool that had fallen to the floor. 'We really appreciate you helping us, Jenny. I know it's a risk for you but you can rely on us to keep it secret.'

I didn't like the feeling of being completely at sea in another culture. Something was happening here that I did not understand and I did not want Jenny putting herself in danger. I was responsible for her after all. 'You must tell me, why is it a secret? Why is it dangerous?'

'Buckra try and stop us if dey know about de brotherhood,' explained Jenny calmly.

Georgie continued, 'The planters feel threatened by their slaves, particularly any sign that they are organizing themselves. You have to remember, Cat, the buckras are outnumbered ten to one and would love to crush anything not under their control.'

Jenny snapped off the thread and handed me my mended stockings. 'White men be de skin of dis island, but we be de heart. Dey rip it out if dey could.'

'We all promise not to tell a soul,' I vowed. Georgie and Jim echoed my words.

'Den we go see tatta.' Jenny gave me a conspiratorial smile.

After the depressing confusion surrounding Pedro's whereabouts, Jenny had provided a chink of light. And if I was not mistaken, my slave had just taken control. She wasn't as subservient as she liked me to think – a good thing too as I had vowed that she would soon be free, Billy Shepherd or no Billy Shepherd.

The following day was Sunday. With a cloudless sky and scant breeze, it looked set to be scorching hot. Sharing the front seat of the hired cart with Georgie and Jim, I took refuge under my friend's parasol, uncomfortably aware of the perspiration between my shoulder blades. What would I give for a good old London fog! I mused longingly.

Behind us, Jenny sat on a picnic basket in the back; she seemed not to mind the rattling ride, but hummed softly to herself.

Moses was not working in the garden when we arrived at the plantation. Jenny dipped into her old home and came back out at once.

'De hoe's gone. Tatta must be at de polinck up in de hills. It be where he go to grow tings for us.'

'How far?' Jim asked, wiping his brow.

'Five, six miles.' Jenny nodded to the distant line of the Blue Mountains shimmering in the heat haze.

'Hop in then.' Jim whistled to the horse and our little cavalcade set off down the rutted track.

As we jolted along the road, Jenny began to hum again under her breath, muttering a melodious stream of nonsense that sounded like 'ying de ying de ying'. After a few runs through, the tune was well-rooted in my mind and I joined in with a harmony. Jenny gave me a glance filled with delight at my hitherto hidden musical ability and she started clapping the rhythm. I took up the challenge, drumming on my knees in syncopation.

Then, of course, Georgie and Jim could not resist adding their alto and tenor parts. The song got wilder and more inventive as we developed on the main theme. Jenny grabbed my furled parasol and thumped it on the floor of the cart, making a hollow noise like a big drum. Georgie took out her coin-filled purse and jingled it in time. I grabbed two half coconut cups from our picnic and clip-clopped them together.

'I wish I had my flute,' called Jim, though he was too busy with reins and whip to add to our orchestra.

Our little concert party lasted all the way up the winding track. On several occasions we passed men and women walking towards their polincks, tools on their shoulders. They turned in amazement as they heard us coming, greeting Jenny with laughter and some even joining in for the brief time they stayed in earshot. It hadn't escaped me that, though Sunday was supposedly a day of rest, these slaves were still hard at work on the land. From their broad smiles, however, I guessed that labouring to feed themselves was a welcome change from sweating all week for no reward in another man's field.

The landscape closed in as we climbed higher. Trees crowded the track, many bearing broad green leaves sheltering clumps of the fruit that, thanks to Billy, I now knew to be called bananas. Birds whistled in the bushes, skimming across the clearing with a flash of colourful plumage. Huge butterflies, some as big as dinner plates, fluttered from flower to flower, appearing far too large to my English eyes. Bright blue, rose red, sulphur yellow: they looked like trimmings from all the silk ball gowns I'd seen in Bath, now dancing a cotillion in the shafts of sunlight slanting through the tree canopy. The air was laden with the scent of damp vegetation and rich soil, deliciously cool after the heat of the valley.

We reached Moses' polinck. Jenny told us to stay in the cart and, following a well-trodden footpath, she disappeared into the bush. Georgie, Jim and I sat in silence, no longer wanting to sing without our leader. Jim took out one of those segars I'd seen smoked by local men.

'Ladies?' he asked in a gentlemanlike fashion.

'Go ahead. I don't mind,' I said.

Georgie gave him a nod.

Striking a spark from his tinderbox, he leant back and relaxed, blowing plumes of grey-blue smoke into the air.

I passed the time studying the scenery, distracted by a buzzing that I could not locate. Finally I spotted a little swallow-tailed humming-bird bobbing by the gaudy pink blossoms of a bush, sipping the nectar as bees do at home.

Angry voices interrupted our peaceful idyll. Jenny stamped back to the cart, followed by Moses, his face taut with rage. He was flailing his arms and shouting in his own language.

He turned to Jim. 'Whatever dat fool gal say it all lies. Me not know noting about de brotherhood.'

Jim sat up and glanced at Jenny's furious face. 'Sure you don't,' he said mildly, picking up the reins.

But I wasn't coming all this way to give up so easily, not with Pedro in peril. Jumping down off the cart, I confronted Moses.

'Don't be angry with Jenny, Mr Moses. She's only trying to help.'

Moses was struggling to contain his temper. I'm sure he would've liked to be rude, but years of training compelled him to be polite to a white girl. 'Me not angry,' he ground out through gritted teeth.

'In that case, you are a better actor than I am. You're doing a very good impression of a man in a fury and I wouldn't want you to take it out on Jenny when it's all my fault.'

'Not your fault, Missis Cat,' Jenny broke in, hands on hips. 'It be my idea to come see dis pig-headed old man.' She glared at her father.

'Dat buckra gal been noting but trouble since we first met her,' Moses grumbled under his breath, turning his back.

I tapped him on the shoulder. 'I freely admit it. But the kind of trouble I cause is child's play compared to what's facing my friend Pedro for going on the run. I told you about him – the violinist, remember? He's got enemies here. If he gets caught, he'll be punished – maybe even killed.

I can't sit by and let that happen. Can you live with that on your conscience? I know I can't.'

Moses backed away, holding up his hands as if to ward me off. 'Oh no, missy. Don't you go blaming Moses for your friend's foolishness.'

I stared him down. If blackmailing his better nature was the only way to get his help, I was prepared to do it. Pedro was worth it.

'Oh Lord!' Moses cast his eyes heavenwards, his resistance crumbling. He sighed. 'What you want to know?'

'If he is here in Jamaica. And if not, where he went.'

He rubbed his hands over the crown of his head. 'Just dat?'

'Yes. I'm not asking anyone to run risks for him. I'll look after him when I find him.' I'd already planned to humble myself if necessary and beg Captain Bonaventure to smuggle him to safety.

Moses paused, considering my request. 'You really be friend to black boy?'

'He's my brother – we adopted each other.' I

held his eye, willing him to see the truth.

Moses sighed, his mind finally made up. 'Come with me den, missy.'

I gave Georgie and Jim a triumphant look.

'Me bring her back to my house tonight,' Moses explained to my friends. 'Jenny, look after dem.'

Jenny grinned and jumped up on to the cart. She threw me down my bonnet and a satchel containing a flask of water and some food. 'Now you take care of my missis, Tatta,' she instructed her father.

He gave a curt nod and started off into the bush. Anxious not to lose him, I tripped off in his wake, wondering what on earth I'd let myself in for.

'See you later,' I called over my shoulder.

'Bye, Missis Cat.' Jenny waved farewell until hidden by the trees.

Swallowed up by the forest, I stumbled after Moses as he made his way relentlessly uphill. Having once lived with Creek Indians, I was not as nervous of my surroundings as I would have been only a year ago. With them I had learned to read signs in the wild, even the basics of tracking. If I lost Moses, I was fairly confident that I could navigate my way back to the road. What worried me most was his silence. I had backed him into a corner where he felt obliged to help, and now he was probably having second thoughts. I decided it would be wise to try and make him understand more about what was at stake.

'You'd like Pedro, Moses. He's very special,' I began, 'a gifted musician. I'm not lying when I say he's like a brother to me.'

'Buckra don't have black-skinned brothers.' Moses cut at a low-hanging branch with a machete.

'Maybe the buckra here don't, but it's different where I come from. We're both as good as orphans and so we're the only family we have.'

Moses grunted sceptically.

'The first time I met him, he saved my life. I was hanging upside down from a balloon and he climbed up to rescue me when no one else dared.'

Swish! A vine fell to the ground, severed by Moses' sharp blade.

'And together we persuaded Mr Hawkins to grant him his freedom eighteen months ago.'

'Ha! Now me knows you lying, missy. Massa Hawkins give no one freedom!'

'Not true. He does when he has no choice. It was either that or be transported to Australia to join the penal colony.'

Moses stopped and turned to face me. 'What's dat you say?'

I smiled. These were very fond memories. 'It is a rather amusing story. Do you want me to tell you it in full?'

Moses waited for me to draw level and we walked the rest of the way side by side as I recounted the adventures in London that had resulted in Pedro's manumission.

Moses whistled low when I reached the end. 'Massa Hawkins keep dat very quiet. He not want his slaves to know dat two young'uns bested him.'

'But we did, Moses! So you can see another reason why I don't want Pedro to throw it all away.'

I felt Moses' warm hand rest on my shoulder for a moment.

'You are a good gal, Missy Royal. One of us at heart.'

I gave a little curtsey. 'I take that as the highest compliment, Mr Moses.'

Twilight had begun to eat up the forest, reducing my vision to only a few yards in all directions, but still Moses strode on. The air was very cool. I shivered in my thin cotton dress put on in anticipation of a valley excursion, not a mountain ascent. Tree ferns had taken over from banana plantations. Up this high, the forest grew in stunted, twisted form, trunks shrouded in moss. There was a ghostly silence to the place. I felt as if we'd left normal life down in the lowlands and passed into a world where the rules of the planter society no longer applied.

'Is it much further?' I asked.

Moses shook his head and pointed to a wooden cabin situated at the head of a little gorge. A light twinkled in the window. 'Home of Obeah man.'

'Obeah man?'

'Our wise man. He call on de spirits for us.'

I nodded my head in understanding. The Creek Indians also had their wise leaders, intercessors between the tribe and the ancestors. 'So he's a kind of priest?'

'You can say dat,' Moses conceded, though he seemed to think the term inadequate.

As we approached the hut, I saw that we were not the only visitors that evening. Already seated around the door were a score of black men and women, chatting in a relaxed mood; one couple played an intriguing-looking game with stones on a wooden board.

Moses did not seem pleased to find we were not the only ones there for an audience with the Obeah man. He motioned me to fall back. 'Stay. Me go tell why you are here.'

All too ready to obey his instruction, I lurked in the shadows. During the afternoon I had felt not a moment's concern being on my own with Moses, but now I wondered anxiously what these folk would make of a buckra infiltrating their private world. I had no right to be here.

My guide disappeared into the hut. I shrank

further back into the darkness. Insects whined in my ear and the squeak of the night crickets filled the forest with an incessant noise. I closed my eyes for a moment, seeking a way to control the fear uncoiling in the pit of my stomach. By slowing my breathing, I willed myself to disappear into my surroundings like my Indian friends used to do just prior to the hunt.

I obviously hadn't spent long enough with the Creeks to learn the skill properly, for a woman's cry rent the air. 'A duppy!'

My eyes flicked open and I saw a plump lady turn tail and run back towards the hut. Looking for a private spot to relieve herself, she had instead stumbled upon a pale shape under the trees. I stayed still, hoping that either the others would be too scared to investigate or Moses would return. But that was not to be.

'Where?' asked a tall haystack of a man, grabbing the woman and giving her a shake.

Still too panicked to speak clearly, she pointed a trembling finger right at me.

Five men left the doorway and advanced

towards my position. One picked up a stick and held it in front of him like a sword.

This was not looking good.

'What you want from us, duppy?' shouted the haystack man.

Unclear exactly what a duppy was, I could not be sure if their fear would keep them from harming me long enough to allow time to explain. Not wishing to test them, I decided to retreat and took a few steps further into the undergrowth.

'Duppy, tell us why you no sleep. We help and you no haunt us,' the man continued. So the duppy was some kind of unquiet spirit. He evidently thought it possible to strike a bargain with a ghost – an intriguing idea and one that seemed to promise me a degree of safety.

I remained quiet, trying to look as ethereal as possible, knowing the game was up if I spoke. But I was so intent on keeping my eye on the stick-wielding leader that I had not noticed the boy circling round behind me. Suddenly, an arm appeared out of the darkness, trapping me around the throat.

'It no duppy!' the boy cried exultantly, laughing at the shocked faces of his elders. 'It be a buckra gal!'

I struggled against the throttling pressure on my throat but he had muscles of steel. Pushing me forward, we staggered into plain view of our little audience.

'Let go, boy!' hissed the leader. 'You must be mad touching white gal!'

The boy laughed again. 'She's alone. Me tink no one know you here to spy on us. Is dat right?'

I shook my head, meaning to deny the charge of spying, but he took it to mean that I was on my own.

'Best kill her quick so she carry no tales.' The boy increased his hold on my neck. I was going to black out if I didn't take action. Kicking him in the shins to make him relax his grip, I swivelled round and administered Syd's emergency manoeuvre. The boy doubled over with a howl as I sprang clear, grasping my throat as I gulped air.

'I'm with Moses,' I panted. 'He'll explain.'

The stick-wielding man motioned to his fellows

to watch me as he strode to pound on the door of the hut.

'Moses, you traitor, get out of dere!' he roared. 'What you be doing bringing white gal with you?'

The door opened slowly. A tall figure stood in the doorway – not Moses but the Obeah man, robed in a long cloak trimmed with beads. The muttering crowd fell silent as he swept past them to where I stood. He cast one scornful look at the boy I had felled and then turned to inspect me. I had imagined an elderly wrinkled witch; I saw a warrior in his prime with haughty stare and wide, flat nose. Like Moses, his body was a swirl of tribal markings, giving him a ferocious appearance.

'Er, hello, sir,' I said, dipping in my best curtsey.

His gaze narrowed a fraction. Perhaps he was wondering if I was mocking him, but I assure you, Reader, my gesture of respect was genuine. I'd rarely seen a more awesome sight.

He gave a shallow nod then beckoned me to follow him.

What did that mean? That I was to be dispatched quickly and buried under a tree? That

I'd passed the test? Cautiously following him, I entered the hut and sat down on the low stool he indicated.

Pedro, I thought miserably as I massaged my neck, wherever you are, I hope you're sorry for getting me into this.

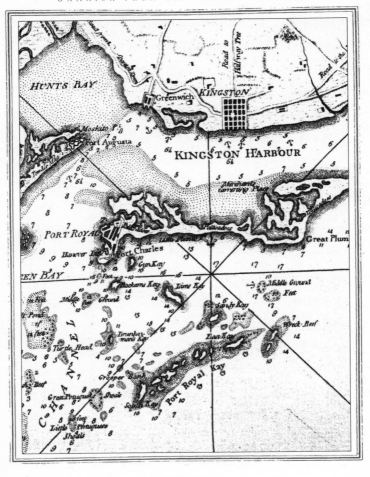

Act III – In which Cat

discovers the colour of her heart…

ACT III

SCENE 1 – OBEAH MAN

Moses remained outside, leaving me alone for my interview with the Obeah man. I would have much preferred to have his company in this strange place, but that was not to be. Silence fell as my host crouched on his haunches and busied himself at the fire. This was built in the middle of the pressed earth floor and surrounded by a ring of stones. The smoke rose up to hang in the rafters and from there found its way out through a vent in the apex of the roof. But the ventilation was hardly adequate: the air in the hut was thick and my eyes were watering. If I stayed here much longer I'd resemble an oak-smoked kipper.

Not wanting to look directly at my host in case he thought me impertinent, I surreptitiously surveyed my surroundings. Through the murk I could make out the interior of his home – a simple affair of wooden pallet bed, stools, and plain shelves suspended by ropes against the walls. Strings of dried plants festooned the room like hundred-year-old Christmas decorations that someone had forgotten to take down. Two chickens, probably destined for the pot bubbling over the fire, clucked sorrowfully in a rough cage by the door.

There was a clatter by the hearth and a black hand thrust itself into my line of vision, holding out a battered tin cup full of a dark liquid. It was thick and sticky and in this half-light reminded me of blood.

'Drink,' ordered the Obeah man. His beaded cloak clicked as it scuffed on the floor.

I took the cup and sniffed. 'What is it?'

He said nothing but pushed my arm up to my mouth. Steeling myself, I took a sip, prepared to spit if it did turn out to be blood. But it was coffee – the thickest, strongest coffee I'd ever tasted, flavoured with sugar. I smiled with relief.

'Thank you.'

The Obeah man poured himself a cup and crouched opposite, perfectly balanced on flat feet, needing no chair to be comfortable. In the silence I could feel him studying me. My pulse pounded in my ears, but this may only have been due to the unfamiliar stimulation of my drink. I was scared but did not feel in particular danger from him, not like from the people outside. If he posed a risk, it was in a deeper way. As the quiet stretched to long minutes, I had the unnerving feeling he was reading me like a book.

'Moses say you have heart of black gal,' he said at last, putting down his empty cup. 'But me tink him wrong.'

This did not seem an auspicious opening but I held my peace. He was not a man with whom one could argue. Or hurry.

'You not part of dis – not black, not buckra.'

He was right, so I nodded slowly.

'Me see someting else me not understand. You are not scared of Obeah.' He waved his arm to the paraphernalia of his craft. 'Why?'

I snagged a braid of dried palm leaves from a bundle on the floor and pulled it into my lap. 'I am an adopted daughter of the Creek Indians.' His eyes widened momentarily before his face resumed its habitual haughty expression. 'They gave me the leaping fish as my spirit guide. My grandmother was the medicine woman of my tribe, the Wind Clan.' I stroked the leaves, filled with fond memories of the little woman's sharp tongue and wisdom.

He laced his long fingers together and studied me again. 'Long years have passed since anyting surprise me. You are a surprise.'

I bowed, feeling secretly rather pleased that I had managed to shock this formidable man.

'So you have heart of red-skinned woman in you.' He chuckled at the image, a most unexpected sound from him. 'Dat explains much, why white colour not fit you. De skin not fit right.'

This seemed about as friendly as he was going to get so it was time to bring matters to a head.

'So, sir, I believe you know why I am here. Will you help me find my friend?'

He nodded. 'Obeah man will ask brothers.'

'Thank you.'

With that, he waved me away with a flick of

his wrist. I backed out, feeling as if I was leaving an audience with royalty, or the Archbishop of Canterbury at the very least. As I closed the door, his dark, low chuckle followed me out into the night.

The crowd was still waiting outside. Moses stepped forward to shield me but no one made any move.

'Let us go,' he said in a rumbling murmur.

I took his offered arm and we beat our retreat back down the mountain. I glanced around once to see all eyes were on us, hostile, calculating stares. I couldn't blame them. I was the trespasser on their secrets. The Obeah man lived in hiding, beyond the laws of the white man. The punishment for consorting with him was doubtless severe. They had little enough as it was and I threatened even that if I betrayed them. Not that I would in a million years, but why should they trust me? What Jenny had called the black heart of Jamaica was not an easy thing to know – I certainly couldn't claim to on the strength of the glimpse I had just gained – but what I did know was that it was beating firm and steady beneath the superficial world down in Kingston. And it pulsed to a tempo that owed more to Africa than to the European settlers who thought they owned the land and all in it.

The Obeah man's network proved impressively efficient. By the end of the following week I knew where Pedro wasn't: not in prison, not in any of the hideouts for runaways, not anywhere that the brotherhood reached.

'Dat mean, missis, he be not on de island,' Jenny said cheerfully as she shook out a clean sheet for our bed.

'Then where is he?' I asked, pinning up Georgie's hair as she sat at the dressing table. We were preparing for an early dinner with our friends from the ensemble before the performance. 'I'm relieved that he's not been caught, but that now leaves me the rest of the world to search.'

'Maybe he not want to be found, missis.' Jenny was quite right, but this was Pedro we were discussing. I couldn't rest until I knew he was safe.

'I can't believe he'd do this to you, Cat,' chipped in Georgie, her eyes flashing with indignation on my behalf. 'He might've been cross with you, but surely he knew you'd worry?'

I dug in the last pin and stepped back to inspect my creation: a thin blue ribbon matching the trimming on Georgie's dress now held her exuberant curls in place. 'Yes, the punishment does seem to exceed my offence, doesn't it?'

My tone sounded overly bright as I tried to hide my hurt from them. I knew I shouldn't doubt Pedro's affection for me – it had been tested enough over the years and never failed before – but his abandonment had hit at my most vulnerable spot. Having been dumped on the steps of Drury Lane, I now had to struggle with the private conviction, learned early on, that somehow this was my due, that no one stayed with me for long.

Georgie, who had known Pedro for so little time, took a more robust view of the situation. 'In that case, Cat, I suggest you forget all about it. If he doesn't want to be found, so be it. We're transferring soon to Antigua, remember. I'm looking forward to showing you around my old home.'

Not wishing to argue, I gave her a smile in the mirror then took my place on the stool so she could have her turn as lady's maid to my unruly red locks. Georgie rummaged through the box of pins and ribbons, preparing her armoury for the challenge of taming my curls into something presentable. Hearing the snap of a sheet being folded behind me, I looked up and met Jenny's eyes. She was studying my reflection, seeking confirmation that I was as committed to Pedro as I had claimed. I grimaced and flicked my eyes to Georgie; Jenny nodded in understanding. She knew I wouldn't give up and I felt sure she had just pledged to support me.

The dinner was held at the Ship Tavern at the unfashionable hour of four. As in London, people were eating later and later these days, taking their cue from high society, known as the Ton, who had abandoned the practice of an early meal. Now only country squires and we working folk ate before six. Thanks to the change in habits, we had to be on stage when most people were just sitting down to dine. This meant that the second or third act was often interrupted by latecomers ambling in after a tardy dinner – an annoyance as much for me in Kingston as it had been for Mr Kemble in Drury Lane.

The compensation was that we had no trouble securing a long table for ourselves in the tavern. Georgie and I, both looking our best in freshly pressed gowns, joined our fellow players who were already seated. We all felt we deserved a treat after a successful run in Kingston, so we'd pooled our wages and ordered up three covers. The dishes came and went quickly. I tasted a little of everything – honeyed chicken, roasted sweet potato, spicy fish, sweet slices of the prickly fruits called pineapples which tasted of paradise. If there was one thing I really enjoyed about Jamaica, that was the Creole cuisine, so much more tempting than the plain diet I had been used to in London.

The noise from our table rose with each course. Theatre folk are not known for their reticence and

I'm afraid we were getting quite boisterous, drunk more on high spirits than the indifferent wine on offer. Jim and his friends were singing snatches of the latest songs doing the rounds of the taverns, Hetty Peabody was laughing raucously at one of Georgie's jokes, and even Mrs Peabody was chuckling at Mr Barker's impression of the governor dancing at a recent ball. It was into this din that Billy Shepherd and Captain Bonaventure wandered. Both were already dressed in evening clothes and showed no surprise to find us all there. I looked away. I'd successfully avoided Billy since our last conversation on the waterfront and saw no reason to change this happy state of affairs. He'd only gloat over my ongoing state of slave ownership. Too late I wished I hadn't put on the cat pendant tonight, but I had succumbed to the temptation to look my finest for the celebration.

On spotting the two gentlemen hovering at the head of the table, Mr Barker jumped up, exchanged a few words, and ushered them over to Mrs Peabody. As her agent, he was always on the alert for any useful connections. I didn't hear what passed but it resulted in them being invited to join our party. Chairs were pulled up to the table. Bonaventure took his next to Georgie, much to Jim's chagrin, I noticed. Billy bumped his over the wooden floor next to mine, clearly delighted to see me. Without pausing for permission, he flopped down beside me and grinned.

'How's things, Cat?' he asked affably, nicking a slice of mango off my plate.

'Fine, thank you,' I replied in clipped tones. 'And you?'

'Gettin' itchy feet. The plantation is sorted out now so I'm thinkin' it's time to move on.'

'Really? How fascinating.' I nibbled a pastry dusted with almonds and sugar, affecting a studied air of indifference.

'I was thinkin' of joinin' you in Antigua. I've 'eard it's a pretty place.'

The last thing I wanted was Billy trailing after me all over the Caribbean. I leant forward confidentially, hoping Georgie wasn't listening.

'Actually, I've heard it's horrid. Full of disease. Snakes and spiders.' I thought hard for a few other things to deter him. 'The hot tip is that there are no business opportunities and the society is very law-abiding: in short, a complete desert for a man of your interests.'

'Oh?' He poured himself a glass of wine. 'Funny 'ow reports differ, ain't it? P'rhaps I should go find out the truth.'

I let the subject lapse. After all, if he took it into his head to go, I couldn't stop him.

'Fine necklace,' he commented, unable to resist mentioning his anonymous gift.

I pretended ignorance. 'Isn't it? Very apt.' I waved my fork expressively in the air. 'In fact, it matches my tattoo.'

He choked on his mouthful. Oh, it felt so good to wrong-foot him again. 'Your what?'

I gave him an enigmatic smile. I was not about to reveal to him the rather bizarre circumstances that left me with a cat tattooed on my shoulder blade.*

---

* But I'll tell you, Reader: it happened one evening in Bermuda when I had a little more to drink than was good for me. I've learned my lesson (see *Cat O'Nine Tails*).

'I'm glad you like the pendant. I was given it by a secret admirer. I rather think the choice of such a sweet animal suggests that the person is a sentimental old biddy, don't you? You know: the kind that has pet cats instead of children.' I frowned thoughtfully and played with the chain. 'Probably overweight and a hypochondriac as well – those animal-loving spinsters very often are.'

Billy looked aghast. 'You think an old lady would send you a gold necklace with emeralds?'

I nodded sagely. 'Yes. I think I can even guess which one she was. She was sitting in the gallery with a white lace cap and steel-rimmed glasses – most attentive to my performance.'

'She wasn't the only one payin' attention,' he muttered, in a foul temper now. He had the choice of owning up to a sentimental taste or letting me labour under the impression that an old lady of Kingston had taken me to her heart. It was fun to watch him suffer.

'Don't you think,' he said after a few moments, 'that it might've been a gift from a gentleman?'

'No, I'm absolutely sure no *gentleman* would've

sent it.' I gave him a look, managing to convey the insult as well as let him know I'd been teasing.

'Humph! You're bammin' me, ain't you?'

I laughed at the puzzled look in his eye.

'I don't normally go sendin' people expensive presents.' He seemed almost hurt by my levity.

My laughter dried up at his serious tone. 'So why give one to me, Billy?'

He rubbed the back of his neck. 'Don't rightly know. I saw it in Sackville Street and took a fancy to it.'

'You didn't steal it off a lady, did you?'

'Nah. I bought it at Thomas Gray's.' He shifted in his seat, embarrassed by the admission of law-abidingness. 'And when you made such a swell job of your debut, I felt you deserved it.'

I nudged him playfully. 'My, Mr Shepherd, you are becoming quite the philanthropist.'

'Philan-what?'

'Lover of humanity, doer of good deeds.'

He looked horrified. 'Nah, not me.'

'I was joking, Billy.' I patted his arm reassuringly. 'I'd say the devil still has you on his books;

you won't be meeting St Peter.'

He relaxed, rocking back in his chair. 'You're probably right, Kitten.'

'Actually, Billy, I wanted to thank you for taking the trouble of coming after me. Even if your motives were as twisted as usual, mixed up with personal profit,' (he grinned), 'I guess somewhere there was a nub of real concern for what became of me.' I held out my hand. 'It seems strange to say it but I suppose that makes us friends – of a sort.'

He took my hand and gave it a firm shake. 'Yeah, of a sort. Until the next round of hostilities.'

'But of course.'

We both laughed at that. Strange how we understood each other so well, despite our mutual antipathy.

'You never did tell me how you came to be here all on your own.' Billy refilled my glass.

'Ah.'

'I'd've thought the Earl of Whatsit would've stuck by you. And Fletcher.'

Seeing it was a good moment to avoid his shrewd eye, I busied myself in watering down my wine. 'They had business back in England.'

'What about the other one – the black boy?'

'Didn't you know they're not letting black freemen on to the islands?'

He took a gulp of his wine. 'Gawd, this is foul stuff. Bonaventure's got a much better cellar . . . So where is 'e?'

'Good question.'

Billy's eyes flicked to my face then slid back to his drink. 'Like that, is it? I wondered what was eatin' at you.'

Surprised that he had noticed my mood, I considered confiding in him. Was there anything for him to gain in this? As far as I knew there was no reward for betraying illegal black entrants to the authorities, and Billy had no personal grudge against Pedro. I needed all the help I could get – even his.

'Pedro's missing, Billy. According to my sources, he's not on Jamaica.'

He cocked an eyebrow. 'Are they good ones? It's a big place, in case you ain't noticed.'

'Excellent ones – better than your network in the Rookeries.'

Billy gave me a sceptical smile but let it pass. 'All right, so he's not here. Wise boy. So where?'

I rested my head on my hand wearily. 'He probably took a ship out.'

'And?'

'He could be going home.'

'But you don't think so?'

'Not really. I think he might've gone to San Domingo.'

'Gawd Almighty! Is 'e mad? The place is in chaos.'

'He wants to fight with Toussaint.'

'Are you sure we're talking about the same 'alf-pint violinist?'

I nodded.

'Ha! They'll make mincemeat of 'im.'

'Billy!'

'Sorry, Cat, but this takes the prize. The little musician fightin' for freedom – 'ow poetic.'

My anger boiled up. 'Billy, if you hadn't forced me to be a slave owner, none of this would've happened!'

'So it's my fault, is it?' A familiar steely glint

returned to Billy's expression.

'Yes. No. Oh, I don't know, Billy. But I don't think he would've gone if he hadn't been furious with me. He believes I betrayed our friendship and running off to Toussaint was a way of getting back at me. But that's not all: he really supports the cause even if he knows he can't be much use to an army.'

'Lord save us from idealists,' Billy said with a hint of bitterness. 'The boy's a fool and you're a fool for carin'.'

'But can you help me find him?'

Billy toyed with his glass for a moment. 'I'll see what I can do, Cat – but no promises.

Having wrung this much out of Billy, I congratulated myself on a good evening's work. With his contacts through the captain, he might be able to discover which ship Pedro had taken and thus give me a hint of his destination port. I was hoping that I could get a message to Pedro – or even go myself – to beg him not to throw his life away. I had no doubt that the slave revolt would soon be forcibly crushed and Pedro simply had to be safe before that happened – I would accept no other outcome.

It took me a while to shake off my worries but nothing focuses the mind quite like the prospect of going on stage. As I shed my street clothes in the dressing room backstage, I felt as if I was putting down my burdens for a short space and putting on only the concerns bound up with the play and performance.

Curtain up for *The Recruiting Officer* and already my mood was much lighter. My character, Sylvia, was a sharp-tongued girl who ignored all obstacles in her way: just the kind of driving spirit that I needed in my plan to bring Pedro back. You couldn't stay gloomy for long in Sylvia's company.

I was well into the swing of the third act when I sensed a disturbance down in the Pit. A party of gentlemen had shouldered their way in – late, of course – and were drawing attention away from the stage with their noise. I risked a sideways look but could see nothing clearly over the glare of the footlights. But the next time I opened my mouth for a speech, someone hissed. Shocked, not clear what I had done to attract an unfavourable reception, I carried on, determined not to let this unsettle me. It got worse: the hissing became booing, and then by my last speech in that scene I was struck between the shoulder blades by a missile. From the crunch underfoot and the wetness dripping down my neck, I realized I'd been hit by an egg.

A rotten egg.

A wave of shame and anger swept through me. I'd played Sylvia several times to great applause so why had part of the audience turned against me this time? From their expressions I could tell that the other actors were as perplexed as I by the reaction, though none wanted to risk getting too close to me as the missiles continued to fly. Every new speech became a torture, each new scene a nightmare. I wanted to run and hide but my gut told me to stay and brazen it out like a professional. And though I stayed, my dreams of theatrical success collapsed around me like a badly built set.

I broke ranks to avoid the curtain call, hiding in the back row near the wings. I remained for one company bow only, then ran for the dressing room.

'Everyting all right, missis?' Jenny asked calmly as I entered. She had been backstage all evening and missed the rumpus out front.

'No, it isn't. I was hissed, Jenny. Me, hissed!' I ripped a seam as I hauled my arms out of the dress.

'Easy now.' Jenny undid the laces to loosen the bodice. 'Do not worry: dere is always tomorrow.'

'But I didn't do anything wrong! It was the same as usual until some gentlemen came in late, then the trouble started.'

'Maybe dey not like you.' Jenny shrugged, not understanding how public appreciation was the very lifeblood of an actress. Not to be liked was fatal to a career.

Georgie burst in and gathered me into a hug. 'You poor darling! What was that all about?'

'I don't know. Did I make a mistake? Insult someone somehow?' I sent my hairpins flying all over the floor as I shook out my braids. My face looked parchment white in the mirror.

Mrs Peabody bustled into the dressing room. I groaned. That was all I needed.

'Mr Garrick would never have put up with a display like that! Most unmannerly behaviour from the gentlemen of Kingston,' she snapped to the room at large before bearing down on me. 'Who have you upset, Miss Royal?'

'No one, as far as I know.' There had been no inkling that my visit to the Obeah man had leaked out, so what other cause could there be for displeasure? I'd done little but rehearse and act since coming ashore.

'Delivery for Missy Royal,' called the porter over the buzz of speculation in the dressing room.

Perhaps the evening was looking up? I could do with the consolation of another gift. Wrapping my robe around me, I went to the door to receive my parcel. It was a beautiful box tied with a bow.

'That's more like it!' said Georgie, appearing at my shoulder. 'See, not everyone was against you this evening. Go on, open it.'

With a smile, I plucked on the long end of the bow and let the ribbon fall to the floor. Levering off the lid, I peered inside – and promptly dropped the box.

'Disgusting!' Georgie expressed my thoughts exactly. My beautiful box contained fresh horse manure. She swept the box up and shoved it into the arms of the porter. 'Take this away at once.'

I'd felt humiliated on stage, but now I was just plain furious. I snatched up the card that had fallen to the floor with the bow.

With fond memories from our time in London.
Kingston Hawkins.

I might've guessed. For the first time since Pedro had run away, I was glad my friend was far from me. I hadn't done anything wrong tonight: the fault lay over a year ago when I had forced Hawkins to free Pedro. Now the slave master was out for revenge.

SCENE 2 – OLD MASTER

Georgie was all for complaining to the city authorities about Hawkins' behaviour but I soon disabused her of the notion.

'A practical joke, that's all,' I said dismissively. 'They'll laugh at you for reading any more into it than that.'

Hetty sponged the back of my costume, trying to remove the egg stain. 'I think it's disgraceful. He should be run out of town.' She too had rallied to my side, not least because the attack had chiefly fallen on her domain of the wardrobe.

'I rather think that's his plan for me.'

'Well, I for one hope that's the last we'll hear of it,' Mrs Peabody said primly. 'I can't have my ensemble embroiled in disputes with the local gentry.'

'Hardly a dispute, Mama,' Hetty countered. 'Cat did not provoke him; he attacked her.'

News of the insulting present had filtered

through to the men's dressing room. When Georgie and I emerged, we were besieged with offers to escort us home to our door. We accepted Jim's arm and quickly left the building, Jenny walking with us. Two of my fellow actors and three of the stage crew fell in behind, self-appointed bodyguards. It was as well that they did because I could see Hawkins was waiting for me at the end of the alley, accompanied by a little gathering of his acquaintances.

'What should we do?' asked Jim, glancing at our back-up to weigh our chances.

'Ignore him if we can,' I replied. I was still wound up tight with fury. There was nothing to be ashamed of in my dealings with Hawkins: I'd beat him fair and square. He was just a sore loser. I would sail past him with my head held high.

'Don't worry, Jim, we're with you,' murmured Bert, the burly stage manager.

'Georgie, perhaps you'd better stay back with Jenny,' I suggested. I'd survived many a street fight but I doubted that she would know what to do if it came to that.

She clasped her reticule firmly, knuckles white. 'No, Cat, we'll stay with you. I wanted adventure, remember?'

Jenny kept her head down but showed no sign of wishing to retreat either.

Trying to lead by example, I marched towards my reception committee, striking up an airy conversation about fashion with Georgie, for all the world as if there weren't ten bruisers waiting for us.

'When I was in Paris, they were wearing sleeves long,' I trilled, quite unlike my normal self. 'With lace. Lots of it.'

'Oh, how fascinating,' Georgie gushed nervously. 'And did they favour plain or pattern silk?'

I was not given a chance to answer that all-important question for Mr Hawkins stepped forward to intercept us. He was an imposing man of forty or so, broad-shouldered, dark-haired and finely dressed, his cravat a testimony to the skills of his valet. Under one arm, he clasped a cane – not the same sword stick that had been tossed into the Thames on our last encounter, but I would not have been surprised to discover it too concealed a weapon. He was like that: a respectable exterior hiding a cruel centre. I gave him the cut direct, eyes sweeping over him as if he wasn't there. But before I could pass, his hand snagged my arm.

'Miss Royal, ain't it? Welcome to Jamaica.' Hawkins didn't remove his hat as would have been polite on addressing a lady, and neither did he remove his hand.

'Mr Hawkins,' I said curtly, 'please let go of me.'

He didn't. 'Got my boy with you?' No beating about the bush with him.

'What boy would that be, Mr Hawkins?' I wrinkled my nose as if he bore the stink of the horse manure he had so kindly thought to send me. 'I don't believe I am acquainted with anyone you *own*.'

His grip tightened. 'Pedro. He's here, ain't he? Never far from you so they tell me.'

Jim gave me a look asking if he should intervene. I shook my head slightly.

'My friend Mr Pedro Amakye is otherwise engaged, sir, and happily beyond your reach. Now please, if you don't mind, I wish to go home.'

'Not yet. I have a few things to say to you, missy.'

'But there is nothing I wish to hear from you. Goodnight.'

'The lady's made herself very clear,' added Jim. 'Good evening, sir.'

A tall man in a maroon waistcoat moved to stand beside Hawkins.

'And my friend's said he's got something he wants to say, so I suggest you stand still, Yankee.'

In a swift move, Bert lunged and grabbed Hawkins' wrist to twist it off my arm. 'And you heard us say "get lost". Miss Cat don't have to listen to no one.'

My whole body was tense, ready for flight. I could see the signs: this confrontation had all the hallmarks of a conversation about to descend into fisticuffs. The men were spoiling for it: you could tell from the clenched fists and challenging glares – Hawkins' nine to my escort of six. And if the local militia was called in to break it up, I could imagine whose side they would take: locals against travelling players – no contest.

I decided to try and redirect Hawkins' ire towards me and away from my protectors. Far better to leave this as an exchange of insults than blows.

I stepped between Hawkins and Jim. 'As you are so fond of messages, Mr Hawkins, maybe you could write me a note?' I said sweetly, giving him my most cloying smile. 'You might find it helpful to put things down on paper, particularly when it appears you have much to get off your chest.'

My supporters chuckled. 'Good idea,' grinned Bert, letting go of Hawkins and giving him a little shove out of my path. 'That's settled that then.'

'No, it damn well ain't settled!' growled Hawkins, brandishing his cane at Bert. 'You'll pay dearly for touching me, you scum!' His men jostled behind him, each trying to gain a good position for the approaching brawl. So much for redirection: I'd only managed to inflame them. Georgie shrank against Jim, Jenny practically clinging to her skirts.

Just as I thought the touchpaper to this particular explosion was about to be lit, a newcomer strolled into the alley, whistling a tune from the play. He touched his hat lazily to Hawkins.

'Evening, Hawkins.' Billy then turned to me with a fiendish smile. 'Miss Royal.' He bowed.

'Mr Shepherd.' I bobbed a curtsey. Did he realize how close this was to an all-out fight? Of course he did: that was why he looked so amused.

'I see you've been renewing old acquaintances,' he remarked, gesturing towards Hawkins.

'Unfortunately, yes.'

'Shepherd, I suggest you tell your little hoyden to get the hell out of Jamaica,' Hawkins said through clenched teeth.

Billy laughed. 'If you are under the impression that Miss Royal will do anything I say then I suggest you think again. She has spent the last ten years defying me and become very skilled at it.'

'If you don't make her leave, then I will.' Hawkins tapped his cane on the palm of his hand.

Billy turned towards him, occupying the ground in between the two parties. 'I think, Hawkins, we discussed this before. I told you then no one harms her without my say-so.'

Hawkins swung his cane between finger and

thumb in a gesture reminiscent of a cat flicking an angry tail. 'That was then. We were on your territory, if memory serves; now you're on mine and I will not let that slave-loving bit of dirt contaminate my town.'

'Contaminate!' I burst out. 'I'm not the one sending boxes of horse dung around town, you snivelling excuse for a gentleman!'

Billy scratched his chin. 'Like that, is it? I don't suppose, Hawkins, that it's a good time to remind you of a mortgage held over certain properties?'

Hawkins glanced nervously at his companions. 'That has nothing to do with it.'

'But I only like doing business with men I can trust. And I'd be seriously displeased if something happened to my little ray of sunshine here. I grant you she's wrong-headed about most things but I find her amusing. I wouldn't want to have my pleasures cut short. Do you understand?'

A pulse ticked at the corner of Hawkins' eye, betraying his fury. 'I understand. But I can't be answerable for everything that happens to her while she's here. She has a talent for making enemies.'

'Oh, don't I know it.' Billy took the cane from Hawkins' rigid fingers and slipped out the knife concealed in the handle. 'Good bit of work that.' He tossed it in the air and caught it deftly. 'If something does happen, if she breaks so much as a fingernail, and the trail leads to your door, you'd better hope you're not home when I come calling. Goodnight.' He thrust the cane back into Hawkins' arms and strode off, tipping his hat to Georgie and me.

With Billy's departure, all the fight seemed to have gone out of the remaining men. With a murderous look in my direction, Hawkins stalked away, barking at his party to follow.

Jim patted my hand. 'Good to see you've got powerful friends, Cat.'

I grimaced. 'I wouldn't call him that exactly. He's more like the lion driving the vultures from his kill. He's very territorial about me – we grew up together,' I added, by way of explanation.

The next few days of the run were nerve-racking. I feared a repeat of the humiliation at the hands of a hostile crowd, adding ten-fold to my stage fright before the curtain rose. Bert had promised to warn me if he spotted Hawkins in the audience again, but to my great relief the slave master did not return. I couldn't wait for the end of our engagements in Jamaica and the transfer to a new island.

Friday morning's rehearsal was interrupted by the arrival of a note carried by one of Captain Bonaventure's crew, a rascal who rejoiced under the nickname of Hog for obvious reasons when you saw his flat nose. It looked like someone had sat on his face, and perhaps they had: it was a rough life on the *Medici*.

'Mademoiselle,' he said in French, 'I'm to wait for an answer.'

I stepped aside from the hurly-burly on stage to break the seal. The writing was a scrawl but just about legible.

My dear Moggy,

I have no doubt that you will be amazed to hear that I've been working hard on your behalf. Thanks to my great talent for greasing the right palms, I found out that your friend shipped out on a fishing boat run by Jamaican smugglers. They're running guns and men to the rebels on San Domingo, so it looks like your guess was correct and your friend intended to add his ha'penny worth to the fight. Bad news is that the boat is captained by a rogue called Tivern. He is as like to chuck Blackie overboard as deliver him safely. If your friend entrusted him with a message for you, don't hold your breath: you'll never get it.

Let me know by return what you want to do now.

Ever your old friend,

Billy

P.S. Don't say I never do anything for you. I'll come by to collect my reward.

Reward? I didn't like the sound of that, but I had no time to worry about it now. The news about Pedro was worse than I had imagined: in his desperation to do something, Pedro had fallen in with a band of piratical smugglers. But what could I do to save him now? He was long gone – either over the side or well on his way to San Domingo.

No, he wasn't dead – I refused to consider that possibility, not till I knew for certain.

I read the message through again, trying to make up my mind. Was it my responsibility to rescue Pedro from himself? This wasn't like the occasion in London when he had been seized by his old master, Hawkins: then he had been blameless. He had needed rescuing. This time he'd headed off on his grand quest without so much as a goodbye. He'd not even honoured his promise to me! If he lived to regret his choice, then so be it: he'd made his bed and now had to lie in it. He couldn't expect me to abandon my chance to succeed as an actress by going on some hopeless errand in pursuit. I'd made friends and enjoyed my first success so I had no desire to leave the camaraderie of the troupe behind.

Cursing Pedro under my breath, I pushed open the stage door and strode towards the parade ground, Hog trailing behind still hoping for a reply. I needed some space, some fresh air, to think – and to cool down. The bond between Pedro and me had been stretched to the limit by his flight but still it tugged on my heart. My bitter thoughts were really only a vent for emotions: I didn't mean them. He infuriated me – but he was still my family, my brother. After all, I reminded myself, he might have tried to get a message to me – smugglers did not make the most reliable go-betweens; I might be blaming him for no reason. As for what I would do next, I didn't really have a choice where he was concerned. If there was the slightest chance I could help him, I would take it.

Briefly I imagined heading back to Philadelphia and explaining to Lizzie and Johnny that I had let Pedro go to San Domingo without even trying to find out if he really knew what he was doing. No, I couldn't see myself having that conversation.

I then pictured finding a boat to take me to San Domingo, hunting down Tivern and discovering Pedro's whereabouts. Unpleasant though the prospect was, I could imagine myself doing just that. It appeared that I was not going to visit the delights of Antigua after all.

Turning to Hog, I passed on my message:

'Please convey my thanks to Mr Shepherd and ask him if he can secure a passage for me to San Domingo on the first available ship.'

Hog touched the peak of his cap in acknowledgement. 'He said you'd say that, mademoiselle.' He gave me a gap-toothed grin and sauntered off in the direction of the *Medici*.

I hadn't realized I was so predictable. But then Billy and I had always understood each other better than other folk. Now all that remained was the problem of breaking the news to Mrs Peabody – her new leading lady was about to duck out of her contract.

'No. Absolutely not. I will not hear of it!' Mrs Peabody was in full flight and had been for the last five minutes. She had scarcely listened to my arguments and pleas, but instead occupied herself in finding as many ways of saying 'no' as she could dream up. 'You are held by your contract and I will not release you. This running after Pedro is a foolish errand and you know it. Your reputation will be ruined if the island audiences discover you've gone off on your own to search for a former slave. And the Peabody Theatrical Ensemble will suffer without you. You must be mad even to contemplate such a step.'

Hetty, standing behind her mother, nodded furiously, no doubt scared stiff that my departure would thrust her back on stage.

'I take it that you are refusing to let me go?' I glanced at the other members of the cast gathered around us. As I expected, I found scant support among them. Jim, Douglas the trumpeter and the other musicians were huddled together in a group around the music stands, frowning; Bert the stage manager had his arms crossed, his expression grim. My fellow actors were looking horror-struck as they anticipated the changes my departure would entail. I knew that I was putting them all to great inconvenience by my untimely decision to bow out. 'Even if I promise to rejoin you at the earliest opportunity?'

Mrs Peabody gave a curt shake of her head. 'Even so.'

'Then I will have to leave without your

permission, Mrs Peabody. I apologize for letting you all down, but my first loyalty is to my friend.'

'But, Cat, it's too dangerous!' Georgie exclaimed, laying her hand on my arm.

I shrugged. 'I'm no stranger to taking risks. I truly am sorry to abandon you all like this,' I said, turning to the assembled company, 'but I hope you'll forgive me.'

'I will pursue you for breach of contract, Miss Royal,' thundered Mrs Peabody.

I took a deep breath. I'd feared as much. 'It is your right. If I do not rejoin you on the tour, I can be reached care of the Duke of Avon in London.'

'If you go, there is no coming back, Miss Royal. I'll make it my business to ensure that you never find employment on the stage again! I am not without friends both here and in London.'

That was going too far. I stepped closer and lowered my voice so it reached her ears alone. 'If you do stoop to such a low revenge, Mrs Peabody, I will make sure it is known that you were more familiar with the wardrobe than the stage when at Drury Lane.'

Her face blanched. 'What do you mean by that?'

'I think you know.' It wasn't in my nature to threaten another but she was forcing me to it. And I had long since guessed that she had never trod the boards herself. I would have to earn my living one day and it was not fair for her to spoil my best chance.

She pressed her lips together, holding her temper barely in check. My own was not in a safe condition either. I felt rather like a coachman trying to restrain a team of six fresh post horses from bolting down the rutted road. If either of us let go of the reins, we would say things we would later regret. A true coach smash of a row.

I silently counted to ten. 'Mrs Peabody, I really am sorry but I have no choice in this matter.' I looked round the circle of familiar faces; they had started to become a kind of family for me. I knew I fitted in here. I hadn't felt that way since leaving Drury Lane; it was a real wrench to give it all up. 'I like being part of this troupe, Mrs Peabody, but I love Pedro like a brother and he must come first. Please try and understand that.'

'I should have you locked up in an asylum, Miss Royal.' Mrs Peabody slapped her script closed, but I thought I saw a brief glimmer of sympathy in her eyes and her threat did not sound very convincing.

'Perhaps you should have,' I agreed. 'I don't want to be doing this, really I don't. I'd much rather come to Antigua.'

'But your heart won't let you.' She bit her bottom lip and put her hand to her forehead wearily. 'I do understand, I suppose.' Businesslike again, she threw her prompt copy on to a box. 'We can't do *As You Like It* without you. We'll have to rehearse *Romeo and Juliet*. Miss Atkins, get learning your part!' She waved the actors away with an irritable flick of her wrist. I thought I too had been dismissed but Mrs Peabody now swung back to me. 'The Duke of Avon to whom you referred, Miss Royal . . .'

'Yes?'

'What is your connection to him?'

'He owes me one.' After all, Reader, the duke had once tried to see me hanged, had been saved from prison thanks to my bright idea to get his wife to sing, and his nephew had had me press-ganged.

'Then I suggest you warn him that I will be applying to him for compensation if you are unable to pay up. Pin money to him, no doubt, but to keep this ensemble afloat I need every penny.'

'I'm sure he will be only too pleased to oblige, Mrs Peabody. His son, the Earl of Arden, is one of Pedro's closest friends.'

From the hum of satisfaction at this announcement, Mrs Peabody was clearly impressed by my aristocratic connections. I could see that her mind was jumping ahead to deal with the new situation and she rapidly formulated a plan to survive my defection. A new play and money from a duke: that should do the trick. I admired her spirit: it wasn't easy to last as a theatrical manager and she was doing an excellent job of protecting the interests of her own people. Even if her acting past was a fabrication, she deserved to be rewarded with success.

'I hope the rest of the tour goes well,' I said, with genuine regret that I would not share in it.

'Thank you. I wish you luck, Miss Royal. You will need it.' She half-turned to go, but then paused, weighing her words. 'Actually, if you do have a chance to rejoin us, I hope you will take it. After Antigua we head for Barbados. We'll stay there until the end of August, hoping to return to Philadelphia before the start of the hurricane season.'

I nodded. 'Thank you. I hope that I can settle this matter speedily. I would like nothing better than to act with your troupe again.'

'We'll see.' She bent towards me, her tone confidential. 'If you return to London, please give my regards to Mrs Reid. Tell her Dotty Peabody sends her love.'

I laughed softly as she swept off to begin the preparations for the new production. Mrs Reid, wardrobe mistress at Drury Lane, an intimate of Mrs Peabody: my guess as to her past had been spot on.

After my final performance in *The Recruiting Officer*, I retired to our chamber to pack my few belongings, not feeling I deserved to participate in the cast party marking the end of our Kingston stay. The troupe was sailing on Monday and I still had no idea how exactly I was to find a smuggler named Tivern somewhere on the seas between here and San Domingo, nor how I was to persuade him to tell me what he had done with Pedro. There was also the problem of Jenny. I couldn't leave her behind after promising to secure her freedom, but neither did I feel it my place to take her into danger. I toyed with the idea of asking Georgie to look after her, but that seemed a shabby way of dealing with them both, offloading the problem rather than facing up to my responsibilities.

In the end it was Jenny who settled the matter. She returned to the chamber shortly after me and placed her small bag next to my valise.

'When do we leave, missis?'

I felt a lump in my throat at her display of loyalty. 'Jenny, you don't have to come with me.'

'Me know. You kind missis, not want make Jenny sad. But me want to help you. Missis Georgie go to Antigua. Who look after Missis Cat now?'

The prospect of having Jenny along to keep me company was very tempting, but still . . .

'You know what I'm going to do, don't you?'

'Yes, missis. Go on fool errand to find your friend.' She gave me a big grin. 'Me like dat about you.'

I gave a half-laugh, half-groan. 'Yes, it is a fool's errand and, to be honest with you, I'd prefer not to face it alone. If you're sure you want to come, then take the day off tomorrow to say goodbye to Moses. Tell him I promise I'll do my utmost to bring you back in one piece.'

She clapped her hands. 'Good. Me thought you make more fuss about Jenny coming.'

'You know me so well already, Jenny? I would have, but I'm too relieved to protest.'

When Georgie returned from the party, looking tired but happy, she tried to talk me out of going after Pedro but her heart wasn't in it: she knew I'd made up my mind.

She watched me in the mirror as I played maid once more, taking out her hairpins. 'I'll miss you, Cat. We've only been together for a short time but already I feel as if I've known you forever. When you catch up with Pedro, tell him I'm furious that he's lured you away like this.'

'I'll tell him – after I've bent his ear on my own behalf.'

Leaning forward, she rummaged in a little sandalwood jewellery box on the table and took out a coral bracelet. 'Here, have this with my love.'

I had nothing to give in return. I kissed her on the cheek and slid the bracelet on my wrist, admiring the warm apricot colour of the beads against the pale skin of my arm. 'Thank you, Georgie: it's lovely. I've had so few things to call my own that with this and my necklace I'm beginning to feel quite the proper lady.'

I paused. 'Georgie, one word of advice before we part: if you're supping with the devil, use a long spoon.'

She laughed at my serious tone. 'And what is that supposed to mean?'

'Keep your distance from Captain Bonaventure. He's a scoundrel.'

Georgie blushed prettily. 'All the most interesting

men are. I could say the same to you about your old friend Billy Shepherd. But don't worry, Cat, I've got his measure. He's not the man to turn my head.' She bent a little closer. 'I've been dying to tell you: Jim has asked permission to court me.'

How could I have been so blind? All the juicy gossip was happening right beneath my nose and I hadn't noticed, thanks to my preoccupation with Pedro. 'Georgie, that's wonderful!' I exclaimed. 'When did this happen?'

'That afternoon when you went off with Moses. We spent a lot of time together.'

I grinned. 'Of course you did. I'm so pleased. I knew someone would snap you up before too long.'

'He says his folks are quite liberal-minded about . . . well, you know . . . my unfortunate ancestry.'

Hackles raised by that comment, it was all I could do not to growl like an irate watchdog. 'I hope he didn't say any such thing! He doesn't deserve you if he did.'

'He didn't say it – I did. I'm a realist, you know – not like you with your fanciful notions of equality.' She patted my arm affectionately.

'Do you feel any less my equal then just because you have mixed blood and I, as far as I know, am all white?' My question was a challenge. I put my chin on her shoulder so she could see us side by side in the mirror, green eyes looking into brown.

She wrinkled her nose. 'Now you come to mention it, no.'

I straightened up. 'And do you think you are inferior to Jim?'

Her smile took on a dreamy quality. 'He is rather wonderful, but no, I don't. He makes me feel like a princess.'

'Then I don't see why my notions, as you call them, should be fanciful.' I began tidying up the dressing table.

'But, Cat, our world doesn't work that way. You only have to look out the window to see that.'

'It's about time it did work my way then.'

Georgie got up and pulled me into a hug. 'That's what I love about you, Cat Royal, always spoiling to take on all comers, setting the world to rights. Don't you ever give up!'

SCENE 3 – YOUR SERVANT, SIR

The following morning my offer to help strike the set with the rest of the troupe was politely turned down. By my own choice, I had cut myself off from them and this was the result. Never one to duck the consequences of my own choices, I tried to accept this with good humour but it was hard, particularly when I watched Georgie set out on Jim's arm, both laughing and chatting happily.

Jenny had left for the plantation early: it was a long walk to her father's hut on Billy's estate and she wanted to be back before nightfall. This left me on my own in Kingston for the first time. I took stock of my resources. I had a reasonable sum – enough to buy passage to San Domingo for two, I guessed, but not much beyond that. Shoving the money deep into my pocket, I promised myself that I would only worry about the next step when and if I discovered Pedro. The biggest difficulty would be finding a vessel heading in the right direction. From what the customs official had said, relations between the two countries were more or less severed due to the turmoil in San Domingo. It would be tricky getting a captain to admit he was sailing there and even Billy seemed not to have suceeded as he'd sent no word that he'd found me passage.

My thoughts touched briefly on the *Medici*. Would Captain Bonaventure go out of his way to help me? Probably not. What if Billy interceded for me? Maybe. But that meant asking him for yet another favour and I already owed him for ferreting out the information about the smugglers. The one hard learned rule in my life is *never be in debt to Billy Shepherd* and it looked as if I was about to break it again.

Deciding I might as well not put off this unpleasant task any longer, I directed my steps to the harbourside. The glare of the sun on the water was dazzling and I soon regretted not carrying my parasol. According to Georgie, the *Medici* was now moored out in the bay and I would need a boatman to take me out if I was to make my request. Being much shorter than everyone else and the only unaccompanied white female in sight, I felt conspicuous mingling with the sailors and stevedores who swarmed all over the harbour, but fortunately no one showed any interest in my presence. I skirted round the edge of a crowd gathered in a dusty market place. I was almost through when I glimpsed what they had come to buy: a line of wretched-looking slaves chained close to an auctioneer's block. My legs wanted to run away as fast as I could but I forced myself to watch. I felt I owed it to those who suffered, people like Pedro, Jenny and Moses; I had to know the worst.

There was nothing particularly special about the auction: no cracking whips or demonic buyers frothing at the mouth. The crowd looked little different from what one would expect to see at Smithfield for a cattle market. A ring of smartly dressed men stood close to the salesman. Most were decently but not splendidly attired, so I guessed these were overseers rather than the planters themselves. Probably few slave owners sullied themselves with the dirty business of standing in the heat and dust to buy slaves. One man stood out as an exception: I recognized Mr Hawkins near the front. I remembered him telling me that he prided himself on his ability to spot a good worker on the block; this was one part of his duties he had not delegated. Knowing the delight he took in humiliating others, he probably enjoyed it too much to give up.

The auctioneer flourished his arm towards the platform. He was dressed in black and had a neat white stock at his throat, every inch the efficient businessman. 'Gentlemen, I bring you the next salt-water negro up for sale: a fine boy only a little worn due to excessive sea-sickness on the passage from Africa. Given decent food for a few days, he'll be as fit as a fiddle and work like a horse.'

An emaciated boy of my own age was prodded on to the block. He stood straight and proud, even though his limbs were stick-thin, barely adequate to hold him up. Sea-sickness all my eye! The boy had been starved. He ignored the auctioneer, betraying no emotion as his finer points – good teeth, wide-set shoulders – were displayed to the onlookers. I was riveted to my spot at the edge of the crowd, watching him dig deep into a stoic endurance that I could barely imagine.

'Thirty pounds. Any advance on thirty?' asked the auctioneer. 'Mr Hawkins, are you in the market for a boy today?'

Hawkins shook his head. 'No, sir. I've boys enough at present.'

That was a relief.

'Very well. Thirty it is.'

This was obscene. I wanted to scream 'Stop!', outbid the last buyer and set every slave free, but the brutal truth was that I didn't have the money for even one. Instead I had to watch the boy's future being sold.

'Going once, going twice.' The salesman slapped down his gavel on a wooden block on the trestle table beside him. 'Sold to Mr Beamish. A bargain for you, sir.'

The boy was led away while another took his place on the block and the whole hateful process began once more. I'd seen enough. My skin was crawling and I felt nauseous. I needed a breath of air, away from this press. I wanted to cleanse myself of the stench of the trade in human flesh but I doubted there was anywhere in Jamaica one could be free of it.

Only fifty yards from the block, people went about their business as normal, oblivious to the life-shattering events a stone's throw away. I slowly made my way through the crowds to the pier. I searched faces, trying to understand why they saw nothing bad about a market in human lives. Did the white population really think that people like Jenny and Pedro were less than them? It seemed so obvious to me that this was wrong; didn't they see it too?

'Wanting to go out on de water, missy?'

Jolted from my thoughts, I turned to find myself addressed by a stocky boatman wearing a red striped neckerchief. Another man, taller and thinner, stood silently at his shoulder. Both were smiling, displaying fine white teeth, but something was not right – the smiles did not reach their eyes.

'Um, yes, I suppose.' My voice sounded feeble.

'Maybe later.' I took a step back but stopped as I was now on the edge of the pier.

'We take you now.'

'Thank you, but really I have to be going.'

'Yes, we take you. Massa says.'

'Who? Mr Shepherd?' I glanced around, hoping to see Billy lounging somewhere close by.

The men just smiled, not moving from my path, prepared to wait me out.

'Your offer is very kind, but I've changed my mind about going on the water this morning. Good day to you both.'

Still they did not move.

'Would you be so kind as to step aside so I can pass?' I fixed my eye on the smaller man, hoping to intimidate him into shifting – not very likely when you're my height and everyone towers over you.

His smile if anything grew broader.

'You're not going to move, are you?'

He shook his head.

'You're going to stand there until I agree to go with you?'

He nodded.

'Then tell me who your master is: Captain Bonaventure?'

While trying to delay them with my questions, I scanned the people on the pier, hoping to find an ally. Would they come to my rescue if I made a bolt for it? Ducking between the tall one's legs seemed my best bet.

I put my hands on my hips, glaring at them as if they were two naughty schoolboys. 'You do know it's impolite not to answer a lady's questions, don't you?'

Over to my right I thought I saw one of Bonaventure's crew. It was an indication of how desperate my plight was when one of the rascals that manned the *Medici* seemed a safe port in a storm. But to reach him, I needed a distraction. Clasping my hands together in pretended exasperation, I slipped the coral bracelet off my wrist. 'I've never met such a quiet pair. If I hadn't heard one of you speak, I'd swear you were mutes.' I flourished my hand expressively, casting the bangle to the pier's boards. 'Oh no! I've dropped my bracelet. Anyone see where it went?'

Obediently, the two men looked at their feet, the bracelet clearly in sight.

'Me get it for you, missy,' the stocky one said, stooping to retrieve it.

Here was my chance. I dived between the spread legs of the tall one, catching them both unawares. He snatched between his knees but came away with nothing. I was already on my feet and running, congratulating myself on my cunning. Prematurely. Suddenly my legs flew from under me and I hit the planks hard, tumbling to land on my chin with a crack. Before I had regained my full senses, a hand gripped my shoulder and pulled me up.

'I do apologize, missy, somehow you seem to have tripped over my cane. I can't imagine how that happened. Allow me to make sure you are not injured.'

The grip did not ease but I found myself turned for inspection by Kingston Hawkins.

'My, my! Miss Royal. What a coincidence.' I glared, fully aware that he had known it was me all along. He pressed his free hand to my forehead. 'I do believe you've banged your head and are feeling faint. Allow me to escort you to my carriage until you recover.'

I don't know about my head, but my chin had certainly taken a knock. I wiped my hand across it and came away with a smear of blood.

'And you're bleeding! Bruised too, probably. How distressing. We must fetch a doctor to look at you.'

'That's quite unnecessary, sir,' I said, still feeling shaken by my nosedive.

Our little scene was attracting some attention from bystanders. Hawkins raised his voice so they could hear our exchange.

'No, no, I insist. You are a guest in my country and I must make sure you are well looked after. Jason, carry Miss Royal to my carriage.'

The stocky slave I'd mistaken for a boatman picked me up before I had a chance to protest.

'Put me down!' I beat on his shoulder ineffectually. A big hand shifted to press my face into his shirt-front, muffling my objections.

Hawkins turned to our audience. 'Not to worry, the lady is a little dazed is all.'

The bystanders returned to their tasks of fishing and net-mending. Clearly, they felt it was quite in order for the only white man in sight to care for a white girl after an accident and they were not about to interfere.

The burly Jason held me tight as he carried me to the carriage. Dropping me on to the padded seat, he quickly retreated. I tried to follow him out the door but found my way blocked by Hawkins.

'Sit down,' he growled, all pretence at politeness gone. He jabbed my shoulder with his cane, forcing me back on to the cushions. 'You should've left when you had the chance.'

I curled up in a corner, minimizing myself as a target. My jaw was aching, but by far and away the greatest worry was his intentions towards me. In London I had baited him in front of the Bow Street Magistrate and forced him to free Pedro – a humiliation he had not forgotten. Bravado was my only option: cowering with fright would not work with Hawkins.

'Strangely enough, sir, I was trying to find a ship out when your men intercepted me. If you would just set me down, I'll do my best to accomplish that before the end of the day.'

His smile stretched, thin and mean. Tossing aside his hat, he ran a hand negligently through his greying dark hair, self-congratulation oozing from every pore. 'Too late for that, I'm afraid, Miss Royal. I've looked forward to having this opportunity to teach you a lesson. Such a shame Pedro ain't here to share it.'

That was the only thing to be grateful for.

'Sir, I don't know what you have in mind, but I should tell you that I am not without friends here. They will worry about me if I do not return immediately.'

'Never fear, missy: I've sent Jason with word that you are visiting people in the country. Your little acting allies will have sailed before your expected return. And when you don't come back, who'll worry then?'

I clasped my hands tightly around my knees, bracing myself against the bumpy road. He was serious. If I didn't do something, he'd make me 'disappear' with no one the wiser.

'You take your revenge too far, sir. We were seen together on the pier. You can't hope to escape suspicion if any harm should befall me.'

'You place too high a value on your own importance, missy. Who'll care what becomes of an actress once her company has left town? And who would have the effrontery to question me about such a matter?'

'Mr Shepherd.' I lobbed the name into the conversation, hoping to provoke some second thoughts.

Hawkins snapped his fingers. 'His threats mean nothing. He won't find you unless I want him to and he's made it clear that he's planning to leave soon. I doubt he'll put off business to look for a chit like you.'

'I wouldn't count on it.'

'Oh, but I do.'

That concluded our conversation for the present. I toyed with the idea of leaping from the moving carriage but discarded it when I realized that I would quickly be recaptured. I could do without broken bones if I was to make my escape on a more auspicious occasion. Clenching my teeth, I concentrated on quelling my rising sense of panic. Hawkins got out a newspaper and made a point of reading it, from time to time casting a contemptuous look in my direction.

'I don't suppose, sir, you care to tell me where we're going?' I asked after an hour.

'To my penn, of course. You can call it my kingdom, if you like.' He chuckled, a long finger stroking the top of his cane that rested on his knees. He would've been a handsome man if his heart hadn't been as rotten as a month-old fish. Traces of that stink marred his features with lines of cruelty around his mouth.

The carriage turned off the main road and entered a shaded avenue leading to a white board house. It wasn't as fine as the residence he had sold to Billy, but it was built in a similar style with shuttered windows on the single storey. The carriage slowed and halted at the steps. Tense like prey crouching before a predator, I made no move, waiting to see what orders Hawkins would give concerning me, looking for a chance to escape.

Flinging the paper on the seat, Hawkins got out and closed the door with a snap. 'To the barracks,' he called. 'Make sure my guest is well secured.'

With a fresh heave on the harness, the horses set off again, taking the carriage round the back of the building. We clattered into the stable yard and the door opened a final time.

'Dis way.' A stern-faced groom waited for me to descend. I hopped out, taking in my surroundings with a quick turn. Stalls for horses stretched one side of the courtyard; the other three comprised cell-like living quarters for slaves.

'I think I've come far enough,' I said brightly as if I did not notice the menace in his stance. 'My morning call is over and I'll just make my way home now.'

Hawkins' lackey had other ideas: he took my elbow and propelled me towards one of the buildings. 'Your room in dere,' he said gruffly. So Hawkins had planned this well in advance. The groom gave me a little shove past a heavy iron-bound door and closed it behind me. I heard the bolt slide home. Footsteps retreated and I was left alone.

For the first time since the encounter on the pier I allowed myself to feel fear. I was in a horrid little cell with no furniture, only a high window and a blanket on the floor. A jug of water stood in one corner, in the other a bucket. It looked as though I was going to be here some time. Lying down on the threadbare blanket, I curled up and pretended to myself that this hadn't happened. Hawkins was just playing with me as he had done before. None of his threats meant anything; he just wanted me scared witless.

Well, he had succeeded. Could I go home now?

It appeared the answer was 'no'. Hours passed and no one came for me. The walls seemed to press closer; I could imagine them squeezing me into a smaller and smaller space like a coffin. I had to get out. Desperate to see what was happening in the world beyond my cell, I turned the bucket upside down and climbed on so I could look out the window. I was just in time to glimpse Hawkins riding by with his overseer, off to check his field workers, no doubt. The barracks seemed empty, apart from an old woman sweeping the courtyard and an occasional groom going about his business. I tried to attract their attention but they were either deaf or under instructions to ignore me.

It was as if I didn't exist.

I returned to the blanket. There was no point beating on the door or exhausting myself with frantic pacing. I would need brains to get out of this and that required a cool head. As I took stock of my unpromising situation, a mad bubble of laughter welled up in my throat. I'd imagined today that I would start out on my glorious rescue of Pedro and instead found myself sorely in need of saving. I had underestimated Hawkins' hatred. As soon as he had found out I was in Jamaica, I should've made plans to protect myself, but I'd been so wrapped up in my own arrangements that I hadn't thought of the very present danger to myself.

Now I knew better.

I wondered what Georgie and Jenny would make of the message that I'd gone to visit friends in the country. Would they assume that meant I'd left for Billy's new plantation? If I'd been planning to go to his penn, Jenny would surely think it strange that I hadn't gone with her and that, if she gave it enough thought, should make her suspicious. Better still, if they checked the story with Billy, then he too would know something was up and I'd bet that he would be canny enough to suspect Hawkins to have a hand in it. My heart gave a small leap. I could almost imagine Billy and Georgie now riding to my rescue. Looked at this way, my situation was not entirely desperate. I'd been in worse scrapes before, hadn't I?

And surely a sane man (and I was praying Hawkins was not mad) wouldn't do away with me just because he held a grudge about something that had happened almost two years ago? I admit, Reader, that I had bitten him then – but only after provocation. Time to let bygones be bygones.

With that piece of philosophy, I allowed myself to doze off, gathering my strength for another encounter with Hawkins.

The next person I saw was not the master but his overseer. He came to my door late in the afternoon, just as the sun bobbed on the horizon. It cast long shadows across the courtyard and threw a menacing orange light into my cell. The heat of the day was beginning to fade but it was still stuffy and airless. A fleshy, shaven-haired white man, the overseer had the look of an escaped convict and fists that promised he'd enforce his will if anyone was foolish enough to disobey. I did not count myself among this group so got up on his order.

'Follow me,' he rasped, jerking his head over his shoulder. His voice sounded as if it was being strangled before leaving his throat.

'Where are we going?'

'You'll see.' He made it sound like a threat. Not that I needed any more intimidation.

Keys at his belt jingling with every step, he led me round to the back of the main house and in through the servants' entrance. The voices in the kitchen faltered as I followed him past the slaves cooking dinner. My eyes met briefly with those of a plump cook holding a ladle over her pots, but no one remarked at my presence. They dared not. Taking me to the wing that housed the estate offices, the overseer opened a door and ushered me into Hawkins' study. The owner was already in occupation, running his finger down a column of figures in a ledger. He did not look up, continuing his work as if we weren't there. Unsure what to expect next, I eyed the chair on my side of the desk, wondering if I should sit down, but decided against it.

'So, Dawlish, she came quietly, did she? I rather thought you'd have more trouble,' Hawkins addressed his overseer.

'She came like a lamb, sir.'

'Good. Then my plan is working.' He closed the ledger with a thump and raised his eyes to mine. 'Learning your place at long last, gal?'

I did not blink. 'What place would that be, sir? As your illegally detained prisoner?'

He shook his head. 'You misunderstand what is happening here. Did you not know that we don't like vagrants on Jamaica?'

'I'm not a vagrant,' I replied hotly.

'Yes, you are. You've broken your contract of employment on which you were allowed to enter the country and now have no means of support. You could be arrested, charged and imprisoned for that. Your sentence would very likely be several years as an indentured servant. In other words, punished by the legal surrender of your freedom in service to a master.'

'There's nothing legal about what you are doing, Mr Hawkins. And I doubt very much the law would be so heavy-handed when it is known that I was about to depart.'

Hawkins raised a sceptical brow.

'Besides, I see no magistrate. You've plucked me off the streets and given me no opportunity to take my so-called vagrant self away as I fully intended.'

'For your information, missy, *I* am a magistrate.' Hawkins lolled back in his chair. 'All I'm doing is just cutting out a few of the annoying and unnecessary intervening steps. I'm sure you'd prefer not to be incarcerated in Kingston gaol. Dawlish, fetch the paperwork.'

Hawkins had the upper hand this time and we both knew it.

The overseer took a roll of parchment from the

shelf by the door and spread it out on the desk to face me, weighing down the ends with an inkwell and a paperweight.

Hawkins gestured to the document. 'I took a long time deciding on a just revenge until I thought of the perfect answer. Let the punishment fit the crime. You deprived me of a slave so you can take his place.'

I clenched my fists. 'Forget it. I'm leaving.'

'Dawlish!'

Even before he spoke, the brute of an overseer grabbed my arm and towed me over to the desk.

'This is a farce! You can't make me your slave!'

'No, not slave.' Hawkins tapped the paper. 'Indentured servant. If you were listening – and that's a quality, by the way, that I demand of all my people – you would've heard me say it already. It's all *bona fide*, believe me.'

I'm afraid I did believe him. I locked my hands behind me.

'I'd prefer to take my chances in gaol if you don't mind.'

'Oh but I do. You'll sign. Dawlish!'

The overseer prised my fists apart and forced my right hand forward. With a callous smile, Hawkins dipped the quill into the ink and pressed it into my fingers. Then, like a rough teacher making a child form her letters, the overseer guided my hand over the parchment, scrawling my name. I had few means of resistance. The best I could do was to spell my name with a 'K', guessing Hawkins would not notice. As soon as we'd finished, Hawkins whipped the paper away and blew on it.

'Excellent. You're mine now for . . . how long is it?' He looked down at the paper. 'My goodness: twenty years! Rather excessive punishment for vagrancy, but I doubt anyone is going to challenge it.'

I shook my aching fingers. 'It won't stand. You forced me – my signature's worth nothing.'

Hawkins turned to his overseer. 'Did I force the gal here, Dawlish?'

'No, sir,' the man rasped.

'Of course not: he did!' I pointed an accusing finger at the shaven-headed man beside me. 'But you ordered him to do so.'

'Changing your story already, are you? That never looks good in court. What did you see, Dawlish?' Hawkins tapped the paper thoughtfully on the desk.

Dawlish smirked. 'I saw the magistrate decide on a punishment and the gal signing the deed, sir.'

'Quite so.'

This was terrifying. Something snapped inside me. Beyond reason, I acted on instinct. I whirled round and bolted for the door, making it out into the passageway.

'After her!' bellowed Hawkins.

I don't know what I thought to achieve by my mad dash for freedom but I couldn't stand there and let them taunt me. Bursting out of a side door, I stumbled over a flowerbed and leapt a fence. My petticoat caught on a splinter but I ripped it free. A field of towering sugar cane lay ahead, cast into deep shadow by the lowering sun. Without hesitation, I plunged in, hoping to lose myself among the thick stalks. Foliage whipped at my face and arms. On I went. Sweat dripped down my back as I grew hot and sticky in my panicked flight.

Chest heaving, I crumpled on to my hands and knees for a moment to regain my breath. Tears and dust tasted salty in my mouth. I could hear shouts behind me but no one was close enough to hear my panting.

Then one voice rose above the others. 'Release the dogs!' shouted Mr Hawkins.

And I had thought things couldn't get worse.

With a sob and a curse, I struggled up and began running again. If I remained on the ground, I did not know what the dogs would do to me when they tracked me down. The field gave way abruptly to another low fence. Beyond stretched a patch of scrub leading down to a cove. The sea, molten gold in the sunset, looked so peaceful as it unfurled like a bolt of silk on to the white sand – a sight completely out of step with the turbulent emotions inside me. I scrambled over the fence, making for the beach. I'd read once that dogs cannot track scent in water: it seemed better than waiting for them to pounce on me up here.

Splash! Splash! Splash! The water drenched my skirts as I ran through the shallows. My shoes weighed me down but I had no time to remove them. Risking a glance over my shoulder, I saw two huge dogs bound down the path, arrowing towards me, baying loudly. They'd reach me in a trice. I turned away to plunge deeper into the water. Briefly knocked back by a wave, I flailed to get beyond their depth. The water was now up to my waist, now my chest. Undeterred by the sea, the dogs followed, swimming through the waves as if this was all some sort of game.

'Stop there, gal!' Hawkins and his men had reached the beach. 'You've nowhere to go.'

Too busy swimming with their paws to maul me, the dogs snapped in my direction, yelping with excitement.

This was not an auspicious moment to learn how to swim but I was too desperate to return meekly to the sand. I struck out for deeper water.

Orders were shouted behind me. A whistle. A wave splashed over my head and I took a mouthful of water and went under. Breaking the surface, eyes stinging, I felt utter despair. I didn't want to drown but neither did I want to be recaptured. But the instinct to survive won out and I barely resisted when an arm caught me round the waist, dragging me the way I'd come. The slave who had been sent to fetch me now carried me back clutched to his chest. Without a word, he released me once we returned to the sand. I staggered a little but then straightened my spine, brushing my hair off my face. Water pooled at my feet as it dripped from my clothes.

A cane prodded my stomach, and I flinched.

'That was very stupid and will not go unpunished. Take her to her quarters, Dawlish.' Hawkins then whistled to the dogs and strolled away, throwing a stick for them to catch.

The overseer marched me to the barracks, sparing no thought for the state of my feet in my squelching shoes or the utter weariness of my body. He opened the door to my cell and pushed me inside, abandoning me there in my wet garments.

Clearly no one was going to offer me any comfort so I would have to deal with my state as best I could. Shivering, I stripped off my dress and wrapped myself in the blanket. I wrung the gown out into the bucket then hung it up by the window to dry. Taking a drink of water from the jug, I curled up in a corner to sleep, too exhausted in body and spirit to think any more. The steady drip, drip from the hem of the gown and the whine of mosquitoes kept me company that night.

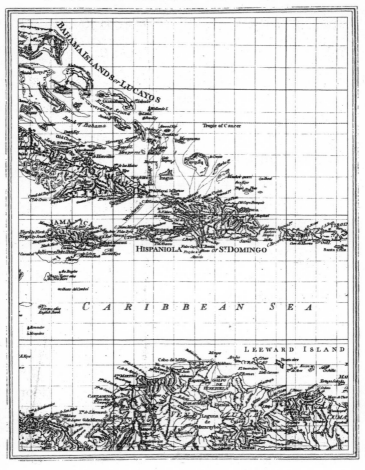

Act IV – In which things take

a bucaneering turn . . .

ACT IV

SCENE 1 – MALARIA

I woke the next morning shaking with cold. My teeth rattled like a brace of dice in a gambler's fist. Surely it couldn't be this cold in my cell? I clutched my arms to my sides, trying to still the shudders that racked my body, but to no effect. I gulped down the remaining water, propping myself against the wall. I don't know how long I remained in this position before the door opened but I sensed rather than saw Dawlish standing on the threshold. He strode across the cell, felt my forehead and swore. To my great relief, he immediately left the room, banging the door behind him.

Time passed and the feeling of cold was replaced by feverish heat. I wished I hadn't finished off the water for I now had a raging thirst. I closed my eyes, too tired to keep up the effort required to remain alert.

My next visitor was a newcomer. I was drifting in and out of a fever-dream but I saw enough to know that it was a slave, carrying a bowl of water, a cloth and a pile of clean clothes. Crooning gently, she removed my damp shift and petticoat, replacing them with a blue cotton blouse and skirt like her own. Her touch was kind as she cooled my burning skin with the cloth. She dipped out of the cell for a moment and returned with a dry blanket and some fresh water. She found me mumbling the song I'd heard on my arrival.

> 'New-come buckra,
>> She get sick,
> She tak fever,
>> She be die
>> She be die.'

'Hush now,' she scolded gently. 'You no die. Dat be wicked song.'

I began to sob. Reader, I'm very rarely ill, priding myself on a sturdy constitution, but this fever was testing my strength to the limit. I needed to be strong to extricate myself from this predicament but here I was reduced to a babbling, weeping wreck.

The fever mounted, took hold and rode me hard. The next few hours blurred into one long delirium broken only by a woman's cool hand and a cup held to cracked lips. Her medicine was bitter, making me vomit, but it did seem to ease the bone ache for a while. I now lay on a mat, scratchy against the skin but better than the cold floor. The sweat poured off me – a sign, my nurse assured me, that my body was fighting the illness. I was too tired to care. My mind played tricks, sometimes making me think I was back in the green room in Drury Lane, or on board the *Courageous* or even in my comfortable bedroom in Philadelphia. Returning to consciousness always brought the returning pain of awareness of where I really was. I preferred the delusions.

The following day, I woke to find my fever had broken. I lay for a long time, relishing the sensation of a clear head and cool skin. I slept, only rousing a whole day later feeling hungry. My kind nurse came in and saw that I was finally awake.

'How be missy now?' she asked solicitously. 'You take malaria bad.'

'Malaria?' I'd heard many frightening tales of this swamp fever and the number of lives it had claimed.

'It hide now. So how you feel?'

'Much better, thank you.'

'Me get you food, then tell Mister Dawlish you well.'

A reminder of the convict-faced overseer made me shudder. 'I wouldn't say I was well, just better than I was.'

Her brow puckered in sympathy. 'Me know, missy, but if me no tell him, me get punished.'

She returned with some broth then left me alone to eat. I guessed that might be the last I saw of her. I doubted Hawkins' servants were allowed to convalesce waited on hand and foot. Deciding it was better I found out my condition before the overseer arrived, I put my bowl aside and hauled myself to my feet. My limbs shook. I felt like a newly birthed foal struggling to stand.

'About time you got up,' Dawlish commented from the door. 'I'll take you to your duties. The master said to start them light until you recovered your strength.'

I leaned my forehead against the wall. 'How kind of him,' I said acidly.

'What are you waiting for?' he growled. 'I told you to come with me.'

'I'm waiting for the ability to put one foot in front of the other.'

Without further ado, the overseer threw me over his shoulder and strode back to the house. Dumping me beside the kitchen table, he gestured to the cook.

'Keep her busy, Cookie. Mr Hawkins' orders.'

'Yessir,' the cook said humbly.

Once Dawlish had gone, I collapsed on to a stool, then tumbled sideways in a dead faint. I didn't even feel my head hit the floor.

When I came to, I found myself propped in a corner with a bowl of peas lodged in my lap. They'd already been shelled. The cook saw my eyelids flutter open. She looked familiar somehow but I couldn't recall where I'd seen her. Not at the theatre, surely?

'You keep busy with dem peas, missy,' she ordered. 'Keep right on shellin' de little devils and me make us a cup of coffee.'

Somewhat revived by her strong, sugared brew, I managed to carry the bowl to the table and took a stool beside her.

'You sure look like duppy now,' she commented, brushing a finger over my pale cheeks.

It now came rushing back to me. So that was where I'd met her: outside the Obeah man's hut. She had been the woman who had spotted me lurking in the bushes. But I knew better than to mention the Obeah man's name here. She had to be able to trust that I would keep her secret.

'Not quite a duppy yet, ma'am,' I agreed, with a weak smile, 'though I feel like one.'

She grinned at my polite form of address. 'No white gal ever called me dat. Mah name's Cookie, noting else.'

'Then I'm Cat, nothing else.'

She chuckled and slipped me a pancake from

the griddle on the stove, a delicious golden coin of feather-light batter.

'Me goin' to fatten you up, gal, so you don't frighten de chillen round here.'

I ran a hand over my ribs. 'Thank you. I think I need it.'

'You sure do, honey. Dat fever come back soon and you need strength.'

My jaw dropped. 'Come back!'

'Malaria – he ride you for a spell, den come back to take you again, sometimes worse, sometimes better. He live with you now so you get used to him.'

'You mean I'm never going to be free of it?'

She shrugged. 'Maybe, maybe not. Me know folk who have de fever all dere lives. No one knows how he come and go.'

I munched my pancake, regretting bitterly my foolish decision to come to the West Indies. Even if I got away from Hawkins, I was now saddled with an illness that could strike at any moment. Foreign travel had sounded so exotic when read about in books; the reality was rather more uncomfortable and costly to health.

'I want to go home.' I hadn't realized that I had spoken aloud till Cookie answered.

'Me know you do, gal, but you must be good servant now. Mister Hawkins is not kind massa.' She glanced at the door. 'How you end up here, missy? All of us want to know why he brung you and treat you so cruel.'

I quickly explained my past dealings with Pedro's old master. I wasn't reassured by her horrified looks as she realized the full extent of Hawkins' hatred for me. Instead of commenting, she pressed another pancake in my hand.

'Keep out of dat man's way,' she whispered. A bell rang above the door. 'Dat be de massa wanting his coffee.' She filled a pot and stuck her head round the door to the courtyard out back. 'Manny, you come take massa his tray!'

A boy bobbed into the kitchen. Cookie wiped his face clean with the edge of her apron and hustled him towards the corridor leading to the breakfast room. A few minutes later, he came back crying, coffee spilt all down his cotton shirt. With a little scream of distress, Cookie whipped the clothes off his back and pressed a cold cloth to his skin.

'Massa say dat de duppy gal should bring it,' sobbed the little boy, fortunately more shocked than scalded.

Cookie darted me a concerned look but quickly refilled the pot. She shoved the tray into my arms.

'You can do dis?' she asked.

I nodded, biting my lip.

She patted my shoulder. 'Den hurry.' She folded the little boy into a cuddle as she watched me leave. Her expression suggested that she doubted she would see me return in one piece.

Standing outside the door of the dining room, I debated what I should do when I saw my tormentor again. Pour the coffee over Hawkins' head to repay him for what he'd done to that little boy? That was my favourite, if suicidal, wish. Keeping my lips firmly closed to prevent my tongue running away with me, I entered, too shivery and weak to stop the cup and saucer rattling as I crossed to the table. Plan B had been to come and go without attracting attention and this was what I was hoping to do.

'Been sick, I hear?' Hawkins' voice cut through the air like a whiplash.

'Yes, sir.'

'You may call me master like my other slaves.'

I put the tray down and poured a cup with a shaking hand. A little spilled into the saucer.

'Clumsy as well as feeble – I'm disappointed in my newest acquisition.'

I still hadn't looked at him. To do so would be to put a match to my gunpowder temper. I wiped the saucer clean with a napkin and set the cup down in front of him. He was sitting alone at a large dining table, the sideboard spread with dishes as if a dozen were to eat.

But I bet, Reader, none of it tasted as fine as Cookie's pancakes hot from the griddle.

I approached him warily, as one would a snake. I was right to be cautious: he had been contemplating his next strike. As I placed the cream jug on the table, he grabbed my wrist, easily circling it with his fingers. He turned my arm over.

'Not malingering then,' he concluded. 'What was wrong with you?'

I stood passively, trying to ignore the fact that he was touching me and my palm was itching to slap him. 'They say it was malaria.'

'Ha!' He flung my arm from him in disgust. 'Damn useless female. Won't get much work out of you if you're sick half the time.'

'I'm sorry for your loss,' I muttered sarcastically.

The cream jug sailed through the air. I ducked in time and it shattered against the door.

'Watch your tongue, gal, or I'll have it removed.' He glared down at his coffee. 'I drink it white – fetch some more cream.'

I retreated to the kitchen. Cookie raised an eyebrow.

'He's in a bad mood,' I explained as I filled a new jug.

'Dat be his usual mood since he lost de other penn to de Englishman.' Cookie stoked the fire, making the kitchen unbearably hot.

I hurried back to the dining room, slowing only as I entered. At least it was cool in here with the breeze whispering through the louvred windows.

'And two sugars!' snapped Hawkins as I stirred in the cream.

'Is that sweet enough for you, sir?' I asked in honeyed tones as I imagined stirring arsenic into his brew.

He took a sip then noticed my expression.

'Why are you smiling? I never want to see you smile again, gal.'

'Very good, sir. I will contain myself in your presence.' Mustering all my acting powers, I pulled my face into a tragic frown. Inside part of me was still laughing that I had so many small ways of annoying him – petty revenges but ones worth taking.

He set his cup back on the saucer. 'What's that expression supposed to mean?'

'Sadness for my inability to appear before you with sufficient gravity . . . sir.' He hadn't yet noticed that I was refusing to call him master. That was a line I had determined not to cross.

Before he could work out if I was being insolent – and Reader, I cheerfully admit that I was – the sound of pounding hooves came from the driveway. We both looked to the window: a young man in a puce coloured coat had just ridden up the drive. When he removed his hat, I realized Billy had come to call. Never before had I been so relieved to see him: my cavalry had finally arrived.

'I thought he'd be here sooner than this,' sneered Hawkins.

I made to run out into the hall but Hawkins barked:

'Stay. You can remain here to see him.'

He was letting me be present for the visit? Why did I not find that reassuring?

The butler opened the door to announce the caller. 'Mr Shepherd, massa.'

'Come in, Shepherd. Do you want some coffee?' Hawkins waved to where I stood by the tray.

Billy paused on the threshold, his eyes sweeping over both of us, then passed the butler his hat and gloves.

'I think I will,' he replied.

Hawkins gestured to me to serve his guest. I hesitated too long.

'Pour the coffee, gal.' He prodded me in the side with his fork. Saucer clattering, I splashed some coffee into the cup and shoved it in Billy's direction. He took it from me with a questioning look.

'What's 'appened to you, Cat? Why are you 'ere?'

'Billy, I –'

'I'd prefer it if you didn't address my staff, Shepherd.'

A muscle twitched in Billy's cheek.

'She's skin and bone! What have you done to her?'

'Nothing. She's been ill. Fever.'

Billy turned to me for verification and I nodded slightly.

'You said she was staff. What the devil do you mean by that?'

'She was picked up for vagrancy and is now an indentured servant,' Hawkins replied briskly, delighted to have delivered this *coup de grâce*. 'I can show you the deed if you wish.'

'He forced me to sign, Billy!' I said in a rush. 'Abducted me – set his dogs on me!'

'Silence!' Hawkins slammed his palm on the table, making the cutlery jump. 'I did not give you permission to speak!'

Billy rose and put his arm around me, pulling me to his side. 'I warned you what would happen if you messed with my Cat. She's leaving.'

'I think not.' Hawkins strode to the window and stood there with his back to us, arms folded. 'It's all legal. You see, there's nothing you can do for her.'

'Just as well I don't care for legal then. And you can expect that mortgage to be called in today, mister.' Billy turned to go, pushing me ahead of him.

'I doubt you'd do that. You forget that I now own your pet cat and if you try anything against me, she'll wish she'd never been born.'

Billy tugged on my arm, still intending to take me with him.

Hawkins chuckled. 'Look outside, Shepherd. Do you think you'd just walk out of here with my property?'

Billy glanced out the window to see his horse surrounded by a dozen of Hawkins' men.

'They've orders to stop you stealing her – and no court will prosecute me for protecting my own so you'd better go quietly.'

Billy swore fluently under his breath. I began to tremble, understanding that my best hope of escape was about to leave without me.

'In fact, I have to thank you, Shepherd. It wasn't until you made your feelings clear on the subject that night outside the theatre, that I worked out a way to control your hold over me. If you make one move to call in that mortgage, then your friend here will know it.'

Billy pushed me aside to square up to Hawkins. I stumbled against the table. 'You think I care enough about her to sacrifice my own business interests?'

'That's the gamble I'm taking. And yes, I do.'

To my surprise, Billy started laughing. 'You're a scoundrel, Hawkins. I like that in a man. You've won this round but you won't win the next. It works two ways this deal: if you harm her, I'll be down on you like a ton of bricks.'

'I look forward to it.'

With a mocking bow to Hawkins and the briefest of nods to me, Billy strode from the room, calling for his hat. I couldn't believe it: he was really going. I thought Billy Shepherd of all people would stand his ground with Hawkins, but it seemed not. Within seconds, the front door slammed and the hoof beats retreated up the driveway.

'There'll be no knight in shining armour for you. Back to work, gal.' Hawkins waved me away. With an effort, I straightened my spine and marched out of the room with all the dignity I could muster.

Over the next few days, I became far more familiar with the workings of a plantation than I desired. Once I regained some of my old strength, I was taken out of the safe haven of Cookie's kitchen and put to work alongside the other women. I was given into the particular care of the slave who had nursed me, a young woman who I now learnt was called Rafie. She showed me how to tend the vegetable and fruit plots. It was backbreaking work labouring for long hours in the hot sun, but I counted myself lucky I wasn't in the cane fields with the men where conditions were much worse. They had the pleasure of the overseer Dawlish's company – him and his bull whip. Few men had unscarred backs.

I was something of an oddity on the penn – Hawkins had no other white female servants. The white men served him in a variety of capacities: there was a carpenter, a manager of the distillery, and half a dozen stockmen. All of them were spared the drudgery of fieldwork. As the days passed and they got used to seeing me about the place, a few of them tried to strike up an acquaintance with me – until warned off by the overseer. Hawkins clearly wanted me kept isolated from any prospect of help or sympathy from free men.

The worst part of the experience – other than the loss of liberty – was, without question, the sun. In addition to sapping all energy with its heat, my pale skin burned after a few minutes outside. I tried to keep covered, wearing a straw hat and long sleeves, but somehow there was always a burnt spot on my neck at the end of the day. High summer – the time to lie in the shade sipping sherbet, not to water the wilting cassava plants, but I had no choice.

The mindless nature of the work left plenty of time for speculation. I wondered with decreasing optimism if anyone was doing anything to rescue me from this little hell. After Billy's visit, I had harboured hope that he would return, but when nothing happened I began to think that he had expended his concern on that one attempt and given up. I tried to tell myself not to be surprised – this was Billy Shepherd after all, not the Good Samaritan – but I was still disappointed that our fledgling friendship had failed to fly. And Mrs Peabody's troupe must be long gone, taking with them any help from that quarter. That left Jenny. What was she doing now? I hoped she had the sense to raid my meagre purse to keep herself in food and lodgings. But when that was all spent, what would she do, slave to an indentured servant? I shuddered to think.

My situation was not entirely hopeless. I had friends who would come looking for me eventually. I took comfort from the fact that neither Frank nor Syd would be content to just let me disappear without trying to discover my fate, but how long would it take them to realize I needed saving? Could I get a message to them somehow? No paper, no pen, no link to the outside world: my chances of succeeding were slight.

Straightening up to rest my aching back from the task of weeding the kitchen garden, my eye fell on Cookie scattering grain to the chickens outside the back door to the house. Emptying the bowl, she looked up and shaded her eyes against the glare. Then, turning her head slowly, she continued until her gaze fell on me some distance away. She gave me a slight nod, a gesture to come closer. My heart gave an answering leap of excitement as I recognized a new possibility beckoning. The white man's world had failed me; what about the black? Would the Obeah man pass a message for me, at least to let Jenny know what had happened? That would be a start.

I volunteered to take a basket of mangoes to the kitchen so that I could grab a private word with my friend.

'Dere you are, Cat,' Cookie said, seeing me standing in her doorway. She tutted. 'Your poor red nose: it look like it be on fire.'

I put the basket down and rubbed a grimy hand over my face. 'It feels like it too. Cookie, there's something I wanted to ask you.'

'What dat be, honey?' Watching my face closely, she poured me some cold water and waved me to a chair.

'Do you remember where we first met?'

Her eyes widened a fraction and she nodded.

'I need to tell my maid, Jenny, what's happened to me. I'm worried she might not know what to do with me gone.'

Cookie smiled now. 'Don't worry about dat gal, Cat. She know.'

'But how do you know that she knows . . .' I paused, working it out for myself. 'I see. The brotherhood knows everything, doesn't it?'

After casting a nervous look over her shoulder to check we were truly alone, she agreed, 'Everyting, Cat.'

'So is she all right?'

'She be fine. Gone back to de Englishman, Moses say.'

Returned to Billy: not a perfect solution but better than starving in my old lodgings.

I sighed. 'That's a weight off my mind. I don't suppose that you can ask her to send a letter for me to a friend in England? The address will be among the papers in my valise. I've got to get out of here somehow.'

Cookie shook her head. 'No need for dat, gal. Me been looking all day for a chance to tell you. Dere be plans for you.'

I felt a quiver of anticipation, a sense of something about to change. 'For me? What kind of plans?'

She winked. 'De brotherhood help de gal who made de massa free a slave.'

I tried to keep a hold on my feelings of relief and

pleasure but my heart was racing. 'Really? How?'

'Dat be secret. Just don't you give up hope.' She leant closer. 'Be ready tonight.'

'Ready for what?'

She shook her head and pressed a biscuit into my hand. 'Get back outside, Cat, before dey notice you be gone. Don't want no problems before tonight.'

That evening I felt strangely light-headed with excitement as I bedded down early, tired out by hours of hard work. Something was finally happening and I cherished the hope that this was the last night I would spend in my cell. Despite my exhaustion, sleep eluded me. The moonlight silvered the wall opposite the barred window, casting long shadows that striped my skin where I lay on the floor, turning me black and white. I shivered and rubbed my arms to get warm. My temples were pounding. When my whole body started shaking, I realized with dismay that my symptoms were not due to the anticipation of escape: my fever had returned. Locked in each night to make sure I didn't run, I had to thump on the door to attract help.

Dawlish shoved it open, none too pleased to be disturbed. 'What?'

'Fever,' I whispered.

He cursed with all the fluency of a sailor. 'You're more trouble than you're worth,' he grunted. 'If you're still alive in the morning I'll send a woman to you.'

He was about to close the door.

'Wait! Your master won't want me to die!'

He laughed. 'I think he would dance at your funeral, gal.'

'Not if Mr Shepherd calls in the mortgage.'

Dawlish slammed the door but my words must have had some effect because, before an hour passed, I was once more back in the care of my kind healer. Rafie gave me the bitter medicine and bathed me in cool cloths to reduce the raging heat that burned under my skin.

Coming out of my delirium for a moment some time later, I heard her debating with Cookie whether to cut my hair to keep me cooler.

'Please don't,' I whispered.

Rafie combed it with her fingers. 'Like de sunset it be,' she said softly. 'Shame to cut it off.'

My hair was given a reprieve but that did not lessen my distress. Cookie had told me that I was to expect help tonight and here I was laid low by malaria. Surely it would be too late to delay the brotherhood?

The little boy, Manny, came running to summon Cookie back to her kitchen. She bent over me and pressed a kiss to my brow. She smelt of new bread, flour puffing from her apron as she moved. 'Trust us, Cat,' she murmured. 'It be all right.'

I had no choice but to put my faith in my slave allies as my fever rose once more, rendering me unable to do anything but groan. Imagine someone drilling into your head, Reader, and you will then have some comprehension of the pain I experienced, tossing and turning on my mat in that miserable cell. My only relief was the snatched periods of deep sleep in which I was unaware of my surroundings.

Reports must have reached Hawkins of my illness because I was honoured with a visit just after supper.

'How's the patient?' he asked my nurse brusquely.

'She need de doctor, massa.'

Hawkins harrumphed. 'Dammit. Move her to the house. I can't afford to lose her just now.'

I felt strong arms – I don't know whose – lift me up and carry me to a real bed in one of the servants' chambers. Sighing with relief, I fell straight back to sleep, this time in more comfort. Sometime later, cold hands started prodding me, feeling for a pulse in my neck. I batted them away feebly.

'Lie still, girl. I'm Dr Hillard.'

Reassured, I quietly submitted to his examination.

'What do you think, doctor?' barked Hawkins from the doorway. 'Will she live?'

'I expect so, sir. But the malignant humours of the swamp fever have taken hold and she doesn't look very strong. I'll bleed her and then we'll see.'

'No.' My protest was so weak I'm not sure anyone heard.

I must have fainted when the doctor made the incision in my arm. Consciousness did not return until the small hours and only because a bell was ringing urgently outside.

'Fire! Fire in the barn!' I heard someone yell – Dawlish, I think – and then banging on the back door.

I could now smell smoke and prayed that it would not spread to the house. It was bad enough burning up with fever without finding my room on fire when I was too weak to move. Yet somehow the danger seemed very distant. I wasn't sure I would even be bothered if the house did burn to the ground. It all seemed so unreal. The only thing I could focus on was my suffering. Added to my headache, my arm was sore where I had been bled. I knew many doctors across Europe and America swore by that treatment but I felt no benefit; if anything I was even feebler than I had been before.

Back I drifted into dreams that curled

through my brain like wisps of smoke.

'Cat?' A hand was shaking me awake.

I groaned. My arm flopped over the edge of the mattress, boneless and aching.

'Gawd, girl, what's the matter with you?'

The thought crystallized in my mind that the voice sounded very like Billy Shepherd. Confused, I imagined I must be back in the Sparrow's Nest in Drury Lane. That was my home after all.

'Leave me alone, Billy. Mr Sheridan won't like you setting foot in his theatre again,' I mumbled.

'What you talkin' about, Cat? I'm not leavin' you 'ere. It's that bleedin' fever again, ain't it?'

'No, no more bleeding,' I moaned.

Billy scooped me up. 'Hush, Kitten. I'm getting' you out of 'ere. Your slave mates 'ave just set light to the barn to create a distraction, so don't waste it.'

I was dimly aware of being carried down the corridor towards the back door. It didn't smell right for Drury Lane but I still didn't understand where we were.

Billy's plan to distract the household with the fire and make away with me unobserved wasn't going to be as simple as that. Not everyone was outside fighting the flames.

'Where do you think you're going with my servant, Shepherd?' Hawkins stepped out of the shadows, a pistol trained on us. The recollection that I was in Jamaica came back to me with a jolt. Gasping, I struggled to sit upright.

'I'm taking her home, where she belongs.' Billy eased me to the floor, propping me against him with one arm.

Hawkins shook his head. 'No you don't. If you take her from this house, I'll have you arrested.'

'Your mistake, Hawkins, was to think I care a fiddler's jig for the law.'

Fever-mad, I was finding it hard to take this situation seriously. Perhaps I was still dreaming? Hawkins looked so cross, Billy so grim – and I was standing in my nightdress. Bare toes – how unseemly. Mrs Peabody would have kittens if she saw me.

The slaver cursed. 'I'll hunt you down, Shepherd. She belongs to me. I have a deed to prove it.'

I swayed drunkenly against Billy's arm, the ground spinning. 'No you don't, mister. Not a deed with my name on it. You own "Kat" with a "K"; "Cat" with a "C", that's me.' Laughter bubbled up – I have no idea what I found so amusing. 'I'm a poet and I didn't know it.'

'Shut it, Cat,' whispered Billy, eye still on the gun barrel.

'You look so silly, Billy,' I chirped. 'Hawkins, Forkins, Porkins – no, I can't think of a rhyme. He is beyond rhyme – or reason.' My chuckles at my own wit subsided into shivering hiccups.

'Are you sure you still want her?' Billy asked Hawkins, raising a brow at my idiotic antics.

'I'm sure.' Hawkins raised the gun level with Billy's heart and cocked it. 'Let her go and step away.'

'All right.'

Without warning, Billy released me and I crumpled to the floor as he knew I would, momentarily distracting Hawkins. With his free hand, Billy now unsheathed a knife and threw, burying it deep in the slaver's arm. Giving a cry of pain, Hawkins jerked back and the pistol exploded; Billy dived left and the bullet passed overhead to embed itself in the ceiling. Billy sprang up and followed through with a punch to the jaw, sending Hawkins reeling. The slaver collapsed against the kitchen door and fell back. Billy leapt after him and I heard another thud, then silence. Too weak to get myself up off the floor, I waited. Within moments, my rescuer returned, brushing his hands off against his jacket.

'Gawd, I've been wantin' to do that for days.'

Picking me up once more, he stepped over Hawkins who was stretched out on the kitchen floorboards and we made our escape through the courtyard.

For some reason, I felt this an appropriate moment to start singing. A large hand settled over my mouth.

'We're not safe yet,' Billy hissed. 'Blimey, Cat, ain't you got a shred of sense?'

Rolls of choking black smoke billowed across the yard. Silhouettes of men darted in front of the flames.

'Are you taking me to Hell?' It seemed quite a reasonable question in the circumstances: I'd always thought Billy a devil and the scene was reminiscent of Dante's *Inferno*.

'Nah, I'm takin' you to the *Medici*.'

Next thing I heard was splashing as Billy waded into shallow water. I was passed over to another man and bundled in a blanket. I felt the boat rock as Billy climbed in and then oars creaked in the rowlocks. I curled up on the damp floor wondering when I was going to wake up from this strange dream. Sea water trickled under my burning cheek; the pains in my bones rose to excruciating proportions. Out of control, my body began to twitch and quiver violently.

'Damnation, what's the matter with her?' I heard Billy ask.

'It is the fever, Shepherd.' That was Captain Bonaventure's voice, I thought distantly. 'It will bring on convulsions. We have got to get her temperature down.'

Before I knew it, I was tipped over the side of the boat and immersed in the water. Mercifully my weak hold on consciousness failed and I slipped away, dreaming that I was drowning in cold, dark water.

SCENE 2 – PIRATE

I woke up many hours later to find myself snug in a cabin on board the *Medici*.

'Not dead then,' I whispered in surprise.

A skirt rustled and Jenny's face appeared, hovering over me like a guardian angel. 'You wake, missis?'

'Jenny!'

She tipped some water to my lips.

'What . . .?' I was too feeble to complete my question.

'You be on board Captain Bonaventure's ship. Massa Shepherd and de brotherhood save you yesterday but you be too bad with malaria to know anytink about it.'

I closed my eyes, remembering in snatches the events of the night before.

'I feel terrible.'

'Me not surprised. But your fever, he go now. Me give you good medicine from the Obeah man. Cinchona bark.'

'How did you . . .?'

'How did Jenny get here?'

I nodded. It still felt as if someone was sticking needles in my head.

'Massa Shepherd, he say you need me. Tell me come with him. No go back to Jamaica.'

'So where . . .?'

'He say we look for your friend. Sleep now, missis.'

I smiled into my pillow. Finally I was back on course.

Two days later I was fit enough to sit up on deck in a chair carried from the captain's cabin. For the moment I was content just to enjoy the sunshine and convalesce. The sailors went about their tasks around me, chatting and joking in coarse French. My appreciation of their skill was all the greater because I now understood what they were about, having a passing acquaintance with sea-craft myself. The *Medici* was an evil-looking ship: sleek lines, small but armed to the teeth, perfect for these waters. As if sensing that she was up to no good, other vessels preferred to keep their distance; we barely saw more than the topgallants before ships ran for a safe harbour in one of the many islands.

'You know somethink, Cat?' Billy came to crouch beside me, arms burnt brown as a berry in the sun. 'I've never seen you like this.'

'Like what?' I pulled my hat further over my face to protect my nose.

'Quiet – a bit yella and weak.'

'I haven't been so ill before.'

'S'pose not. Back in London, you always seemed indestructible – a ball of fiery energy.'

'And now you realize I'm not?'

'None of us are, sweetheart.' He paused, chewing on his lip in an uncharacteristically uncertain gesture. 'What does Jenny say about your illness?'

'She's given me some powder and told me to mix it into a drink if I feel the fever coming back – it should keep it under control.'

'But it'll come back?'

I shrugged, hardly able to bear thinking about it. 'Probably. She says most people learn to fight it and it's never so bad again.'

He cast a covetous look towards Jenny. 'Useful slave that – seems to know a thing or two about the sickroom.'

'You gave her to me, remember!' I warned.

'I ain't forgotten, worse luck. We should get you 'ome.' He tapped my arm. 'Sure you still want to go after Blackie?'

'Yes, Billy.'

'Stupid cow.'

'Devil.'

We smiled at each other in perfect understanding.

'Just don't go and die on my watch, all right?' he said, standing up. 'Fletcher'll skin me.'

'Scared of Syd, Billy?'

'Nah, just don't like failure. Came all this way to get you; wouldn't want to sew you into a hammock and tip you over the side with shot at your feet. Waste of perfectly good ammunition.'

I shivered. My recent brush with death made this too close for comfort. 'Do you have to be so fulsome in your description of my funeral?'

He grinned. 'Annoys you, does it? Good. Now I know you'll survive just to make sure it ain't me that does the honours.'

As I had arrived on board clad only in my nightgown, I was pleased to find my luggage in my cabin, though none of my dresses seemed very suitable for life at sea. Feeling much stronger now, and with no Mrs Peabody to comment, I intended to enjoy myself doing all the things she would have frowned on. In preparation, Jenny rustled up some spare clothes from the sailors but I refused to go about in plain breeches again. Dressing like a boy had always landed me in trouble and I had quite lost my taste for it. We compromised on me wearing breeches under a calf-length skirt – an odd but practical combination. A belted shirt and my sunhat completed the outfit.

Captain Bonaventure bowed gallantly when I appeared on deck. '*Très belle*, mademoiselle. I rejoice to see you on your feet again.'

I gave him a polite curtsey. 'I thank you for

coming to my aid again, Monsieur le capitaine.'

He gave me a wolfish smile. 'I am being extraordinarily well paid, *ma petite*.'

That was only natural. He could not be expected to go to these lengths out of the goodness of his heart – I already knew that he didn't have one. I'd never forgotten that at our first meeting he had offered to sell me into the white slave trade – and meant it.

'Where are we heading?'

'It is said that Monsieur Tivern is in these waters. We plan to have a little tête-à-tête with him.'

'And how are you going to do that?' I squinted at the horizon, wondering where the smuggler's ship was now and if Pedro was still aboard.

'We will intercept his vessel and persuade him to give up the information you require. I hope, mademoiselle, that you have no qualms about turning pirate?'

I gulped. 'You won't kill anyone, will you?'

'Not if they are reasonable, but I should tell you that Monsieur Tivern is not noted for his merciful disposition. We may have to be forceful in our attempts to gain his attention.'

Billy arrived at my shoulder. ''Eard the plan then?' I nodded. 'I've been meanin' to give you this, just in case it don't go our way.' He pressed a dagger into my hand. 'Don't s'pose you know how to 'andle a gun?'

'No.'

'Then best keep below when we board them.' He rubbed his hands together.

Seeing his eager anticipation, I thumped my forehead in exasperation. 'You're enjoying this, aren't you, Billy?'

'Too right. Life was gettin' a bit borin' in London to be honest with you, Cat. I 'ave to act respectable. But out 'ere, a man can take a few risks, get what 'e wants.'

'I always knew you were a born pirate, Billy.'

He laughed. 'And if you're on board a pirate vessel, what does that make you? Anne Bonny?'

'I'm not −'

He folded his arms. 'Then order us to stop the pursuit and leave Blackie to 'is own devices.'

He knew I couldn't do that. I bit my lip.

'See, you're a pirate,' he chuckled.

Feeling almost back to my old self, I spent the next few days exploring the ship and getting to know the crew. My time on board Captain Barton's *Courageous* had cured me of any qualms about heights and I enjoyed the compliments from the sailors when they discovered that, not only could I climb the rigging, but I was faster than most of them at doing so. Noting with amusement my interest in all things nautical, Captain Bonaventure found time to explain the basics of navigation, showing how the sextant and an accurate clock could be used to plot longitude. He was very proud of his own timepiece, made by the finest Parisian watchmakers and 'liberated' from the possession of a Dutch sea captain.

'It is worth its weight in gold,' he told me as he locked it back in a special chest. 'Better than buried treasure to a real pirate.'

By his calculations, we were not far from the western coast of San Domingo when we spotted a vessel matching the description of Tivern's sloop.

It was alongside a fishing smack and appeared to be relieving the owners of its cargo.

'Is it him?' Billy asked as Bonaventure handed over his telescope.

'Maybe, maybe not,' shrugged Bonaventure. 'Let us invite him to a parley and then we'll see.'

Cramming on more sail, the *Medici* surged into pursuit. Our quarry was in no hurry to accept our invitation and it too made all speed to outrun us, abandoning the fishing boat to its fate. When we passed the fishermen without pausing to harass them, they gave us a cheer – the little fish applauding the shark that had chased off the predator.

Bonaventure doffed his hat to the captain of the fishing smack. 'What ship?' he called, pointing to the sloop.

'The *Merry Meg*, sir!' called back the fisherman. 'The blackguard stole my rum!'

'Consider yourself avenged!'

'Merci, monsieur.'

The two vessels passed beyond hailing distance.

'It is Tivern,' confirmed Bonaventure with a hungry grin.

'Small fry if he steals from fishermen,' Billy said in disgust, not alarmed by the stealing but by the lack of ambition in the target.

'Sounds to me as if the crew have drunk him dry,' I suggested. 'I wonder what state they'll be in.'

'We'll soon find out, mademoiselle.' The captain pointed to the *Merry Meg*: we'd already closed on her and could now see the crew scurrying around the deck preparing to mount a defence. 'I suggest you get below.'

It seemed a churlish thing to do when they were risking their necks to help my friend.

'Is there nothing I can do to help?'

Billy laughed. 'Always knew you were a blood-thirsty wench. Can't bear to miss the excitement, eh, Cat?'

I wrinkled my nose at him. 'You know that's not so.'

The captain raised my hand to his lips and gallantly kissed my knuckles. 'You are a brave girl, mademoiselle, but you can do nothing up here. It will be no place for women and my crew will only be distracted if they have to worry about you. Stay below.'

It was an order. 'Aye, aye, captain. Keep your head down, Billy,' I urged.

'How about a kiss for good luck?' Billy said with a smirk as he loosened his short sword in its scabbard.

'Don't push it,' I growled, retreating to my cabin.

Not knowing what to do with ourselves, Jenny and I spent the next ten minutes trying to pretend that nothing out of the ordinary was happening on deck. When the first shots were fired, I gave up even that pretence and took to pacing. It was so frustrating: our window looked out the wrong way on to an empty ocean; all the excitement was taking place a few feet away and we had no inkling which way the fight was going. What if Pedro was caught up in the battle and no one realized who he was? He wouldn't know that it was we who had come to save him and he would assume that he had to defend himself against pirates. He might get injured.

'I can't stay here!' I announced. 'I'm going on deck.'

Jenny grabbed my arm. 'But, missis, de captain say –'

'I know what he said.' I tucked up my skirts and gripped the dagger. 'I'll keep out of sight but I have to see if I can find Pedro before something happens to him.'

Shaking her off, I slipped out of the cabin and cautiously made my way up on deck. No one tried to stop me as they were all too busy with the attack to spare a thought for what I was doing. I found myself in the midst of a scene of confusion with men running to and fro, rifle shots splintering the spars, shouts and cursing. It was ugly – bloody and brutal, like a gang fight back in the Rookeries. No wonder Billy felt in his element. Crouching down behind a barrel, I took stock of the situation. The *Merry Meg* was alongside us; the crew of the *Medici* had just thrown grappling hooks to prevent her slipping away. The other crew were trying to sever the lines binding the two ships together but were hampered by snipers up in the rigging.

'Boarders!' yelled Bonaventure, giving the signal.

Twenty men, the captain and Billy included, jumped or swung across the narrow gap, aided by the fact that the *Merry Meg* sat lower in the water. The deck of the smugglers' vessel became a battlefield, short swords flashing in the sunlight, pistols cracking with sharp reports. A quick survey revealed no boy among the fighters. As far as I could tell, Pedro was taking no part in the defence, if he was even still on board.

A gasp and thump behind me – I spun round to see the sailor manning the wheel fall forward, a dagger between his shoulder blades. A boatload of Tivern's men had made a surprise attack on the starboard side of the *Medici*, trying to take the advantage while most of the crew were engaged in the boarding party. Three of those left behind tried to shout a warning to Bonaventure but they were soon engaged in a fierce defence of the ship. I dashed to the rail.

'Captain! Billy! The *Medici*! Look starboard!'

My voice was lost in the bellows and screams of the battle. Abandoning this attempt, I shoved the dagger in my sash, raced to the ship's bell and rang the alarm with both hands. All eyes turned to me, including those of the men who had boarded our ship. One finished off his opponent with a slash of his cutlass and charged in my direction, arm raised to strike.

'Hell, hell, hell!' I ran for my life, heart beating wildly. The only place I could hope to out-manoeuvre him was in the rigging. I leapt up the shrouds with a speed that even my old captain, Barmy Barton, would not have been able to fault. Glancing down, I saw that my pursuer had sheathed his sword but was now after me with a dagger in his teeth. My aim was to reach one of the snipers up in the crow's nest, hoping he would pick off my hunter for me. But when I reached the lookout I found the sniper had himself fallen victim to a bullet: he was bent double over the rail, arms limp. I squeezed past him, stifling a shudder, and grabbed his rifle: it had been fired and I had not the slightest idea how to reload it, even if I'd had the luxury of time. A quick look down confirmed that my pursuer had not yet given up. What now? I waited until the man came within reach then swung the rifle butt down on his head. My aim was poor: I only succeeded in landing a glancing blow to his shoulder. He grunted, seized the butt and tore it from my hands, flinging it on to the deck below.

'You'll pay for that, you cur!' he swore, his face livid.

Marvellous: I'd just made him angry. I belatedly wished I'd stayed in my cabin.

Retreat was my only option. I began to edge along the yardarm. The sailor, a great brute of a fellow, heaved the body of the sniper out of his way and gained the platform. With his dagger now clenched in his fist, he got his first good look at me as I shuffled across the footrope.

'A girl!' he grunted in disgust. Then, seeing the humour in the situation of nearly being brained by a lass half his size, he grinned and took a step on to the yardarm, beckoning me back with his fingers. 'Come here, darlin', I won't harm you.'

'Oh no?' I gave a wry laugh and went as far as I could to the very end of the yardarm.

'I don't hurt girlies.'

'And why don't I believe you?' I searched for a way off my perilous perch. The deck looked no bigger than a tabletop from this height – no promise of a soft landing on those planks.

He feigned a look of innocence, tapping his cheek. 'Maybe because I'm standin' here with a dagger and you got nowhere to go?'

'That's where you're wrong.' Leaping for the nearest halyard, I slid all the way down to the deck, skinning my palms in the process. I landed in the middle of battle and this time had the sense to duck back into the cabin. On guard inside the door, Jenny almost knocked me out with the chamberpot but stayed her hand just in time.

'I wouldn't go out there just for the moment,' I said, chest heaving as I collapsed with my back to the door. 'It's turned a bit nasty.'

A quarter of an hour later, the sounds of battle faded to be replaced by gruff voices shouting commands.

'Who won, do you tink?' Jenny asked, wide-eyed.

Biting my lip, I shrugged, assuming a calm I did not feel. 'I suppose I should go and see.' My plan was to poke my head round the door to discover which way fortune had leant.

Jenny lunged and grabbed me around the waist. 'No! Me no let you out again. You be stupid once already.'

'But Jenny –'

She squeezed harder. 'No, Cat.'

My jaw dropped. 'You . . . you called me "Cat".'

Jenny let go and put her hands to her mouth in horror. 'Me sorry, missis. Me mean no disrespect.'

I chuckled. 'Of course not. No, I love you calling me by my proper name. You're forgetting that silly piece of paper that says you're my slave.'

Jenny wrung her hands. 'Me no forget.'

I clasped her fingers in mine and pulled her into a hug. 'But you must forget. Hawkins has a piece of paper saying I'm his servant for twenty years and do you think I care a jot? In my opinion, that piece of paper is only fit to be used in the privy. The same goes for yours.' I measured my palm against hers, fingertips touching. 'See, we're the same.'

A knock at the door returned us to our situation. With a shared look of understanding, we positioned ourselves either side of the entry, armed with a chamberpot and a knitting needle I'd grabbed from Jenny's sewing bag. The door opened and I leapt forward to poke my weapon in the back of our visitor, hoping, if our worst fears were realized, that he'd mistake it for a knife.

'Hands up!' I ordered.

A man in a torn shirt, smeared with dirt and blood, swivelled round, twisted the needle from my grasp – then burst into laughter when he saw what it was.

'You two have some guts!' said Billy approvingly. 'Planning to defeat all boarders with that?' He waggled the knitting needle in my face. 'What's wrong with the knife I gave you?'

'Thank goodness, Billy!' I slumped against the bulkhead in relief. 'I'm so pleased to see you. I thought we might've lost.'

'Never. The scum put up more of a fight than expected – lost three good men – but that was because they 'ad somethink to hide. Bonaventure's over the moon.'

'Not Pedro?'

'Nah, nothink to do with your friend. Come and see.' He paused at the door. 'Don't open your trap though, Cat. Bonaventure's spinnin' them the yarn that we're privateers acting on behalf of the French Navy, tryin' to restore order on San Domingo.'

I followed him up on deck. Much of the debris from the battle had been cleared but my gorge rose when I saw the three bodies laid out by the rail. Billy seemed to treat the deaths as all part of life at sea, but I couldn't help feeling guilty that they had died in an attack I had tacitly approved. It did not salve my conscience to know that both the crews of the *Medici* and the *Merry Meg* had been through many such encounters and did not blame this one on me. For the first time I began seriously to question my determined pursuit of a friend who might not even want saving.

Bonaventure was striding to and fro in front of a line of bound men, all of whom looked battle-scarred and angry: the survivors of the *Merry Meg*. He was speaking in rapid French, waving a piece of paper in front of the nose of the largest of the men – the captain, I assumed. Tivern was built like a barn: a wild crop of black hair, broad shoulders, thick neck, fleshy face, and fists like hams. Next to him stood the man who had chased me up the mast – not someone I wanted to meet again. I moved closer to hear what was happening.

'Rifles!' Bonaventure was declaring. 'You, monsieur, take arms to the enemies of France!'

'You have no to show of that,' muttered Tivern in poor French.

'I have your letter of understanding with the rebels.' Bonaventure flourished the note. 'Taken from your own cabin. Six hundred rifles and a hundred boxes of ammunition, powder, *et cetera, et cetera*. Do you know the penalty for gun running?'

'No.' Tivern looked mutinous.

'A life spent in prison – or on a plantation. I

hear prison is more comfortable.' Bonaventure licked his upper lip, his expression that of a cat whose whiskers drip with cream.

Behind this impromptu court, the crew of the *Medici* began transferring the rifles to their hold. Billy gave me a wink.

'What are you doing?' Tivern asked, his fists clenching.

'Commandeering the evidence.'

'Stealing, you mean.' Suspicions roused, Tivern glanced around him. His eyes fell on me standing next to Billy. 'Wait a moment, this is no government ship.'

'Non?' Bonaventure frowned. 'And I thought it was going so well.' He gave a Gallic shrug of resignation.

'I saw that girl on stage in Kingston.' Tivern jerked his head towards me. 'What would she be doing on a customs vessel?'

'Mademoiselle Royal's business is no concern of yours,' Bonaventure said smoothly.

'Miss Royal?' The pieces were falling into place for Tivern. 'You didn't know about the arms, did you? It was the boy. You want the boy.' He stood up straighter. 'I have a letter for her.'

'For me?' I squeaked in excitement. 'From Pedro?' So he did think to send me a note!

Tivern switched to English. 'Aye, for you. If you get this pirate here to untie me, I'll give it to you.'

Not trusting the smuggler further than I could throw him, I glanced at Bonaventure uncertainly. This annoyed Tivern.

'Ain't it enough that he's stolen my guns? All that rubbish about putting me in gaol – I don't believe a word of it. He's a thief – a pirate.'

I refrained from pointing out that it took one to know one.

'You can tell him he's won this round, but I'll get my revenge next time.'

'I speak English, monsieur,' Bonaventure slipped in with his vulture smile.

'A damn sight better than I speak French, I've no doubt.' Tivern's resentment was growing and I feared that he would withhold the message out of spite.

'My letter!' I pleaded.

'*Bien sur*, mademoiselle.' Bonaventure turned to the crewmen guarding the prisoners. 'Return them to their ship. I will detain Captain Tivern but a moment longer.'

The captives were led away. I approached Tivern warily.

'Captain, what have you done with Pedro?' I asked.

Tivern gave me an assessing look but didn't answer the question. 'You were the wench up in the rigging. My bosun told me about you, said you slipped down the ropes like a monkey, but I didn't believe him. Where did you learn to climb like that?'

'Same place as Pedro.'

Billy gripped my shoulder – I hadn't realized he was hovering just behind me.

'What the 'ell were you doin' on deck during the fightin', Cat Royal?'

'Do you know you sound just like Syd when you talk to me like that?' I brushed his hand off. 'It really doesn't suit you.'

Tivern seemed amused by our exchange. It was fortunate that his anger at Bonaventure did not appear to stretch to me. He grimaced at Billy. 'Who do you think spoiled my little attempt to board behind your backs? This wench here rang the bell before I could get to her.'

'That was you, Cat?' Billy clearly didn't know whether to admire or curse me for my foolhardiness.

'Yes. I told you I wanted to help. My letter?'

Billy gave a bark of laughter and held his hands high. 'I give up. You're too much even for me to 'andle. Give the girl her message or she'll plague you to death, Tivern.'

The smuggler flicked his eyes to me; I moved a step away. 'Untie me first. I can't reach it without my hands free,' he demanded.

'Actually, Billy, maybe this can wait.' My instincts warned me that Tivern was planning something.

Distracted by the sight of the weapons being offloaded, Billy patted me on the shoulder absent-mindedly. 'It's all right, Cat. 'E don't 'ave a weapon – 'e's been searched.'

'Perhaps if he gave it to you?'

'No, I promised the boy I'd put it in your hands,' Tivern said with an unconvincing air of self-righteousness.

Billy shrugged. 'You've come all this way, don't you want that letter?'

'Of course, but –'

Billy sliced through Tivern's bonds and waved him on. 'Give the girl what she wants.'

The smuggler reached inside his jacket and pulled out a folded piece of paper.

'I left the lad on Tortuga. He asked me to make sure you got this.'

'So he's safe?' I took a step closer, eager to have the evidence that Pedro was alive.

'If he ain't now, that's none of my doing. I was going that way so I delivered him as he asked. A clever fellow – he entertained us all voyage. The crew didn't want to let him go.'

My face broke into a smile. Of course, Pedro's gift as a musician had saved him from any poor treatment – I should have guessed. Half my worries had been for naught.

'So he's really all right?'

'Got some damned fool idea to fight for Toussaint, but other than that he's safe enough.'

'Thank you, sir. I can't tell you how relieved I am to hear it.'

My fingers brushed the edge of the letter. Suddenly, Tivern struck, yanking me to his chest and relieving me of the dagger I'd earlier tucked into my sash and forgotten. Billy muttered an oath, made to move forward, but froze when he saw that Tivern had no intention of releasing his hostage. Billy held up his hands in a placatory gesture.

'Let the girl go, Tivern. Bonaventure was about to return you to your ship – you'll gain nothing by this.'

'My guns, mate. Tell him to put them back or she gets it.'

'Do you think he cares what you do with that troublesome bit of baggage?' Billy waved at me dismissively. I glared at him, making sure he knew whom I blamed for releasing Tivern in the first place.

'Let's find out, shall we?' Tivern grasped me by the waist and carried me to the rail. Billy followed and gave a piercing whistle.

'Oi! Bonaventure! We've got a problem.'

The French captain looked up from the task of unloading the *Merry Meg* and frowned.

'How –?'

'Does it matter?' Billy shouted back in exasperation. 'He wants the guns or he'll kill her.'

With catlike agility, Bonaventure scaled the plank connecting the two ships.

'So, monsieur, you take little girls captive now. Is there no end to your cowardice?' he asked disdainfully.

'It's business,' Tivern said, a little defensive. 'Don't make a habit of it but what do you expect?'

'A little more gallantry perhaps? But no, you Anglo-Saxons were ever the boors of Europe.'

The insult made Tivern's grip on my waist tighten, squeezing the air from my lungs.

'If you don't mind,' I gasped, 'could you save the discussion for later? Just now I'd like this situation resolved peacefully.'

'Listen to the little lady. I'm not a patient man,' added Tivern.

'How did this happen?' Bonaventure asked Billy, ignoring my protest. I felt no more significant than a sack of meal.

Billy ran his hand through his hair in frustration, incredulous that he had let the smuggler get one over on him. 'Brainless female had a blade in her sash. When she got close enough, he grabbed it.'

'Only after you cut him free,' I snapped, thinking Billy's explanation cast my part in far too unflattering a light. I was already cursing myself for forgetting the weapon, but then I was not used to going about with daggers in my belt – that was more Billy's style.

'Now here's what I'm going to do,' announced Tivern, none too pleased to be excluded from our bickering when he thought it should be his grand moment of turning the tables. 'I'm going to take her back to my ship and watch while you put my cargo back in the hold. When I'm satisfied, I'll cast off and resume my voyage. You will not interfere.'

'And the girl?' Billy asked.

'I'll let her go when I'm sure you won't trouble me again.'

'*Non.*' Captain Bonaventure's single syllable cut through Tivern's self-satisfaction like a hot knife through butter.

'What!' I squawked.

'Take the girl if you like but I'm not giving you the guns.' He turned his back on Tivern in contempt and strode away. Billy took one look at me then set off in pursuit.

The smuggler flushed with rage. Realizing he had met with a cold-hearted scoundrel like himself who wasn't going to give even an inch, he muttered an oath then bundled me along the plank and on to the deck of his ship, shoving a sailor out of his path. Forced to drop his load, the sailor lost his balance and tumbled into the water, now in serious danger of being squashed between the two vessels as they rode the waves. Thankfully, the last glimpse I had was of him hauling himself hand over hand up the *Medici*'s anchor cable.

With a glance into the hold, Tivern quickly

ascertained that half the guns were still on board the *Merry Meg*. Maintaining a death grip on my neck, he sliced through the ropes tying his men. Bonaventure gave no signal to stop him. I could see the Frenchman watching us coolly from the wheel of the *Medici*, taking no steps to help or hinder Tivern as he resumed control. The smugglers' bosun hacked through the ropes tethering the vessels together and the two ships slowly began to drift apart. The last members of the *Medici* leapt overboard to avoid being stranded among an enemy crew.

My gaze raked the deck of my ship, desperate to see some sign that Bonaventure wasn't really going to abandon me like this, but there were no preparations to come to my rescue. Billy was arguing with the captain, fists bunched, yet the Frenchman was unmoved, happy to accept three hundred rifles in exchange for one useless passenger. As I watched, Billy lost control of his temper and threw a punch at Bonaventure. The Frenchman went down, but sprang up immediately and ordered Billy to be restrained by two crewmen and dragged below.

Thus ended their friendship.

That would teach me to sail with pirates.

Tivern seemed almost to have forgotten he was still holding me as he issued orders to make sail. I was in no hurry to remind him so remained quiet, dangling like a doll in his iron grip. When more than a thousand yards separated us from the *Medici*, he suddenly remembered me and dropped me to my feet, tucking the dagger into his belt. His expression was murderous. I'd proved almost useless as a hostage – he was sure to think me of no further value. It looked as though I was about to be jettisoned.

'I'm . . . er . . . sorry,' I blurted out.

Surprised out of his anger, Tivern raised a bushy black eyebrow. 'You're sorry?'

I nodded. 'Sorry that Captain Bonaventure didn't care more for me than the guns. That's French gallantry for you.' I attempted a wry smile.

Tivern burst into laughter and slapped me on the back with his meaty palm. I staggered.

'You're made of stern stuff, my girl. Most females would be having hysterics by now but no, not you. You apologize for the blackguard who abandoned you.' He scratched his unshaven chin, then folded his arms. 'I'd say you've got even more cause to hate him than I have.'

I rubbed my bruised ribs which ached as if they'd been squeezed in a vice. 'I suppose I have.'

'Don't feel too insulted, miss: it's something that he didn't try to stop the *Meg* leaving, knowing what it would mean for you. You must've counted for something. Here.' Tivern shoved Pedro's letter into my hand. 'You suffered enough to get this. Read it while I decide what to do with you.'

With a nod, I took myself off to an out-of-the-way corner of the deck and unfolded Pedro's message. The sailors glanced towards me curiously from time to time, but otherwise seemed happy to ignore my existence. That suited me.

Onboard the Merry Meg
31st July 1792

Dear Cat,
What can I say? I'm sure you are furious with me. I'm

sorry I went off without a word but the chance came along and I had to make a quick decision – the **Merry Meg** was sailing that night and the captain would not wait. I know you will have fretted about me a little but please stop worrying: I've always had to look after myself and am quite good at it now, despite what you might have thought when you first showed me round London!

As you may have guessed, I've decided to throw in my lot with the rebels on San Domingo. You don't need me now you've got Mrs Peabody's Ensemble so my conscience tells me that I should fight for what I believe in or live with the shame for the rest of my days. Such a chance comes but once in a lifetime. I don't know if you'll understand, Cat – please try – but it is something I just have to do. Even if I can't be much help at the very least I can lighten spirits with my music – a far better thing than entertaining fat slave owners and their wives as I had planned to do in Kingston.

I'll write to you care of Frank as soon as I can. Forgive my harsh words on our last meeting. No doubt you were only doing what you thought best, but promise me you'll never forget that slave-owning harms both the slave and the master.

With love,
Your friend and brother, Pedro

Stroking the paper that had so recently been in Pedro's hands, I folded the letter. Pedro sounded well: determined and clear-headed. He hadn't run off in a pique as I had feared but had been drawn to something far more important. Seeing history unfolding before his eyes, his conscience had told him to play his part, no matter how small, in the struggle for freedom. Who was I to try to stop him?

As the wind tugged on the letter, threatening to blow it to San Domingo, the extent of my own arrogance dawned on me. Despite everything, I had assumed I knew best for Pedro and had been trying to manage his life for him. My reaction may have been rooted in the concern of a sister, but it reminded me of the lording instincts of the white man. Pedro's dedication to a cause humbled me, making my own aims seem so very petty. He deserved my support, not my attempts to nanny him.

I tucked the letter away in my pocket. Not that any of this mattered now: I was a hostage on board a hostile vessel heading into unknown waters. Perhaps I should start worrying for myself?

SCENE 3 — MERRY MEG

'You know, girl, I'll be damned if I know what I should do with you.' Tivern had returned and stood towering over me. He scratched his head, dislodging his battered hat so it sat aslant on his curly dark hair. The odour of drink and dirt rose from his clothes when he moved — a perfume he shared with the rest of his grubby crew. 'It's been a godawful day but you were the only piece of luck that came near me — halved my losses. By rights, I should chuck you over the side and be done but I wouldn't like to spit in the face of Lady Luck.'

Nor did I want to be thrown to the sharks.

I managed a small protest. 'I can't swim.'

'Don't matter out here: nowhere to swim to. What's your Christian name?'

'Cat.'

He gave me a grin that displayed his blackened teeth. 'I've heard cats don't like water.'

I shuddered. 'You've heard right.'

'Little actress, aren't you? I saw you do that Shakespeare play the other week.'

'I am, but I left the company to go searching for Pedro.' I rubbed my arms – despite the sun my skin felt very cold. Fear, I realized, not malaria this time. 'It was the stupidest idea I've ever had.' Remembering some other foolish behaviour on my part, I amended my remark. 'One of the stupidest.'

'Tell me, girl, why do you want to find Pedro? He left of his own accord – no force on my part, I promise you.'

'I know that now.' I gestured to the letter.

'So what you doing out here? Ain't no place for a lady.'

I shrugged. 'Just doing what I always do.'

'And what's that?' The smuggler took a swig from a bottle he held loosely in his fist.

'I think I've been far too protective of Pedro. I'm stopping that now. I see that he doesn't need me to survive.'

Tivern grunted and handed me the drink – a gesture of fellowship that I could not refuse. Not wanting to taste the contents, I took a sip with closed lips, feeling the burning touch of undiluted rum on the tip of my tongue. Definitely not my favourite tipple.

I passed it back. 'I could murder a cup of tea right now,' I muttered more to myself than to him.

Tivern called over his shoulder to a sailor on the lower deck. 'Oi, Kai, fetch the lady some of your dishwater.'

A sailor with the pallor of the Orient and a whip-like black braid dangling over his shoulder put down the sail he'd been mending and disappeared into the galley. He returned moments later carrying a bowl of steaming liquid. Despite looking a blackguardly fellow, he gave a polite bow that would not have shamed a Mayfair butler. I took a cautious mouthful then sighed as my taste buds rejoiced in the heavenly savour of tea.

'I think I've just fallen in love.' I cradled the bowl and inhaled. The clench of fear in my stomach was unknotting in the steam; surely a crew intending to do away with me would not bother to pamper me first?

'Hear that, Kai? The lady likes your brew.' Tivern appeared to be enjoying the simple pleasure I was taking in the first decent cup I'd had since Philadelphia. From his bemused expression, I think he couldn't quite believe that he was being so kind to me. Long might it last.

Kai touched his heart. 'Missy have good taste. Not like them.' He gestured to his crewmates.

'We give him a lot of grief for refusing to drink rum,' explained Tivern, propping himself against the rail and taking another swig.

Kai squatted down beside me. 'I only one not a drunken sot.'

I took another gulp, marvelling at the contrasts this day had brought. At one moment, this crew had been the enemy, chasing me up the mast at sword-point; next they were my captors, dragging me off my ship; now they were discussing the virtues of tea-drinking as if I were a treasured guest.

'Seems you've found a soul-mate, Kai,' remarked Tivern. 'How do you fancy an extra pair of hands in the galley?'

Kai inspected me then nodded.

'So you're not going to throw me to the sharks?' I'd guessed as much but it was still a relief to have this confirmed.

'Not yet.' Tivern toasted me with a third swig.

Unfortunately, it was at this moment that an old acquaintance arrived – the man who had pursued me along the yardarm.

'Captain, seems like the *Medici* is following us after all,' said the bosun, casting an unfriendly look at me. 'P'rhaps we've got something they want back.'

'Maybe.' Tivern took the offered spyglass and trained it on the sails just appearing over the horizon behind us.

'We could leave her for them to pluck out the water.'

'She can't swim and I won't wait for them to get so close again,' Tivern said with an air of finality.

'So what if she drowns?' The bosun had not forgotten or forgiven the bruise I'd given him with the rifle butt. 'She won't be the first.'

'I thought you said you didn't hurt girlies,' I said accusingly, putting down my tea in preparation to resist any attempt to chuck me over the side. If necessary, I was planning to cling like a barnacle to Tivern's leg.

Tivern roared with laughter. 'He told you that, did he?'

'He did. And I'm sure he's an honourable man – a man of his word.' I scowled at the bosun.

'Are you saying you doubt my honour?' the bosun challenged.

'No. Will you give me reason to change my opinion?'

Tivern clapped his hand on the rail. 'She's got you there, Mickey. If you hurt her, you're dishonoured. How on earth did she wriggle round that one so fast?'

I began to feel more confident. From the relaxed stances of the three men it was apparent that the bosun's threat was not about to be carried out. In fact, it occurred to me that I was strangely at home among this group of cutthroats. They reminded me of my friends in London, the same ease of a gang that had known each other for a long time, through good times and bad.

'I'm a wriggler, you say? That's no mystery – I grew up in London. It'll be all those jellied eels I ate when I was little.'

'Well, you're not so big now.' Tivern pulled me to my feet. I only came up to his chest. ''Bout the height of my daughter when I last clapped eyes on her. She lives in London too.'

'Wish I still did,' I said, thinking of my snug berth in the Sparrow's Nest.

''Fraid I'm not going that way, minnow. Too many enemies waiting for me.'

I sighed. 'Oh well, it was worth a try.'

'I thought we threw the little ones back,' grumbled the bosun, but he too appeared to be mellowing towards me.

Tivern shook his head. 'Not this one. We'll take her to our next port, then let her go. For now, let's put our minds to giving the Frog-pirate the slip.'

My future on board the *Merry Meg* decided, I followed Kai to the galley. I had not even bothered to ask Tivern to try to return me to the *Medici*. After Captain Bonaventure had cheerfully traded me for the rifles, I trusted him even less than this bunch of smugglers. It was enough for now that no one appeared to be planning to harm me – a nice change – and that I had some allies on board in the captain and the cook. I would worry later what to do when I was cast off in a strange port with no more than the clothes on my back. At least I had my cat necklace tucked away under my shirt – that should fetch something if I was desperate.

Touching the pendant, I wondered what Billy was doing now. If the *Medici* was following, it was possible that he had managed to bribe Bonaventure once more in an attempt to rescue me. But as the distance between the two ships increased, that looked increasingly doubtful. The *Medici* did not act as if determined to waylay us; she merely looked to be heading in roughly the same direction. After a while, she dropped below the horizon. I found myself worrying about Billy and Jenny – would they be all right? I laughed sardonically when I caught myself at it, chewing my lip as I stood at the rail scanning the ocean. I had never imagined I would ever be anxious about Billy Shepherd of all people.

'Little missy, are you going to dream all day?' Kai called from the galley. 'There is work to do.'

Feeling hungry after my adventures, I was more than happy to be cook's mate. We spent a couple of sociable hours preparing the food on deck in the sunshine before he chucked it all in a big pan sizzling with oil. The actual cooking took no time at all. Kai's method impressed me immensely – it was just the sort to suit my impulsive nature. Now I saw that it was possible to prepare a meal in this way, I wondered why anyone bothered with baking.

As the crew settled down around us to eat, I filled my own bowl from the pan.

'Where did you learn to cook like this?' I asked, savouring the gingery taste of the chicken meat. I was using a spoon but Kai was picking his meal up with two long sticks like extensions to his fingers. I'd never met anyone from so far away before and his exotic habits intrigued me.

'I come from China – this how we eat.'

'So fast?'

'Yes.' He shovelled in a clump of rice, speaking with his mouth full. 'Tell me how little missy get on board bad Frog ship.'

We passed the next few hours sipping green tea and recounting tales of my recent travels interspersed with anecdotes from Kai's epic journeys. The off-duty men who lounged within earshot chipped in with the odd comment or joke, usually at Kai's expense, but he gave as good as he got. No one was spared a taste of the crew's cruelly friendly banter – if you were ignored, that meant they didn't see you as one of them. So I decided it was comforting rather than insulting when they started referring to me as the freckle-faced midget and other less flattering names.

The stars had been lit for the curtain-up of night by the time we finished clearing away from supper, the sky an astonishing display that put any spectacle created by the theatre to shame. The ship's bell rang, the signal to turn in. Kai led me below deck. Those not on watch were slinging their hammocks and removing their boots in preparation for sleep.

'Little missy hang her hammock next to mine,' Kai announced, pointing out two hooks in the ceiling of the lower deck. 'Captain, he decide he like you, but not all crew can be trusted.' He drew his finger across his throat in an expressive gesture.

Casting nervous looks at the men, some already snoring in their bunks, I hung mine as instructed. All too aware how the tolerant mood could change in a blink of an eye, I was grateful to accept Kai's protection. Thus, swinging gently next to the Chinaman, I fell asleep dreaming of his stories of pandas and pagodas.

The following evening we made landfall off the north coast of San Domingo to rendezvous the rebels waiting for their guns. I guessed my time on board the *Meg* was coming to an end.

'Are you going to leave me here, Captain?' I asked Tivern as he supervised the unloading of his cargo.

He patted my head absent-mindedly. 'I don't think so, minnow. There is no "here". This is as far from "here" as you can get. No port, no ships to take you home.'

I watched the boats rowing to shore. In the darkness with only the moonlight to show the way, men dashed out from the trees to help haul the keels on to the beach. A line formed to pass the cargo so it could be packed on the backs of a dozen mules – all done without a word being spoken. A tall man stood to one side directing operations, a dark silhouette against the pale sand.

'Who are these people?'

'The rebel leader Toussaint's men. I don't think they're going to be too pleased when they realize I've only brought them half what they paid for.' But Tivern didn't seem to be worried by this. He filled a pipe, struck a spark and began to smoke calmly, blowing the fumes into the air to disperse the humming mosquitoes.

'Will they do anything – anything bad, I mean – when they find out?' I asked anxiously.

'No. They need me too much. They're in a desperate way and I'm one of the few prepared to stick my neck out and get them what they want.'

I looked at Tivern with new respect: I hadn't expected this noble side to his character.

'So I take it you hate slavery too then?'

He raised an eyebrow. 'No, little'un, it's the way of the world. I have no quarrel with it.'

'Oh. Then why help the rebels?'

'Damn good money, that's why.' He scratched his belly lazily.

I mentally scratched out 'noble' from my list of Tivern's attributes, sticking with mercenary.

Shipment complete, the man who had directed the offloading on the beach came on board to complete payment. He must have been at least six feet tall and carried himself like a soldier on parade. With his shaven head and sharp eyes, he made an imposing leader, despite his tattered clothes.

'Monsieur Tivern, you have tricked us!' he announced angrily as soon as his foot hit the deck. 'General Toussaint will not be pleased!'

'Not at all, sir,' Tivern drawled. 'It was a blasted Frog who took your guns.'

The rebel scowled, finding Tivern's English hard to follow. 'Who is this "frog" you speak of?'

Recalling my fluent French, the smuggler decided to save himself the bother and waved me forward. 'Minnow, explain to the man what happened.'

I rapidly acquainted the soldier with the pertinent points of our encounter the previous day.

'And if you still need the arms, sir,' I added on my own account, 'I imagine Captain Bonaventure would be happy to sell them to you. He has no loyalty but to money and his ship is heading this way.'

The soldier gave me a surprised look, followed by a curt nod. 'Thank you, mademoiselle.'

He was about to leave but I couldn't pass up this chance – I wouldn't get a better one.

'Sir, do you know if a boy called Pedro has joined you recently?'

He reassessed me contemptuously. It was clear in his estimation I had quite cancelled out my good deed of tipping him off about Bonaventure. 'Runaway slave of yours, is he?' he asked coolly.

'No!' I made a move towards him but drew up short when I saw his hostile expression warning me off. 'He's my friend. You might know him because he plays the violin like an angel.'

The soldier paused, examining my face more closely. 'I know him. What of it?'

'Is he safe?'

'None of us are safe. This is a rebellion, mademoiselle, not a tea-party.'

I glanced at Tivern, who was following the gist of our conversation with a frown, then turned back. 'Will you take me to him?'

Tivern stepped forward. 'Not a good idea, minnow. You'll be heading into a war.'

'Why you want to see him so badly?' the soldier asked, running a hand over his bald head a little wearily. I could see that I was a complication he could well do without.

'I just want to find him, see that he is all right.'

The soldier appeared to accept this. 'I'll take you – if you come immediately. I've not got time to waste.'

'I'm ready now.' I nodded to my abductor. 'That's the benefit of travelling with no luggage.'

The soldier turned away, but added as an

afterthought over his shoulder, 'Be warned: make any move against us and I'll kill you.'

Tivern took me aside as the rebel disembarked. 'Are you sure about this, minnow? I can take you to a proper port. Don't seem right to let a little lady go gallivanting off with the likes of them.'

'I'm not sure of anything, Captain Tivern, but I came all this way to find Pedro so I'd better go ahead and finish it.' I reflected a moment, then went up on tiptoes to give him a quick peck on the cheek. 'You're not as mean as you make out, did you know that?'

He looked sheepish. 'Don't let on or my name will be mud.'

'I won't.' I bowed to Kai then kissed him also. 'Thank you for everything.'

'You mad girl,' Kai said, shaking his head.

'I know.'

He pressed a little packet in my hand.

'What's this?'

'The best medicine.'

An order to hurry was shouted from the boat. I clambered swiftly over the side and dropped down near the bow. As the rowers took us to shore, I sniffed my present.

Green tea!

The journey from the coast to the rebels' base was far more arduous than I had anticipated. I hadn't thought much beyond getting on dry land but, of course, I should have realized that the slaves had to hide far from the centres of white men's power. This meant a long, foot-blistering tramp into the highlands, travelling mainly in the dark. Once the soldier – called Colonel Deforce by his men – had agreed to my presence, he appeared to forget all about me, assuming I'd either keep up or give up. It was all the same to him – he had an army to think about. He organized the arms train so that most of the guards were deployed as scouts on either side of the little trail we were following, checking ahead and behind for problems. I had only to look at their grim faces when they came back to realize that they were serious about the likelihood of meeting with trouble – another aspect of the journey to which, in my ignorance, I hadn't given much thought. As I counted my blisters each night, Reader, I reflected that my recklessness had gone too far this time. What was I going to do if it came to a skirmish?

Feeling the acute need for an ally in this crowd of warlike strangers, I made friends with the man in charge of the mules, a kind-looking runaway from Le Cap. With twinkling brown eyes and a smile that could light up a dark room, he walked with a limp at a pace that I could match. After boldly introducing myself, we shook hands. As our palms clasped, I noticed that his right hand was maimed.

'Don't mind that,' said Caesar, my new friend, when he caught me flinching. His French was good – he'd obviously had some schooling. He tucked his hand into his jacket pocket. 'I lost several fingers to my old master; it could've been worse.'

Shocked as I was by the cruelty of slavery, I was also impressed by the man's acceptance of the lot life had dealt him.

'He sounds a nasty tyrant,' I commented.

'That he was. I bided my time. He could take

my fingers as a punishment but he couldn't steal my thoughts. When Toussaint and the others put the call out to rebel, I was ready.'

I prodded a mule away from a bush that it had taken a fancy to in large mouthfuls. As usual it was the most stubborn of the creatures, the one that I'd christened Mr Pitt in honour of our illustrious British prime minister. 'No you don't, Mr Pitt, no time for that now. I think that was very brave of you, Caesar, to join up. And your family? Are they safe?'

'Don't have no family, mademoiselle. The only girl I cared for was sold on to another master. I hope we'll find each other again, but I doubt it.'

His company greatly lightened the hours spent walking. I think I would have been forced to give up if he hadn't extended the care he showed to his animals to me. The sole of my shoe disintegrated halfway through the second day. Caesar walked barefoot on big leathery feet but refused to allow me to do the same.

'It takes a good few years to toughen up, mademoiselle. Your feet will be in shreds if you risk it and you'll never keep up with us.' Perching me on the back of an obliging mule, he cobbled together a temporary solution with a piece of bridle and a bit of bark stripped from a tree. 'That should last for a day or two.'

'I am most obliged to you, Caesar.'

'My pleasure, mademoiselle.'

A shrill whistle echoed from the trees ahead. Without a word, Caesar turned swiftly and led the mules from the path. We plunged into the cover of the undergrowth, shielded by the broad rubbery leaves and trailing vines. With wide eyes, I tapped his arm, making a silent enquiry as to what was going on. He shook his head and put a finger to his lips. I guessed that meant that we had company. A shot creased the canopy overhead, bringing foliage fluttering down upon us, soon followed by more gunfire, cracking away in the distance like a Vauxhall Gardens fireworks display. If only it had so peaceable an explanation. Pushing me to the ground, Caesar tugged his rifle off the lead mule and crawled on his belly to the edge of the road. My heart pounding, mouth full of dirt, I lay as still as possible, praying that this would soon be over.

A shot rang out much closer now and Mr Pitt, the stubborn mule, took it into its head to panic. Pulling on the tether that bound it to the animal in front, it began to drag the string of mules into a jogging trot towards the road. It was like watching the inexorable slide of pearls tumbling off a broken necklace as each animal caught the fear and jerked into flight. Caesar spun round too late to catch Mr Pitt. Someone had to do something or the rifles would be in enemy hands. Without thinking, I leapt to my feet, dashed to the head of the line and threw my arms around the foolish creature's neck, fumbling for the bridle to turn it before it reached the open and got shot to pieces. Too late. Mr Pitt staggered on to the road and the bullets ripped into the ground around us. One ball struck the mule in the shoulder and the creature went down so quickly that it crushed me under it, my legs trapped. Jerking and braying in agony, poor Mr Pitt tried to struggle up but the wound was mortal. Still the bullets pinged around us, spraying me with dirt and chips of stone.

Help was at hand – at least for the other mules. Caesar appeared behind me with a machete. Swiftly he sliced through the tethers to free the surviving pack animals and lead them off the road – his priority to save the shipment of arms. Desperate now, I tried to heave Mr Pitt off my legs but the animal was too heavy. Each distressed movement the creature made ground my thighs against the stony ground. I had been left a sitting duck; it would surely be no time at all before a marksman hit me.

Then two hands grasped me under the shoulders and heaved. With a painful scrape of shins against stone, I was tugged from under Mr Pitt and hauled off the road. Caesar dragged me ten yards into the undergrowth and buried me under a bush.

'Stay there!' he ordered, returning to his rifle.

I wasn't going to argue. The last few minutes had just revealed that courage under fire was not my strong suit. I had come close to all-out panic when pinned out there under that poor mule. In any case I had serious doubts I could move my legs even if I had wanted to. Cautiously feeling down their length, I discovered long bleeding scratches through the ripped material of my sailor's breeches. They stung like fury. Mercifully, no bones were broken.

Eventually, the gunfire subsided. Caesar waited for the all-clear, then strode back on to the road, shouldered his rifle and took aim. Mr Pitt was put out of his misery with an efficient bullet in the brain. Next my friend came in search of me.

'Let me see,' he ordered, gesturing to my legs. I turned on to my stomach to allow the examination. I felt a splash of liquid on my cuts and the smell of brandy.

'I hope that wasn't your finest,' I commented once the sting had worn off a little. 'Hate to waste it.'

'Not wasted, little soldier. If I don't clean it, your legs might go bad and have to be chopped off.'

I grimaced. 'Fair enough. But if it comes to that, promise you'll put a bullet in my brain first.'

He helped me up and it was then that we discovered both my shoes were still under Mr Pitt's carcass, having parted company with my feet when I had been dragged to safety. Caesar went back to retrieve them, bloodstained and battered. It turned my stomach to put them on again, but, as I was rapidly discovering, there was no time for squeamishness in war. Caesar pulled the string of mules back on to the road, minus one of their number, and insisted that I perch on the back of the lead animal until my wounds stopped bleeding. It was only as we plodded onwards around the bend in the trail that I saw the other casualties and realized that I had got away lightly. Four dead white men, local militia from their uniforms, lay on their backs. Two rebels were stripping them of their weapons, clothes and boots, making sure nothing was wasted.

'War,' grunted Caesar. 'Ugly, *n'est-ce pas?*'

'Ugly and terrible,' I agreed with a shudder, sending up a silent prayer for the victims.

Caesar sighed. 'The way I see it, we have a choice between two bad paths. Either we carry on being killed as slaves or we take our chances as rebels – I've chosen to fight. But I'd prefer to be tending my own animals on a little farm where the soil is rich and the climate kind.'

'Maybe one day you will.'

He shrugged. 'I'm not holding my breath. I fear we've a long dark road of fighting and hiding out in the hills to travel first. The odds of us coming through this alive are slim.'

'But there's a chance?'

'*Oui*, mademoiselle, as long as the sun rises each morning, there's always hope.'

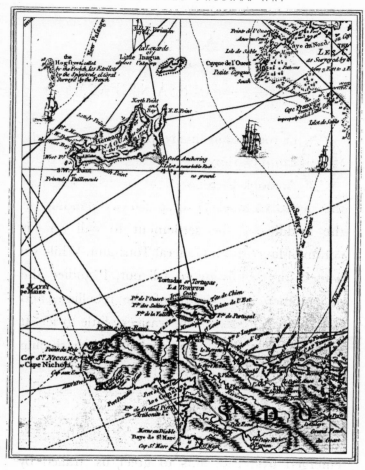

Act V – In which Cat expresses her feelings towards Captain Bonaventure…

ACT V

SCENE 1 – TOUSSAINT'S ARMY

Our mule train finally arrived at the rebels' camp two days after the attack on the road. Anxious to report that he had only half the arms, Colonel Deforce left us standing in the middle of the settlement to call on his commanding officer, General Toussaint. While we waited for permission to fall out, I studied the encampment, the centre of the rebellion, and quickly realized that there was very little to see. It was a sad jumble of cabins on the steeply sloping ground – not an inspiring sight. General Toussaint would have to pray that his troops turned out to be more disciplined than this dilapidated camp.

News of our arrival spread rapidly. Women emerged from the huts to greet us, trailed by children hanging on their skirts or held to their backs in cloth slings. Soon the air was filled with the soothing sound of greetings and laughter. I was given a wide berth, but attracted many curious glances. It felt very odd to be the only white face among so many. I now knew what it must have been like for Pedro when the children of London followed him about the streets, bemused by the novelty of his skin. However, I was too weary to care very much what they thought of this dirt-streaked English girl. Relieved to have finally stopped travelling, I sat down on the ground, took off my tattered shoes and wriggled my toes, letting the fresh air get to my blisters.

A bold infant in a ragged shirt crept up and tweaked my hair.

'It's all right – it's real,' I said, collapsing back on to the grass, eyes closed. 'You can play with it if you like, just make sure no one treads on me for the next few minutes while I sleep.'

The child took me at my word. With a giggle, she settled down beside me, the gentle tugs on my scalp reassuring me that she was still there as she plaited it.

Suddenly, the ground thudded under my head and a body launched itself on top of me, knocking the air from my lungs. Gathered up into a hug, I was squeezed hard against a familiar narrow chest.

'You stupid, idiotic, reckless girl! What on earth are you doing following me here?' cried Pedro, giving me a shake.

'Pleased to see you too, Pedro,' I gasped, feeling as if the sun had risen inside me, warming me from head to toe with joy. 'Would you mind letting me breathe, please?'

His arms relinquished a little of their hold, but not enough to let me escape – not until he'd finished telling me exactly what he thought of my decision to chase him into a war zone.

'You don't deserve to breathe, Cat. I told you not to worry about me – you should've stayed with Mrs Peabody – I can't believe you've got here in one piece – you should be thrashed for being so foolish!'

Hugging him close, I waited for his stream of words to dry up. Pedro was usually so self-contained; it was decidedly odd to see him like this, spilling out his worry on my behalf.

'They said you survived an ambush. Dammit,

Cat, I don't know what I would've done if you'd been killed coming after me!'

'Probably chased me into the afterlife to tell me off.'

'Very likely.' He squeezed me tighter. 'But, hang it all, Cat, it's good to see you. I hated going off without saying goodbye but you'd understand if you knew the captain of the *Merry Meg*. I wasn't given a choice.'

'Oh, but I do know him,' I interjected. 'A very sweet man.'

Pedro pushed me to arms' length. 'Captain Tivern, sweet? I don't think we're talking about the same person at all.'

'Yes, we are. He gave me your letter. That was after he abducted me and then signed me up as galley hand. I got on famously with most of the crew, with the possible exception of the bosun who chased me up the main mast of the *Medici* with a dagger between his teeth.' I twirled a curl between finger and thumb reflectively. 'He seemed to warm to me eventually though.'

Pedro caught the twinkle in my eye and

realized I was teasing him. He burst out laughing and hugged me again.

'You'll have to tell me all about it. Doubtless it is some tall tale worthy of Cat Royal at her most inventive.'

'It's all God's honest truth, sir!' I protested. 'You didn't think I managed to get here without a story or two to tell you, did you?'

'I suppose not.' He sat back and studied me. 'Why are you sitting on the ground?'

'I'm exhausted. You'd have to be as blind as a brickbat not to notice that my feet are a battlefield all of their own – the blisters being the victorious army in case you wondered. My legs are scraped and in danger of rotting off, according to Caesar, and I could sleep for a week. Other than that, and the fact that I'm still supposed to be recuperating from malaria, I've never been better.'

Hearing my plight, Pedro stood and scooped me up from my grassy bed, staggering slightly under my weight. I squawked but he wouldn't put me down. Secretly I was impressed he could manage me, but then he had always been strong for his size.

'Come on then, Trouble – let's get you fixed up and we can talk.'

'Yes, I'd like that.' I sighed, content just for the moment to let someone else look after me.

An hour later, cup of green tea in hand, I sat on a patch of earth in front of Pedro's cabin, gazing down on the mountain slopes, an effective rampart hiding the camp from the San Domingo planters and their militia. Pristine forest clung to the hillsides, low clouds straggling over the highest peaks. The air was full of the sound of birds calling, hammering, and the shouts of men at their exercises. Down at the bottom of the valley, a fast-flowing stream slipped like a silver snake gliding northwards to the sea. A group of women washed clothes on the banks as children played beside them, the occasional laugh or cry reaching us.

As I looked more closely, I saw that the trees had been cleared from the lowest slopes around the camp and the red earth, free of restraining roots, now bled into the river like an open wound.

The sight of the forest's fertility being washed away reminded me of the fragile peacefulness of the scene. It was all temporary, a pause before more bloodshed. Would those children live to see a time without war, a day when they would be truly free? Or would the dream that Toussaint had planted be cruelly cut down and crushed before it had a chance to flower? If I was a gambler, I'd put my money on the latter.

'Penny for your thoughts?' Pedro asked as he came to crouch beside me.

'You don't want to hear them. I was feeling melancholy.'

He snorted. 'Cat Royal is never melancholy. Angry, yes. Rude, definitely. Cheerful, most of the time.'

'Maybe I've changed.'

'Doubt it – not if you coming here is anything to go by.' Pedro gave me a fond but exasperated smile.

'What do you mean by that?'

He chuckled. 'I should've guessed you'd come after me. I imagine you browbeat everyone to get your way so that you could give me a piece of your mind and then drag me home with you. But it won't work, Cat – not this time.'

I put my cup down. 'That's where you're wrong, Pedro.'

He waved my words away. 'No, Cat, I'm serious. I appreciate you coming all this way, but this is my fight, my struggle; I'm not leaving while I still feel I can help.'

'I know that. I'm not here to stop you.'

'What!' Pedro looked almost disappointed that he didn't have to convince me of the rightness of his decision. 'So why are you here then?'

'I don't know really. To check you're all right, I suppose. I started out just as you said. Until I got your note from Tivern I wasn't really sure what had happened to you. But I realized a while ago that I can't live the rest of your life by your side, trying to keep you safe, I've been too . . . too managing. I just didn't want to lose you.'

'But you haven't lost me, Cat. The only difference is that I've found myself. General Toussaint says I can help maintain morale and give the men the words they need. I've put one of their songs to a new tune. It's about Moses leading the Israelites out of Egypt. Do you want to hear it?'

'More than anything.'

Pedro took his violin out of its case and set it under his chin. He gave me a smile totally free of the reserve that had always clung to him in London, then stood up to play. After a few bars, a woman ambling by with a basket of fruit began to sing along. Her voice was joined by a carpenter working at his bench down the hill. As I listened, more and more voices added to the chorus until even the women down at the stream were part of the choir. The harmonies were exquisite, resonating deep inside me in a place rarely touched by such feelings – the bottom of my soul if I had to put a name to it. Even more moving was the fact that this was the song of a free people – men and women who had claimed their liberty from God, not from any man, just like the people of the Old Testament. I knew I had to give up my friend to this cause and I was proud of him, even though the sacrifice felt like a limb being amputated. When I left – as I had to do very soon

– I would be leaving Pedro behind with scant chance of seeing him again.

Pedro finished with a flourish and the song died away as his comrades returned to their tasks with a smile on their faces. He looked at me expectantly, head cocked to one side.

'What do you think?'

What could I say? I'd watched him receive standing ovations for his performances in Drury Lane, but this outshone anything he'd done before – a true gem to the paste jewels of the theatre.

'Speechless?' Pedro laughed. 'Then that's praise indeed from Cat Royal.' He gave me a bow.

I tweaked his ear, struggling to regain my usual manner with him. 'You know it was brilliant, you rogue! You've always been disgustingly talented. You put the rest of us mere mortals to shame.'

He laid the violin back in its case. 'But you have a more important talent, Cat, for loyal, unswerving friendship. See where it's brought you.' He waved an arm at our surroundings.

'Humph! To the back of beyond and a ragtag army that hasn't much chance of surviving the winter.'

'But the chances are a mite better with my music to encourage them.' He gave a gesture as if conducting an orchestra on the hillside.

I smiled. 'With your music hitched to the wagon, I imagine they'll be able to drive this rebellion all the way. You made them sound like gods and goddesses. And if they sing as well as they fight, then you can't fail.'

He gave me an ironic look. We both knew that it was not going to be as easy as that. 'So what are we going to do about you, Cat? You know you can't stay.'

His question reminded me that I had to make some decisions.

'I don't belong here – and I wasn't joking about recuperating from malaria. I've not been well and it might come back at any time, according to Cookie. I'd be a burden.'

'Who's Cookie?'

'Mr Hawkins' slave-cook. Oh yes, I forgot to mention that I am now your old master's indentured servant, still with twenty years to serve.'

'No!' Pedro rocketed to his feet in indignation.

I tugged him back down. 'Don't worry – I couldn't care less what he thinks. Billy burned down his barn to get me away so it cost Hawkins dearly to entrap me. But it did make me think that perhaps I should head back to England where I can rely on the Avons to protect me should Hawkins decide to try and enforce his poxy bit of paper. I could rejoin Mrs Peabody's troupe, but what if Hawkins gets wind of this and pursues me to another island? I don't think I fancy that as the authorities might well side with the local man.'

Pedro nodded. 'No, I wouldn't risk it. Shame though.'

'Yes, I know. I wanted to see Georgie again, but I suppose I'd better be sensible for once. As for going back to Lizzie and Johnny, that seems just a retreat as I have no intention of settling with them – I'd still have to decide what to do next. No, looking at it now, I think my future is in the old world, not the new.'

Pedro tapped his fingers on the violin case for a

moment before agreeing. 'I think you're right. You promised you'd go back one day so it might as well be now. The only problem is how to get you there.'

'Well, I'm sure as the devil is in London not going to swim. I thought the only thing I could do was find a ship heading that way and bargain my way on board with this.' I held out Billy's necklace.

Pedro touched it reverently. 'That's lovely. Wherever did you get it?'

'From Billy.'

'Really? Well, wonders will never cease – that's something else you're going to have to tell me about. Shame to lose so pretty a thing but you're right: it should buy you passage. When your feet have recovered, I'll take you to Tortuga – you'll find a ship there without having to tangle with the French authorities.' That settled, he picked up a stone and threw it down the hill to click against a larger rock. 'By the way, Cat, what did you do with your slave?'

'I did nothing, I'm afraid. As I said, I was taken hostage off the *Medici*. She's still with Billy, I expect. But I promise you, as soon as I can, I'll find her and make sure she's all right.'

Pedro gave a disgusted 'harrumph' but even he could not blame me for my unplanned excursion on board the *Merry Meg*.

Several peaceful weeks passed on the hillside. Knowing this might be the last time we would be together, Pedro and I spent as much of it as we could in each other's company, chatting about the past and planning for the future. I helped him with his French, sang with him as he composed new tunes, and tried not to grieve already for the loss of his friendship. Even though he said I would not be losing him, I knew that in truth the next separation would be like a death. Divided by thousands of miles of sea and a country at war with itself, it would be impossible for us even to correspond with any frequency, if at all.

The journey back to the San Domingo coast was less arduous than the one I had made to reach the camp, but no less nerve-racking. Word had reached the rebels that three hundred rifles had mysteriously turned up with a merchant on

Tortuga who was willing, if the price was right, to sell them to the rebels. Caesar and his mules were dispatched once more, this time carrying Pedro and me as passengers. The armed guard followed separately to rejoin the pack animals once the guns were loaded. There was no point alerting the white authorities to the suspicious nature of the mule train with an unnecessary show of force.

Instead, we were to pose as an innocent party of refugees. To this end, I had been donated a dress, slippers and petticoats stolen from a planter's daughter on one of the rebel raids. It felt strange to be back in frothy skirts after the liberty of my pirating gear, but I quickly adapted, and even began to enjoy pretending an elegance I did not naturally possess. Riding side-saddle on a mule, a parasol twirling above my head, I wondered if I would convince anyone that I was a San Domingo lady. We were to find out at the first road block.

'Excuse me, mademoiselle, but can you tell me who you are and where you are going?' The soldier inspected my escort of two 'slaves' with a suspicious eye. 'And why, do you mind me asking, do have you no chaperone?'

'Yes, I do,' I rapped out curtly in my best Parisian French, trying to disguise my shaking fingers with an artful spin of the parasol. I drew on my experience of outraged aristocrats and decided that the demeanour of the Duchess of Avon would best suit my purposes: attack better than defence.

'Do what, mademoiselle?'

'I do mind you asking, monsieur.' I pursed my lips, the picture of offended maidenhood. 'I'm sure that it is not part of your duties to interrogate young ladies fleeing for safety. But I will tell you in any case: the rebels attacked my home –'

'The blackguards,' cursed the soldier, looking more sympathetic now.

'Quite so. My father is sending me to my aunt in Le Cap. Having a plantation to salvage, he could not come himself so entrusted me into the care of his two most loyal slaves.' I gestured imperiously to my friends.

'And who is your father?'

I said the first French name that came to mind. 'Monsieur Jean-François Thiland. Have you heard of him?' I felt a curl of concern in my belly, wondering if my subterfuge was about to unravel.

The soldier shook his head. 'No, mademoiselle, can't say that I have, but I don't know everyone in these parts.'

That was a relief.

'Do you have any more questions for me or will you allow me to reach safety before it gets dark?' I cast a significant look up at the fading skies.

The soldier took another glance at my escorts – one crippled, the other a boy – then at the mules burdened only with provisions for the journey, and dismissed us as posing no threat.

'Hurry along then, mademoiselle. You won't make Le Cap tonight but there's a friendly welcome to be had at Widow Perigord's three mile or so further on.'

'Thank you, monsieur.'

He lifted the barrier and Caesar tapped the mule train into motion, Pedro shuffling meekly along at the rear.

Once out of sight, Pedro swung up on to the mule next to me.

'That was very well done. You'd better get back to the stage as soon as possible: it's clearly your destiny.'

Caesar chuckled.

'Thanks. It's pleasant to hear I have one.'

Pedro patted my shoulder. 'Whatever you choose to do in the future, Cat, I know it will be a triumph.'

But what, I wondered, was the point of a triumph when my brother would not be there to witness it?

SCENE 2 – SWEET ENDING

As the mules were staying on the mainland to await their load, we had to part with Caesar before taking a fishing boat to Tortuga. My kind friend gave me a hug by way of farewell.

'You are one fine girl, Mademoiselle Cat. I'm pleased you're getting out of this madhouse before the whole thing explodes.'

'Is it going to be that nasty then?' I wondered fleetingly if it would be possible to kidnap Pedro and take him to safety. But no, I'd already decided not to interfere.

'I'm afraid it will be. Poor whites against rich whites, mulattos standing up for their rights, we black men wanting our freedom – it's a cauldron full of trouble just waiting to boil over.' Caesar grinned. 'And if there's trouble for the white man on so many fronts, then we have a chance.'

'Will you look after Pedro for me?'

'No need to worry about that. We won't let

anything happen to our musician.'

Pedro tugged on my arm. 'Are you coming, Cat? The boat's ready to leave.'

'I am.'

Pedro tipped his hat to the mule-driver. 'See you in a few days, Caesar.'

'I'll be waiting, son.'

Pedro had promised me an experience in Tortuga and I wasn't disappointed. Though he had prepared me for the wildlife of the taverns and lodging houses of the waterfront, it wasn't the same as seeing it for myself. We arrived at midnight to find the drunken party had only just begun – the kind of celebration where Blackbeard and William Kidd would feel right at home. Sailors staggered down the waterfront arm in arm with strangers, fights broke out at random intervals, fortunes were won and lost in gambling. But the thing that made it different from all other ports I had visited was the prevailing sense that Tortuga was a ship sailing out of control: no man at the wheel, no one caring if they were headed for the rocks.

'Is it always like this?' I whispered, clutching Pedro's arm as a man spun past and reeled into a puddle.

'Only for the last hundred years or so. That's why pirates used it as their base – there was no law to call them to order. But the pirates have more or less been driven out of business by the naval patrols – it's much less dangerous now.' He backed me into a doorway to avoid a gang of carousing seamen.

'But it doesn't appear to have grown any more respectable.' I gave the sailors a pointed look.

'No – and it's got worse since the authorities have lost their grip on the mainland. Can't expect Tortuga to behave if the master has his eye elsewhere.'

All in all it did not look a very promising place to find a safe passage home.

'And you think we'll find a ship going to England from here?' I asked incredulously. 'I mean one I'd last five minutes on?'

Pedro grinned. 'You might not like the nightlife, Cat, but I assure you that many crews look forward to coming here as the high point in their voyage. Just trust me.'

Taking my hand, he pulled me into the largest tavern on the waterfront. Tables, chairs and patrons spilled out on to the veranda. The noise was deafening as each drinker shouted louder than his neighbour to get his voice heard.

'What are we doing here?' I yelled into Pedro's ear.

'The captains of the vessels in port tend to gather over there.' He gestured to the end of the bar where a few cleaner tables could be seen, less densely packed by customers. A couple of beefy men stood on guard, denying entry to this hallowed zone to any common sailor.

'Will we be able to get in?'

'That is why I brought my violin.'

We slid through the tables, avoiding out-stretched legs and barmaids bearing trays of drinks.

'Here, darlin', let me buy you a drink,' called a sailor to me, patting the seat next to him.

'Thank you, but no,' I said politely, a little

annoyed that he had mistaken me for the kind of girl who frequented these places.

He hooked the hem of my skirt with a bunched fist. 'Sure I can't change your mind? I feel awful lonely.'

'My heart aches for you, sir. Perhaps you should get yourself a parrot – I hear they make very good company.'

The sailor's mates laughed at my suggestion. There was a moment's pause while my admirer decided if he felt offended, then he let go of me.

'Don't want no damn creature that answers back,' he growled.

'Then you certainly wouldn't enjoy my company.' I gave him a sweet smile.

His mates howled with laughter at his expense and even my sailor smiled.

Pedro tugged me away. 'You took a risk there, Cat,' he whispered.

I shrugged. 'Not really. He meant no harm – you can tell from their eyes if they're going to turn on you. You can't live round Drury Lane all your life without knowing a thing or two about drunks.'

We reached the captains' corner with no further interruptions. The two guards, bronzed Hercules the pair of them, gave us a hard stare.

'What do you want?' one challenged us.

Pedro produced his violin. 'Just the chance to entertain.'

While Pedro continued his negotiation, promising a cut to the guards if they let us in, I peeked round the nearest of the two muscle-mountains to survey the prospective audience. At a quick count there seemed to be around a dozen captains in port, hopefully at least one of them bound for Europe. And the back of one man looked somewhat familiar . . .

Rage blew up inside me with all the force of a small hurricane, destroying self-control. I leapt over the bench separating the captains from the rest of humanity before any of the guards could stop me. I grabbed the tankard of ale out of the man's hand to cast it in his face.

'Captain Bonaventure, you are a foul wart on the derrière of French gallantry! You didn't care what happened to me, did you? I could've been chucked overboard, had my throat slit, but all you thought about was swiping those guns!'

The Frenchman wiped the ale from his eyes, momentarily robbed of speech to find a little red-haired fury berating him in front of his peers. Pedro tugged at my sleeve.

'Er, Cat, this isn't what I had planned to persuade someone to give you passage,' he hissed.

I shook him off, too busy prodding Bonaventure in the chest. 'If J-F ever finds out what you did, you can bet that your business dealings with him are over!'

Bonaventure frowned, picked up the remainder of his tankard and toasted me with the dregs. 'He'd understand the provocation, mademoiselle.' Splat! He threw the contents over me.

Incensed, I raised my hand to slap his face but I found my wrist restrained from behind.

'Cat, I really wouldn't do that.'

I spun round. 'Billy! Are you still drinking with this blackguard after what he did to me?'

Billy Shepherd shrugged and wiped the ale off my nose, still holding my wrist as a precaution.

'It was business. I realized that when I cooled down. I'd've done the same in 'is position. No 'arm done.'

'But . . . but I was almost thrown overboard. I've been shot at, walked my feet to bloody ruins, abandoned in a foreign country with no money, no way to get home –'

Billy winked. 'Sounds like you've been 'aving a fine old time – *and* you found Blackie.'

'His name is Pedro as you well know.' Pulling my wrist free, I folded my arms across my chest.

Bonaventure rose, ale still soaking into his once spotless shirtfront. 'Monsieur Shepherd, you will deal with the punishment for her insult to me?'

'You deserved it, Bonaventure, and you know it.' Billy didn't take his eyes off me in case I did anything else rash.

The Frenchman picked up his hat, twirling it on the end of one finger. 'Perhaps. But if she's going to make problems for me with my Parisian business contacts, maybe I should deal with her myself.'

'Leave her be. She won't – I'll make sure of that.'

'I'd like to see you try,' I growled.

Billy held my eye for a moment, a familiar hard glint making him seem far more dangerous than of late. But he couldn't intimidate me any longer.

'You won't like it if I have to persuade you to keep your mouth shut,' he warned.

I hadn't really meant to carry through my threat to tell J-F; the little King of the Palais Royal Thieves would probably not care enough about me to harm his business empire. But that didn't mean I couldn't gain something from this situation. Devil take me – I'd spent so much time in Billy's company, I was now even thinking like him!

'It'll cost you, Billy.'

He cocked an eyebrow.

'Jenny's papers.' I held out a hand, fingers waggling.

'Blackmail?'

'You should know all about that as you're the past master.'

With a snort, Billy felt in his jacket pocket and pulled out a sheet of parchment from a document wallet. 'Your promise?'

'I'll forgive and forget Captain Bonaventure's

scandalous lack of chivalry to a female in his care.'
I shot the Frenchman a poisonous look.

Billy turned to the captain. 'Satisfied?'

'*Oui*, monsieur. But don't look to me for passage back to Europe. I will not let that little vixen on board my ship for any money.'

'Then please unload my belongings. I will be escorting Miss Royal home.' Billy placed the document in my palm. 'Jenny's waiting in the kitchens, in case you wondered.'

With a grin, I pushed past the guards and made a dash for the rear of the tavern. I found Jenny seated at a long table, chatting companionably to some black women servants. She squealed with surprise on seeing me.

'Cat! You be alive!'

'Did you doubt it?' I gave her a hug.

'No, but me not expect to see you again. Mr Shepherd, he said we go back to London and wait for you to turn up dere, but me no want to go.'

'Well, you don't have to do anything now.' I stuffed the parchment into her hand. 'There you are.'

Jenny unfolded it and gave me a questioning look. 'What is it?'

Of course, she couldn't read. 'Your papers.'

She laughed. 'Cat, me not need them.'

'What?' I was a little disappointed that her gratitude was so muted.

'You tell me already – dey fit only for privy paper. You cannot give me my freedom – it always belonged to me.'

What was I thinking? I clapped my hands. 'In that case, into the fire with them.'

'Yes, missis.' With a roguish grin, Jenny tossed her papers into the kitchen hearth and, with great satisfaction, we both watched them blacken and burn.

Pedro appeared at my shoulder. He'd witnessed the whole scene from the doorway.

'I was wrong, Cat,' he said in a low voice, giving me a congratulatory kiss on the cheek.

'Wrong?'

'You made a good mistress if that's what you taught her. Will you introduce me?'

'Jenny, this is Pedro Amakye. Pedro, Jenny.'

Pedro bowed. 'Delighted to make your acquaintance, Miss Jenny.'

'You be de boy dat give Cat so much grief?' she asked, her indignation undermined by her twinkling eyes.

'I'm afraid to say I am, miss.'

She shook her finger at him. 'You should be ashamed of yourself.'

Pedro held up his hands. 'I am, I am.'

'But we've made up,' I explained, smiling at the sight of my former slave coming to my defence.

'And what now for you, Cat?' Jenny asked. 'You go back to England?'

'Yes.'

'And your friend?' Her eyes strayed to Pedro.

What was this? Was she thinking what I thought she was thinking?

'He's staying,' I replied innocently. 'He's got things to do here. What about you? Do you want to come with me to England?'

Jenny shook her head. 'What would me do in dat cold place? Me thought maybe . . .' she bit her lip . . . 'maybe me go with dat fool boy of yours and keep him out of trouble.'

'But Jenny –'

'Me want to be part of de rebellion. It be de one place me can be free.'

Pedro gave her an understanding look and took a seat by her side. I remained standing, not wanting to give in so quickly.

'And your father? What about Moses? What will he think?'

'He understand. He join us if he could.' Jenny waved to the place opposite her. 'Sit down, Cat. Eat someting. You look hungry.'

'But –'

'Me be free now, remember? You cannot do noting to stop me being a fool like your friend.'

I sat down, feeling thoroughly deflated. I had no right to stand in their way – not that I could. Nor did I really want to.

'I'll shut up.'

Jenny passed me a hunk of bread and cheese. 'Put dat in your mouth instead save you havin' to bite your tongue.'

I broke the roll apart and slapped on the

dried-up piece of cheese. 'Was that a joke at my expense?'

'Me tink it was.' Jenny appeared delighted by her own wit.

'Proof you're a free woman,' laughed Pedro, taking her hand and kissing it gallantly. She did not pull away.

EPILOGUE

TRIANGULAR
TRADE

Billy found us passage on a ship carrying cotton and sugar to England.

''Ere you go, Cat. My bunk's next door,' he explained, showing me the tiny cabin I'd been allocated. 'I said we were brother and sister. Saved answering too many questions.'

'You're probably right.' I shivered. I didn't like this ship: it had an evil smell. Billy had promised me that it was not carrying slaves, but I guessed that it might have done in the recent past. The barrels of sugar and bales of cotton were now packed where people had been crammed. The crew looked no better than brutes. Give me Tivern's honest dishonesty rather than this respectable cruelty any day. But at least with Billy Shepherd as my travelling companion, I knew that I had no need to worry for my safety – he knew the minds of such people, as under normal circumstances he was one himself. Slave owner and London crime lord – the perfect chaperone.

Pedro and Jenny did not step on board (who could blame them?) but waited to say their farewells on the dock.

'Look after each other, won't you?' I said in a choked voice.

'We will,' vowed Pedro. 'You're not going to cry on me, are you, Cat Royal?'

I sniffed and shook my head. His eyes looked very bright too.

'Good, because I want my last memory of Cat Royal to be of her smiling.'

I tried to oblige but it was a terrible performance.

'Give my regards to Frank and Syd. Tell Signor Angelini "thank you" for all his kindness towards me.'

'I will.'

Jenny moved off a few paces to give us some privacy for our final farewells. Pedro and I hugged for a long while, both silently remembering the last few years and the friendship that had given us two orphans someone to love like family.

'When my task here is done, I'll come find you,' Pedro promised, his voice hoarse.

'I'll be waiting.'

'Don't let Billy bully you on the journey home.'

'He doesn't stand a chance – those days are gone.'

Pedro squeezed my upper arms, then set me apart. 'Do you mean I should feel sorry for the poor brow-beaten villain?'

'Perhaps.' I couldn't help a watery smile at the thought. 'A month with me will certainly kill or cure his attachment, don't you think?'

'If you really put your mind to it, there's no contest. He'll be crying mercy before you leave port.'

'I love you, Pedro.'

'I love you too, Cat.'

With that, he turned and walked away before he disgraced himself with a display of tears. Jenny gave me a final hug and ran after him. It was good to know that I had left him with a friend. I felt no embarrassment as I wept. Pedro was really gone.

'Well then, Cat, time to get you back where you belong, don't you think?' Billy hooked my arm and led me up the gangplank.

I blew my nose on the handkerchief he offered me and straightened my shoulders. In truth there was nothing to grieve for: my friend was only doing what he felt he had to do, making a free choice as all men should.

'Yes, Billy, I'm ready to go home.'

Curtain falls.

CAT'S GLOSSARY

(Including many Creole terms)

ALL MY EYE – what a load of rubbish (hopefully not your conclusion about my story)

ANNE BONNY – famous female pirate, not my role model

BAM, BAMMING – to tease or hoax someone (what, *moi*? Never!)

BLIND AS A BRICKBAT – very dense or blind about something

BLOCKING – planning of moves on stage

BONA FIDE – Latin for genuine, in good faith

BOSUN – sailor in charge of sails and rigging, right-hand man to captain

BUCKRA – white man or woman

CHICHONA BARK – treatment for malaria, a Godsend

CHILLEN – children

CUT DIRECT – to snub or ignore

DONS – university tutors

DUPPY – A spirit or ghost

FIDDLER'S JIG (to care a . . .) – not care a jot

FLAT – person who it is easy to fool

GUINEA BIRD – term for newly arrived slave from Africa

HOYDEN – boisterous girl

INDENTURED SERVANT – someone legally bound to a master by contract, sometimes used in place of a prison sentence

MASSA – master

MICHAELMAS TERM – first term of academic year at Cambridge University

MISSIS – mistress, a swear word in my vocabulary

MULATTO – a person of mixed origins

OCTOROON – a ridiculous – and I think insulting – term for a person with a black great-grandparent

PACERS – smart carriage horses

PENN – an estate or a plantation in Jamaica

POLINCK – small-holding for growing of extra food

QUADROON – a person with a black grandparent (I hope you will never use this word in my hearing or you risk having your ears boxed!)

QUARTERDECK – raised deck to the stern of a ship

RED-LETTER DAY – special or holy day, referring to the custom where such dates are highlighted in red in almanacs and calendars.

SAN DOMINGO – French colony in a spot of bother

SALT-WATER NEGRO – slave that has just stepped off ship

SEGAR – a strange tube of tobacco for smoking, much liked by Jamaican gentlemen (I can't believe it'll catch on)

SHARP COVE – clever gent

STEVEDORE – man who loads/unloads ships

STRIKE THE SET – dismantle scenery, pack up

SURE AS THE DEVIL IS IN LONDON – to be very certain of something

TATTA – father

THOMAS GRAY'S, SACKVILLE STREET – top-notch jewellers

TOGS – clothes

THE TON – Society, the top people, only apply if you have a title or stacks of money

TOPGALLANTS – topmost sails

TORTUGA OR ILE DE LA TORTUE – lawless island off north coast of San Domingo

ALSO BY JULIA GOLDING

THE CAT ROYAL BOOKS

The Diamond of Drury Lane
Cat among the Pigeons
Den of Thieves
Cat O'Nine Tails

THE DARCIE LOCK NOVELS

Ringmaster

THE COMPANIONS QUARTET

Secret of the Sirens
The Gorgon's Gaze
Mines of the Minotaur
The Chimera's Curse

The Ship Between the Worlds

Dragonfly

A Sparkling Diamond Mystery
Starring Cat Royal

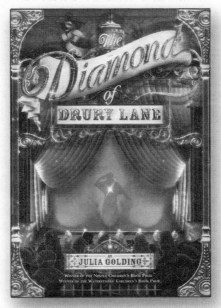

At the Theatre Royal in Drury Lane, Covent Garden,
This present day, being 1st January, 1790,
Will be presented

THE DIAMOND OF DRURY LANE
(written by Miss Cat Royal).

PRINCIPAL CHARACTERS

Miss Cat Royal - orphan and ward of the theatre

Mr Johnny Smith - prompt with a secret

Mr Syd Fletcher - leader of the Butcher's boys

Mr Billy 'Boil' Shepherd - evil leader of rival gang

And a HIDDEN diamond!

CAT GOES TO SCHOOL

Herewith another thrilling adventure. . . In which
Cat must save Pedro from being shipped off to a
slave plantation, is obliged to wear the breeches
and cap of a boy, and once again comes face to
face with her nemesis, the evil *Billy Shepherd*!

CAT IN REVOLUTIONARY PARIS

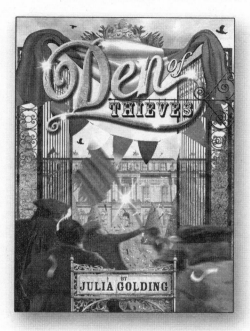

Herewith another captivating volume
from our favourite heroine Cat Royal . . .
In which the French Royal family flee as
Cat takes her first steps as a dancing spy
and witnesses the power of the people.

VIVE LA RÉVOLUTION!

ALL ABOARD,
CAT'S GOING ABROAD

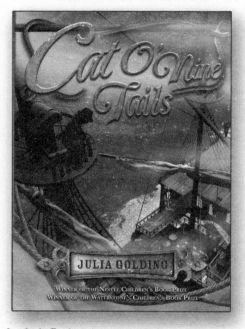

In which Cat becomes an unlikely recruit for the
British Navy, takes passage to America and unravels
a fiendish plot to do away with Lord Francis, heir to
a dukedom. From the grand Assembly Rooms of Bath
to the wilds of a new frontier, Cat finds she is for
once quite out of her depth . . .

COMING SOON ...

 New Lanark Cotton Manufactory

 REQUIRES

Young persons of sixteen years and under To work as Spinners and Weavers. Must be industrious, polite and well-behaved.

Apply to *David Dale Esq.*

Cat's Cradle

In which *Cat Royal* spins a tale about the search for her family, weaving in friends and foes, old and new. Her journey takes her from riotous London to a revolutionary cotton mill on the River Clyde in Scotland.

And introduces a mysterious newcomer. All will be revealed.

So take your seats, ladies and gentlemen: The Industrial Age has arrived!

Dear Reader,

Over time we have shared enough confidences for me to feel quite safe entrusting you with the story of how I came to be published. You may remember that I had an awful experience with a certain Mr Tweadle who stole my manuscripts and sensationalised them*. From that day on I determined that my literary career was not going to be ruined by another such scandal, and fortune later favoured me when my stories were discovered by a lady scholar, *Dr Julia Golding*.

Julia (she has given me permission to be on first name terms) was once a diplomat in Poland and I feel that she is a kindred spirit, as I was once an envoy to a foreign country – France – myself. You cannot imagine how delighted I was when Julia, acting on my behalf, accepted awards for my first book, *The Diamond of Drury Lane*. It won both the Waterstone's Children's Book Prize and the Nestlé

* For full details of his wicked exploits see *Den of Thieves*

EGMONT PRESS: ETHICAL PUBLISHING

Egmont Press is about turning writers into successful authors and children into passionate readers – producing books that enrich and entertain. As a responsible children's publisher, we go even further, considering the world in which our consumers are growing up.

Safety First
Naturally, all of our books meet legal safety requirements. But we go further than this; every book with play value is tested to the highest standards – if it fails, it's back to the drawing-board.

Made Fairly
We are working to ensure that the workers involved in our supply chain – the people that make our books – are treated with fairness and respect.

Responsible Forestry
We are committed to ensuring all our papers come from environmentally and socially responsible forest sources.

For more information, please visit our website at
www.egmont.co.uk/ethicalpublishing

Children's Book Prize. Julia, being something of a bluestocking, has also penned her own prose: *Ringmaster*, the *Companions Quartet*, *The Ship Between the Worlds* and *Dragonfly*. If ever perchance I visit Oxford, she has assured me that she, her husband and children will always welcome me into their home.

Cat Royal

P. S. If you'd like to know more about my 18th century world, go to www.juliagolding.co.uk.